THE SKY BLUE TEE SHIRT

With best wishes
Jenny Whitfield.

The sky blue tee shirt

ONE LIFETIME – TWO DIFFERENT LIVES

JENNY WHITFIELD

Copyright © 2018 Jenny Whitfield

The moral right of the author has been asserted.

Apart from any fair dealing for the purposes of research or private study, or criticism or review, as permitted under the Copyright, Designs and Patents Act 1988, this publication may only be reproduced, stored or transmitted, in any form or by any means, with the prior permission in writing of the publishers, or in the case of reprographic reproduction in accordance with the terms of licences issued by the Copyright Licensing Agency. Enquiries concerning reproduction outside those terms should be sent to the publishers.

This book is a work of fiction. Names, characters and incidents are a product of the author's imagination. Any resemblance to actual people, living or dead, is entirely coincidental.

Cover design by Lisa at The Art Partnership

Matador
9 Priory Business Park,
Wistow Road, Kibworth Beauchamp,
Leicestershire. LE8 0RX
Tel: 0116 279 2299
Email: books@troubador.co.uk
Web: www.troubador.co.uk/matador
Twitter: @matadorbooks

ISBN 978 1789014 020

British Library Cataloguing in Publication Data.
A catalogue record for this book is available from the British Library.

Printed and bound by CPI Group (UK) Ltd, Croydon, CR0 4YY
Typeset in 11pt Minion Pro by Troubador Publishing Ltd, Leicester, UK

Matador is an imprint of Troubador Publishing Ltd

MIX
Paper from responsible sources
FSC® C013604

*Once again, I must thank everyone who has helped me with this book. My Grandson Miles, Toyah, for all her ongoing support, and Lisa, for her advice and another eye-catching cover design.
Oh, and my husband Martin.*

PART 1

CHAPTER 1

1991

The sisters stood close together, taking comfort from each other. They were quite different, both in looks and temperament. Chris was the eldest by two years, tall and slim with fair curly hair, while Rose barely came to her sister's chin and her hair was short and dark. But they were close and had always been there for each other. Never more so than today. Chris put her arm round Rose's shoulders.

"Are you alright Rose?" There was a pause and a sigh.

"Yes, I'm OK, but I'll be glad when everyone has gone. I've been thinking Chris, how's Mum going to manage? Dad did everything for her, she didn't have to make any decisions, only about what flowers to put in the garden. She's going to be really lost now he's gone." Her voice wobbled and she dabbed at her eyes. Chris gave her shoulders a little squeeze.

"I'm not so sure about that Sis. I think Mum may surprise us. She'll manage just fine, you wait and see."

Rose looked doubtful.

"Well I hope you're right." She glanced around the room. "Where is she anyway? We'd better find her, and make sure she is OK."

They left the lounge and walked through the hall and it soon became clear that their mother was in the kitchen washing up. Chris tutted as they walked through the door.

"What are you doing Mum? We can load the dishwasher later."

Isabelle raised a tear stained face. "I've nearly run out of cups and saucers and I thought people might like another cup of tea."

"Oh Mum, please don't encourage them to stay any longer." She handed her mother a towel. "Here, dry your hands, I think Aunt Dorothea and Uncle George are about to leave."

"Thank the good Lord for that." Isabelle said with feeling. Which made Chris pull a face and Rose stifle a giggle. Right on cue their aunt swept into the kitchen.

"There you are Isabelle. George and I must be on our way now. We've got that arduous journey ahead of us."

"Alright Dorothea, and thank you so much for coming."

Dorothea looked at her sharply.

"Of course I came, Bernard was my brother after all." Isabelle ignored this remark and reached up to kiss her sister-in-law on the cheek, then smiled at George and kissed him too.

"Have a safe journey home."

The girl's favourite uncle, Rob, was next to leave. Not officially an uncle, he was in fact Bernard's cousin. But there was no family resemblance, Bernard had been tall and dark and almost too thin. Rob was shorter and stocky with fair hair. He had an open and friendly face and a warm smile. The girls adored him and Isabelle was fond of him too. He was an agent for a company manufacturing plastic ware in Swindon and when visiting the Oxford area, he would drop in for a cup of tea. If Isabelle was out he would call in on Rose instead. He hugged Rose and Chris, then turned to Isabelle.

"Now then my dear, let me know if there is anything I can do for you. I'm not too far away and my work brings me to this area as you know."

Isabelle hugged him. "Dear Rob, I'll be fine but I will remember what you said. Off you go now and take care."

Over the next half hour people left steadily until there were just Rose, her husband Dave, Chris and her other half Steve, and Isabelle's lifelong friend, Bubs. Chris carried a pile of plates through to the kitchen and slotted them into the dishwasher.

"I think Steve and I had better be off now Mum, if you're sure you'll be alright." Then she added with more than a hint of sarcasm. "After all we've such an arduous journey ahead of us."

Isabelle tapped her lightly on the hand. "Don't be naughty dear."

"Well honestly Mum, she's only got to go to Birmingham and it's a good road all the way. She'll easily be home in an hour and a half."

Bubs had been listening to this conversation. "Yes, you go now Chris if you want. I'll look after Mum if you need to get home. She'll be fine with me."

There were hugs and kisses all round and Chris promised to ring the next day when she got home from work.

Dave put the furniture back where it belonged, while Bubs, Isabelle and Rose cleared away the remaining bits of food. Isabelle rummaged in a cupboard and found a large plastic container.

"Here Dave, fill that up for your lunch tomorrow and put enough in there for Rose and the kids as well. I'll never eat all this. Take some of the egg sandwiches, they don't freeze very well." Dave did as he was told with pleasure and Isabelle put the rest in the fridge or the freezer. "Here, you can take this red wine as well Dave, it's virtually a full bottle and I won't drink it.

Dave's face lit up. "Ta Mother-in-Law, I'll enjoy that."

When all was done Rose came and gave her mother a hug. "It was a nice service wasn't it? I think we gave Dad a good send-off don't you?" Her eyes filled with tears. "Oh Mum, I'm going to miss him so much. I know he could be an old grump but we always got on OK."

"I know dear. You always did get on with him better than Chris. She would argue with him and it was guaranteed to annoy him. You are right though, it was a nice service but I'm glad it's all over. Thanks for all your help dear and I'll see you tomorrow I expect."

"Yes Mum, I'll pick the kids up from school and come straight here for a cup of tea."

Isabelle watched them walk down the path, hand in hand, with the box of goodies tucked under Dave's arm. As soon as they had gone Bubs took Isabelle's arm and propelled her into the lounge, gently pushed her into an armchair and lifted her feet onto the pouffe.

"Now just you stay right there Belle, and don't move." They smiled at each other in complete understanding. Bubs disappeared into the kitchen and Isabelle heard the fridge door open and close and the chink of glasses. Bubs came back and handed Isabelle a glass of white wine.

"Now you can really relax Belle." The friends lifted their glasses and gently touched them together. "Here's to the first day of the rest of your life." Bubs said with a smile.

"Oh Bubs, thank goodness everyone was so kind and sympathetic. At least it got me crying and behaving like a grieving widow. But nevertheless, it was sad. Nobody should die that young. I know I didn't love him, but I wouldn't wish that on anyone. He did keep himself fit but it was the stress of work that—" Her voice trailed away.

They sat quietly for a few minutes, sipping their wine and thinking about the day.

Bubs broke the silence. "Have you any plans Belle, or is it too soon?"

Suddenly Belle's face was animated. "Have I got plans did you say? You wouldn't believe how many plans I have. They have been whizzing around in my head for days. I know I've had other important things to think about, but I just couldn't help it Bubs."

Bubs looked at her expectantly. "Well. Are you going to share them with me or are they all secret?"

"Nothing is secret from you Bubs, but you will never guess in a million years what the first thing is." "What? Come on tell me" Bubs said.

"I'm going to try and stop calling everyone 'dear'. It makes me sound like an old woman who can't remember anyone's name, and I'm not an old woman. I'm 48, well for a few more weeks anyway."

"Good idea, I agree." Bubs said as she emptied the remaining wine into their glasses. "Then what?"

"Well, in a nut shell, I'm going to sell this house, it's far too big for me. Then I'll buy a small apartment. Something nice, you know, in a good area. Then I'm going to travel. Bernard would never go abroad, would he? Every year it was just one week either in Wales or Norfolk. I liked those places and so did the girls, but when they grew up I thought Bernard might try somewhere different. But no, he wouldn't. I longed to explore different places, abroad maybe, or even different areas of the British Isles. So that's what I'm going to do now and I can't wait."

Bubs smiled at her. "Well good for you Belle. If you want company I'll come with you, but if you want to explore alone I quite understand."

Belle leaned over and hugged her. "You're the best friend anyone could wish for. You've kept me sane over the last twenty years or so. If I hadn't been able to confide in you I think I would have lost my mind."

"That's what friends are for." Bubs replied.

Belle looked thoughtful. "It's easy to talk about all I want to do, but will I have the confidence Bubs? I've been crushed for so long."

At nine thirty Belle yawned and confessed to being exhausted. She said goodnight to Bubs and went upstairs to shower and prepare for bed. Bubs followed soon after, going into the bedroom she always used when visiting. Belle snuggled down in bed, but sleep would not come. For more than thirty years she had shared a bed with Bernard and it still seemed very strange to be alone. Bernard had always been a sound sleeper. He would lay down, say goodnight, roll onto his side and go to sleep. He hardly moved all night, although the last few months he had been more restless, the stresses of work playing on his mind. Now Belle had started to think of the past and she couldn't seem to stop. Her mind went back to the first few years of their marriage when they had been so happy. Then further back to their courtship. She had just been so young and innocent, but she had fallen madly in love and could think of nothing but being married to Bernard. There were so many 'ifs and buts'. What if her parents had been younger and more easy going? What if she hadn't met Bernard? Would she have had more boyfriends and made a happier choice? But her parents had been in their forties when Belle came along, and they were keen to see her settled and happily married. Bernard had seemed perfect to them, and as Isabelle was an only child, there were no siblings for her to talk it over with. As far as she knew she had no other relatives. You couldn't change the past anyway and she couldn't have wished for more kind and loving parents. Belle sighed, rolled over and tried to sleep.

PART TWO

CHAPTER TWO

1958

Belle weighed out flour and fat into a mixing bowl while her mother watched.

"Now rub it in Isabelle, while I grease the tin."

Belle was just about to do so when the front door bell rang.

"Oh, that will be Mr. Johnston. Let him in please and show him into the living room. You'd better call Father, I think he's upstairs."

Belle opened the front door and a tall, dark haired young man stood there.

"Mr. Johnston? Please come in."

"Thank you, I've come to see your father as requested." Belle took him into the living room and indicated that he should sit down. There was no need to call her father, he came in at once and the two men shook hands.

"Thank you for coming Mr. Johnston. Isabelle dear, could we have some tea please?"

Belle smiled at her father. "Yes of course." She went back to the kitchen.

"Father wants tea. I'll get back to the mince pies in a minute Mother."

"All right dear, there's no hurry. I expect they will be in there for hours." She smiled at her daughter. "I expect you are curious."

"I did wonder who Mr. Johnston was."

"Well, Father is retiring soon as you know, and Mr. Johnston is an accountant. He has agreed to come here for an hour or so to help Father sort out his savings and pension. He's been rather worried about it all and he didn't want to go into their office, he felt it would be more private at home."

Belle poured a little water into the pastry mix and kneaded it together. "He looks a nice man Mother. I'm sure he'll be able to help Father." She rinsed her hands and poured boiling water into the teapot. "Will you have a cup Mother?"

"Yes please dear, but pour the men's first. Put a few custard creams on a plate and take them in too."

Belle put the brass tray on the table and placed the plate of biscuits beside the two cups of tea and the sugar bowl. She picked up the tray and walked through the tiny hall and, nudging the living room door open with her hip, went through and put the tray on the coffee table. She smiled at her father, then at Mr. Johnston. A pair of solemn brown eyes looked back at her. Belle's heart gave a little leap and then steadied.

The mince pies were soon in the oven, and fifteen minutes later they were cooling on the rack.

"Let's try one dear." Her mother said with a twinkle in her eyes. "We're sure to eat later than usual. If they are good, which I am sure they will be, you can take some in to the men."

Mother and daughter sat down at the table and each cut a steaming mince pie in half and carefully sampled them. Mrs. Pope brushed the crumbs from her fingers. "Well done Isabelle, they are delicious. You will make someone a good wife in a few years."

"Oh Mother, don't try and marry me off yet, I'm only sixteen and a half."

Her mother sighed. "I know dear. But your father and I are not getting any younger. He will be retiring next year don't forget. We would like to see you settled with a nice young man, but don't worry, you have time yet to enjoy your teenage years." Mrs. Pope turned the oven down to low and put a casserole in that had been cooked earlier.

"Mother, is it alright if I go to the youth club tonight? I'll be home before ten."

"Of course dear, are you going with Leonora?"

"Yes, I said I would call for her between seven and seven thirty."

***

All Leonora's friends called her 'Bubs', she was a friendly and lively girl and somebody at school started to call her 'Bubbles'. The nick name had caught on and then after a while it was shortened to 'Bubs'.

It was about seven forty-five when Belle knocked at her door. It opened immediately "I thought you had forgotten." Bubs said with a frown.

"No, of course not. Grab your coat and I'll explain on the way."

They linked arms and headed for the community hall. Belle began to explain. "You see, Father had an accountant call at home to help him with his pension. You know Mother is not very strong and I helped to make them a cup of tea and guess what? I made my first mince pies and they were yummy."

Bubs grinned. "So, what was this man like? Was he young and good looking or old and grey?"

"He was good looking" Belle replied "But old."

"What, old like your father you mean?"

"No silly. Probably getting on for thirty, but he was very serious and that might have made him seem older than he actually is. Oh Bubs, he had the most gorgeous brown eyes. They made me go all funny."

"Oo'er, don't tell me you've fallen in love Belle."

"Of course not, but I bet he earns loads of money. He must be very clever. Anyway, I expect he's married at his age." They walked up to the door of the hall, "Here we are, let's get in out of the cold and warm up with a bit of dancing."

Mr. Johnston called twice more on a Friday evening, before both men were happy with the financial arrangements. Each time he came, Belle took tea in and smiled shyly at him, and each time those brown eyes looked back at her. Then Mr. Johnston disappeared from their lives and everything went on as before.

★★★

Belle worked hard at her job, and with her shorthand and typing. She was soon good enough to have a small rise in her wages and take on more of the work in the office. Another school leaver came to take her place as the office junior. At just seventeen years old, Belle's parents were naturally very proud of her.

One lunchtime in October, needing a breath of fresh air, Belle decided to walk down to the river which was only ten minutes away. The weather was fine, although windy, and Belle felt invigorated after a morning in the stuffy office. Being a modest young lady, she had no idea how pretty she looked with her fair hair blowing around her face and her cheeks rosy from the wind. She stopped close to the river and watched the boats, some leisure boats, some working craft, bringing goods and people to where they needed to be. She was brought out of her reverie by a deep voice just behind her.

"Hello Isabelle."

Belle jumped and swung round, then to her annoyance she felt herself blush. It was Mr. Johnston.

"Err, hello." She stammered.

Mr. Johnston smiled. "How lovely it is here. I often come here in my lunch hour. I presume you're on your lunch break too?"

Belle returned his smile shyly. "Yes I am. It's noisy and stuffy in the office," She looked at the busy river, "I never get tired of this, do you Mr. Johnston?"

"Indeed not," He replied. His eyes admired her, "I hope you don't mind me saying, but you look charming today."

Belle felt herself blush again. She put her hand up to her windblown hair, then glanced at her watch. "I must get back to work. Goodbye Mr. Johnston."

"Goodbye Isabelle. Perhaps we'll meet here again sometime."

Belle walked back to work, the meeting with the young man going around and round in her mind. She felt drawn to him despite thinking him rather old. He was probably married with children, although somehow she didn't think so. Anyway, she didn't feel ready for romance. A chat and a laugh with the boys at the youth club was enough.

She told nobody of her meeting with Mr. Johnston, not even Bubs, and soon it was all forgotten, until four months later. On a bright sunny day in February, once again Belle was walking by the river. This time Belle saw him first and was just about to turn away when he looked up and saw her. His face, usually so sombre, broke into a smile and he came over and shook her hand.

"Isabelle, how lovely to see you. How are you my dear?"

"I'm very well thank you Mr. Johnston."

"Oh, please call me Bernard, Mr. Johnston sounds so formal. May I walk with you for a while?"

Belle could hardly say no and anyway, did she want to? So, with a nod she agreed and they turned and walked beside the busy river, silent for a while. Then, haltingly, Belle asked him about his day. Bernard sighed. "I'm helping a solicitor on a very complicated case at the moment. Obviously, I can't give you any details, but someone passed away, someone very wealthy, and there is no will and no wife or children. But as is often the case, people come forward, so called friends, distant relatives, business associates, all claiming some of the money is theirs. It's a headache and will probably go on for months, even years, before it's all sorted out."

Belle glanced up at him. "Oh dear, that sounds like a lot of work and rather frustrating I should think."

"Yes, but I can't complain. I chose this career and most of the time I enjoy it. People will always need accountants so it's a secure profession to be in." They walked on a little further, then Bernard stopped and took her arm, turning her to face him. "I'm sure I can rely on you not to mention any of this conversation to your friends or family. You do understand don't you Isabelle?"

"Of course, Bernard." Belle reassured him.

He looked at her for a few moments, then said. "I just find you easy to talk to my dear. I'm naturally rather shy you see, but I wouldn't normally talk about my work anyway, not even to my mother – especially my mother." He smiled crookedly, "She does so like to boast about me to her friends and I know things would slip out, so I find it best to say nothing."

They turned and walked back alongside the river and Belle told him about her rather boring morning in the office. "The office manager lost her cool because there were no biscuits left to have with her coffee." She rolled her eyes. "She's like a spoilt child. So, I had to leave my desk and go out and buy her some. Then this afternoon she will be cross because I haven't quite finished my work."

Bernard nodded. "Yes, I know. I find women in authority can sometimes be like that. Best just to keep your head down and get on with your work."

They had now got back to the spot where their walk had begun, and Belle glanced down at her watch.

"Oh gosh, look at the time. Bye Bernard." She ran off down the road, leaving a bemused Bernard watching her until she was out of sight.

On the same day the following week, they met and walked beside the river again. They chatted for a while and then Bernard fell silent.

Belle glanced up at him. "Are you alright Bernard?"

He smiled at her and her heart gave a lurch. How handsome he was when he smiled.

"Yes, I'm fine, but I do have a small problem you see. I would like to ask you out Isabelle. But I'm aware that you are much younger than I am, and I don't think your parents would approve. But if I spoke to them and they don't mind, would you like to come to the cinema with me?"

Belle only hesitated for a few seconds. "Yes, I would. That would be lovely. But you are right. You will need to speak to Father and Mother. If they say no, then so shall I. They are very sweet but rather old-fashioned and I wouldn't go against them."

"No, of course not, I wouldn't expect you to. Besides, I am rather old-fashioned myself. Perhaps too old-fashioned for you, but we shall see. Now I think we should turn back before we make you late again. When shall I call to see your parents?"

"Oh, any evening except Wednesday, they go to a prayer meeting then. Oh, and I go to the youth club on Fridays, so that's not good either."

"How about Tuesday then at seven thirty?"

"Yes Bernard. That would be the best time."

To Belle's embarrassment her parents had made Bernard promise to take her only to the cinema or to other places where they were not alone. Then to bring her straight home afterwards. Bernard listened politely, then promised to take great care of her. So, their first date was made in front of her parents to make sure that they were happy with the arrangements. When all was settled, she went to the door with him and wished him good night.

"Goodnight Isabelle. I'll see you on Thursday. I'll pick you up at seven." He bobbed his head and stepped out into the night. Belle gave a little wave and then closed the door.

★★★

"You're what? Am I hearing you correctly Belle? You've got a date with Mr. Johnston? I can hardly believe it." Bubs had stopped short in the middle of the road and clutched Belle's arm.

Belle pulled her onto the pavement. "Are you trying to get yourself run over you silly thing? Yes, we have got a date. Come and sit in the bus shelter for a minute and I'll tell you all about it. But please don't say anything at the club."

They sat down and Belle told her everything from when she had first bumped into Bernard by the river, right up to Tuesday when he had been to see her parents. "I was shaking like a leaf Bubs. I had sort of told my parents what it was all about. I think they were a bit shocked at first, but they had time to think about it before Bernard came around. I quite expected them to say no, but they didn't. Now I don't know whether to be pleased or sorry."

Bubs looked at her, a slight frown wrinkling her brow. "Are you sure about this Belle? From what you've told me, he seems rather old and boring."

"Yes, I know." Belle's face took on a dreamy look. "But there's something about him Bubs. I can't explain it."

Bubs shrugged. "Oh well, just be careful. I would imagine he's a lot more experienced than you. Don't let him take advantage of you."

"That's just it Bubs, I'm sure he wouldn't. He's like an old-fashioned gentleman. To be honest I don't think he's had a lot to do with ladies." She giggled. "I think he's as innocent as me!"

Bernard rang the doorbell just as the clock struck seven, and, heart thumping with nerves, Belle opened the door.

"Hello Bernard. Come in and say hello to Father and Mother while I get my coat."

A few minutes later she pulled the front door closed and walked to the car. Bernard opened the door and Belle got in and made herself comfortable. He was a very steady driver and soon they were pulling in to the car park near the cinema. The film was good and they both relaxed a little, but only exchanged a few words all evening. Belle began to think that maybe Bernard was as shy as she was. He was obviously confident at work, in familiar surroundings and doing a job he was good at, but this was different. As they walked back to the car Bernard cleared his throat.

"It was a good film Isabelle. Did you enjoy it?"

"Yes, I did," Belle replied, "It kept me guessing right to the end."

He drove her home and saw her to the door where he shook her hand and thanked her for her company.

"Perhaps we can do the same next week, what do you think Isabelle?"

Belle agreed, gave him a wave and let herself into the house. She slipped her coat off and went through to the sitting room where her parents were quietly reading. Her father smiled up at her.

"Well, how did the evening go dear?"

"The film was really good, but do you know we hardly said two words to each other all evening. I felt so shy and nervous and I think Bernard did too. I don't feel I know him any better. When we bump into each other by the river we are much more relaxed. It must be because we were on an actual date."

Mrs. Pope smiled and said. "Well that's better than talking all through the film."

Bubs followed Belle into the youth club on Friday evening. So far Belle had said very little about her evening with Bernard, despite Bub's probing. They slipped their coats off and sat in a corner away from the other young people.

"So aren't you going to tell me anything about your date Belle?" Bubs queried. "I thought I was your best mate."

"You are Bubs. But there's not much to tell. We just went to the pictures and then he took me home."

Bubs rolled her eyes. "So, you didn't talk I suppose? He didn't hold your hand or kiss you goodnight? Is that what you're saying?"

"That's about it," Belle told her "We hardly talked and he certainly didn't kiss me, unfortunately."

Bubs laughed, her grumpy mood gone. "He will next time I bet. Are you seeing him again?"

"Yes, next Tuesday. He's picking me up at seven, but I don't know where we're going."

"Oh well." Bubs said. "Perhaps you'll see more action next time!"

★★★

It was early spring, and the days were lengthening. Bernard and Belle continued to meet once, sometimes twice a week. They were much more relaxed with each other now. Bernard would take her arm as they crossed the street and sometimes Belle would take his as they walked back to the car. But they were both rather shy and their friendship could hardly be called a romance, despite the brief kiss on Belle's cheek when they said goodnight. One evening Belle decided to talk to her mother about this.

"Is it normal Mother, for him to be like this? I thought he might want to give me a hug or a kiss. Do you think he just wants a friend, not a girlfriend?"

"Don't worry about that dear. I can see he's very fond of you just by the way he looks at you. He just knows how young you are and doesn't want to rush you. I'm rather relieved actually, that he's taking his time." She gave a little laugh, then asked "Do you care for him Isabelle?"

"Yes, I do Mother. I can't explain it. There's just something about him."

It was early April and Bernard and Belle were walking to a small restaurant which had become a favourite of theirs.

"I'm always glad when April Fool's Day is over Isabelle. I'm not one for practical jokes I'm afraid."

Belle laughed. "Well the old dragon in our office wouldn't allow them anyway. Nobody would dare to play tricks on her." She paused and then said something she had been itching to say for weeks. "Everyone calls me Belle, except my parents of course. Will you do that please?"

"I'm afraid not my dear, I don't like shortened names and Isabelle is a pretty name and it suits you."

Belle wasn't surprised by his answer and just accepted it. He always frowned when she mentioned Bubs.

They arrived at the restaurant, which served traditional English food, expertly cooked. Bernard pushed the door open and stepped back for Belle to enter.

The waiter came forward. "Hello again sir, table for two?"

Bernard nodded and they were led to a quiet corner and he handed them a menu. "Can I get you a drink while you study the menu sir?" They ordered drinks and then looked at the food on offer.

"Do you know what I fancy tonight Bernard?"

He smiled at her. "I think it's going to be fish and chips. You looked longingly at mine the last time we were here. Am I right?"

"Yes, you are, you clever old thing. Are you going to have the same?" Bernard agreed and beckoned the waiter over. As they waited for the food to come, Bernard reached over and took Belle's hand.

"Do you remember the promise I made to your parents two months ago? They said we were never to be alone. But wouldn't it be lovely to walk in the countryside? It's April and getting warmer and everything is beginning to look spring like." He gazed at her lovingly. "It would be nice to be alone with you, but I don't think your parents trust me."

"Oh Bernard, I'm sure they do."

He shook his head. "No, I think it's the age difference and the fact you are still so young. But I can be trusted dear, please believe me."

"I do believe you Bernard, and you're right, it would be lovely to go for a walk," She squeezed his hand. "I'll have a chat to Mother when the moment is right. She may be old fashioned but I can talk to her about anything and not feel embarrassed. I'm sure she'll understand."

Belle laid in bed that night trying to think of the best way to broach the subject with her parents. It was so difficult. They would think immediately that Bernard had 'ideas'. In the end it all came out quite naturally over breakfast the next morning. As they sat at the table with tea and toast, her father looked up and said to his wife.

"What a beautiful morning. We're so lucky my dear, now I'm retired we can go for a walk whenever we like. Do you feel well enough?"

"Yes, I do Harry. That would be lovely. Can we go to where the primroses are? That's a pretty walk and not too far for me."

"Yes, that would be good. Shall we leave about ten o'clock?" He smiled at his wife, then glanced at Belle. "What a frown Isabelle. Don't you think we should go?"

Belle sighed. "Of course you should go, but I envy you. Bernard and I were just saying yesterday how much we would like to go for a walk, but you don't want us to so that's that. We shall miss all the spring flowers and the leaves coming out, and my favourite flowers are the bluebells in May." She was aware she sounded rather petulant but couldn't seem to help it.

Her father answered. "You are still very young Isabelle and Bernard is a man of the world. But Mother and I will talk it over while we are walking. Now don't you think you should get to work?"

Belle was relieved that evening to find her parents had relented.

"But in the daytime Isabelle. Remember we are trusting you."

Belle rolled her eyes. "Oh Father, I'm nearly eighteen and I'm an adult now. I can promise you there is nothing to worry about. Bernard would never do anything bad, he's too much of a gentleman. Gosh we've been going out for two months and all he's done is kiss my cheek!"

The next evening Bernard picked up Belle in his car and they set off for the cinema. He parked the car and turned off the engine, then smiled at Belle. "You're looking pleased with yourself this evening. Have you got good news?"

"Oh Bernard, yes. My parents have agreed we can go for a walk in the country. Isn't that wonderful?"

Bernard's face lit up. "It certainly is. Don't lets go to the cinema. Let's find a quiet pub somewhere and have a drink. Then we can talk about where you would like to go." Then to Belle's surprise and delight, he leaned across and kissed her softly on the lips. They smiled into each other's eyes for a moment, then Bernard started the engine and drove away from the city and into the Oxfordshire countryside.

Belle woke on Sunday morning, yawned and stretched, then remembered. A thrill of anticipation ran through her. She mentally went through the day ahead. Breakfast, church, Sunday roast. Then at two o'clock Bernard would be calling for her. She just couldn't wait! The church service passed in a blur, and then lunch was over. She was drying the dishes when the front door bell rang.

Her father wagged a finger at her. "Now remember everything we said Isabelle, and home before dark please."

Belle nodded, then turned away with a silent groan before hurrying to the door to greet Bernard.

"Come in. Father and Mother want to say hello." Then she thought to herself 'If they embarrass me, I'll leave home'. But she needn't have worried.

Bernard shook her father's hand. "Good afternoon Mr. Pope. How are you?"

"Very well, thank you Bernard."

Then Bernard turned to Mrs. Pope, dipped his head and shook her hand gently, a smile transforming his face. "Are you well Mrs. Pope?"

"Yes, thank you. Quite well."

Bernard addressed them both. "I thought we might drive out beyond Wheatley and walk by the river. It's not too far and there are tea rooms where we can refresh ourselves. We should be back about seven o'clock. Will that be acceptable?"

Mr. Pope was all smiles now. "Of course, Mother and I will have a quiet afternoon. We'll see you later."

Bernard locked the car door and took Belle's hand. He glanced down at her feet, "I'm glad you have sensible shoes on my dear. The path is tarmac for the first few hundred yards but then it gets a bit uneven." He smiled down at her. "It's so lovely to see you, and it's good to be in the fresh air."

They walked on, chatting about their work and Bernard had a little moan about his mother. "She's sulking because I'm out. She gets lonely since my father died and because I'm at work all week she expects me to stay in with her on Sundays."

Belle glanced up at him. "So, does she get annoyed with you playing golf on Saturdays?"

Bernard grinned, "Yes she does I'm afraid. I can understand it really. She only sees me Saturday afternoons and several evenings a week. She belongs to the Women's Institute, but she needs to do more. Volunteering or something like that."

The path narrowed and moved slightly away from the river through a small copse of trees. A family passed them, heading back to the car park. Bernard glanced over his shoulder, then pulled Belle gently into his arms.

"Come here you lovely girl and let me kiss you." He lowered his head and kissed her gently. Belle felt herself respond. Bernard kissed her again, this time more ardently. Belle's knees felt weak and she put her arms around him and hung on, wanting him to go on kissing her and never stop. But Bernard pulled away and took a deep breath.

"I've wanted to do that for months." He lifted her hand and brushed her fingers with his lips, "You are so beautiful Isabelle, but I must be good. Come along, let's walk a bit further." They walked on, silent for a while, both rather overwhelmed by their emotions. After a short distance the path widened again as they approached a small village beside the river. The tea rooms came into view and it was clear that they were very busy. However, Bernard managed to find the one free table and led Belle to it.

"Tea, Isabelle, or would you prefer a cold drink?"

"Tea would be lovely please."

"Are you happy to sit in the garden my dear, or would you rather be inside?"

"I'm happy here Bernard, by the river."

He disappeared inside to order the tea, returning after a few minutes to sit down close to Belle.

"The waitress will bring it out in a few minutes." He took her hand. "I have ordered a plate of cakes as well. I hope that's alright?"

"That will be lovely. Oh Bernard, I'm so enjoying the afternoon."

They smiled, then Bernard said softly. "I feel we have something special darling girl. I know there's a big age difference between us, but although I'm twenty eight, I haven't had many girlfriends. I'm rather fussy I'm afraid, but with you everything seems right somehow. I'm very fond of you and I think you may feel the same. Am I right?"

They were interrupted by the waitress bringing tea and the plate of assorted cakes. After she had moved away to clear another table, Belle smiled at him and admitted that she did feel the same. She dragged her eyes away from him and poured the tea, then chose a cake. As they sipped their tea, both were oblivious to all around them. There were just the two of them, with thoughts only of each other. Later, as they drove back to Belle's home, Bernard reached over and took her hand.

"I've had a wonderful afternoon. I hope we can do this again soon."

"Oh yes Bernard, I hope so too, it's been lovely."

★★★

It was Friday evening and Belle and Bubs headed for the community hall where the youth club was held.

They linked arms and Bubs asked. "Well, how did you get on with Bernard at the weekend?"

Belle was silent for a few moments, then looked at Bubs, her face serious. "Oh Bubs, I think I'm in love with him and I'm pretty sure he's in love with me."

Bubs gasped "Has he said so?"

"Well no, not exactly but-but- oh Bubs, I didn't want this to happen, I'm too young to get all serious.

But when we kiss each other it's just so wonderful and it's hard to stop."

"Look Belle, let's not go to the club. We're getting too old for it anyway. It's a lovely evening, let's just go to the park where we can talk in private." They turned off down a side road and walked the few hundred yards to the park, where they found a seat near the lake. Bubs looked at Belle earnestly.

"You will be careful won't you? Don't get carried away. It would break your parent's hearts if anything happened."

"Don't worry Bubs, Bernard has terrific self-control." She suddenly giggled "More than me actually."

Bubs couldn't help laughing as well. "Oh Belle, I can't believe you said that."

★★★

As the weeks went by Bernard and Belle continued to meet on a couple of evenings a week and most Sunday afternoons. April and May passed and June came in with hot, sunny weather. Belle had begun to notice that Bernard seemed to be reluctant to be alone with her and she desperately missed his kisses. Her heart plummeted. Had he grown tired of her? Was she after all, too young for him? Did he want their romance to end? In the end, as they walked in the local park amongst other couples and families, the time seemed right to broach the subject. But Bernard had sensed she was worrying over something.

"What is it my dear? Is something bothering you?"

Belle squeezed his hand. "I hope you don't mind me saying this Bernard." Her voice shook a little. "But you don't seem to want to be alone with me anymore. Have your feelings changed? Do you want to stop seeing me?"

Bernard stopped and swung her round to face him, his hands gripping her arms.

"Don't ever think that, my darling Isabelle." Oblivious to other people nearby, his eyes swept longingly over her face. "I love you, don't you know that? I want you more than I can say. If we were alone, I'm not sure that I could trust myself. Oh Isabelle, please say you love me too, I couldn't bear to lose you."

Belle put her hand up and touched his cheek. "Yes, I do love you and I understand now."

He led her into the shade of some trees and they fell into each other's arms and kissed hungrily. "Marry me darling, please, I want you to be my wife."

Belle's heart sang. "Oh yes Bernard." They kissed again. Then Belle pulled away.

"I shall have to speak to my parents. They are bound to say I'm too young. But I'm eighteen next month. If I wait till then it will seem better somehow."

"Yes, that's a good idea. Eighteen does seem more grown up. Do you think they will agree?"

Belle bit her lip. "I'm not sure, but I think there's a chance. They are both elderly as you know and Mother is quite frail. I think they would like to see me settled with someone they approve of, and they think a lot of you Bernard dear."

"I know they do and I get on very well with them. They know I have a good job and I'll take good care of you. Oh darling, we'll have a good life together, I know. I'll always look after you and you'll never go without the essentials, I promise you." He pulled her close and they held each other for a few moments, then reluctantly pulled apart and walked on.

"Talking of parents, darling, I think you should meet my mother. Once she knows what a sweet girl you are, she'll understand why I like to be with you."

"I'd like to meet her Bernard. She sounds rather lonely. I expect she still misses your Father. How long has he been gone?"

"Oh, about five years. She certainly misses someone to boss around." He gave a wry smile. "She's a dreadfully bossy woman Isabelle. But then, I suppose I take after her to a degree, and my sister Dorothea certainly does."

Belle chuckled. "I'm sure she can't be that bad."

Bernard grimaced. "Every bit as bad. Poor George, I don't know how he puts up with her. Children might have softened her but she doesn't want any."

Belle had been dreading meeting her future mother-in-law, but the moment had come. Bernard had picked her up in the car and driven them to a quiet street fifteen minutes away. The houses here were substantial, with large gardens. He pulled into the drive of the third house along and switched off the engine.

"Well, here we are. Isabelle, you're shaking! Don't be nervous, Mother is harmless I can assure you. Just a bit overbearing at times. But I'm sure she will be perfectly charming to you. Come along dear." He took her arm and they walked to the front door. It opened as they approached and a tall well-dressed woman stood there, a smile on her face.

"Mother, this is Isabelle as you will have guessed. Isabelle, my mother."

Mrs. Johnston shook Isabelle's hand warmly.

"Come in Isabelle. Oh it's so lovely to meet you at last, let me take your coat. Bernard, take Isabelle into the lounge while I make the tea."

As Bernard had said, his mother was charming and Belle relaxed a little. She was asked about her family and her work, while they drank tea and nibbled biscuits. Then the ordeal was over and Bernard took her home. He turned onto the main road and sighed.

"Mother will say how young you are, I can guarantee it. But she can't argue about how lovely you are darling."

★★★

A week after Belle's eighteenth birthday, the right moment came along. It was just after six o'clock on Sunday evening and Belle and Bernard had just come back from a walk. Occasionally Bernard would risk his mother's sulks and accept an invitation to tea with Belle and her parents.

"Come in lad." Mr. Pope ushered him into the living room. "Isabelle, put the kettle on please love, I could do with a cuppa. How about you Bernard?"

"Yes please, I am rather dry. We walked quite a long way and it's warm today."

Belle looked at her mother, "And one for you?"

"Yes please dear."

Belle disappeared into the kitchen and Bernard decided to speak. He cleared his throat nervously.

"I wanted to speak to you Mr. Pope, I think you can probably guess what I'm going to ask." He paused, while Belle's parents waited patiently. "I've fallen deeply in love with Isabelle and she feels the same about me, I would very much like her to be my wife. I know she's young, but she's sensible and mature and well, these things happen and we couldn't help falling in love."

Mr. Pope looked at his wife and seemed lost for words. After a few moments he squared his shoulders and said.

"Well, Mrs. Pope and I will need to discuss this Bernard. We knew you were growing fond of each other but well, it is a bit sudden."

"Yes of course sir, I quite understand."

Belle appeared with a tray of tea, smiled and put it on the coffee table, then returned to the kitchen for some biscuits. She put them beside the tea and looked around, a puzzled look on her face.

"Everyone looks so serious. Is everything alright?"

Mrs. Pope grasped her daughter's hand. "Bernard has just asked for your hand in marriage dear, and Father and I are a little stunned."

Belle felt herself colour up, but didn't know what to say. She looked at Bernard, then at her parents.

Mr. Pope was the first to speak, "Your mother and I will discuss it dear, but you are very young."

Belle looked at her father, "I know, but it's what I want too."

"As I said, we will discuss it. Now pour the tea, there's a good girl."

Later, Belle said goodbye to Bernard and ran upstairs to prepare for bed.

Her parents looked at each other, "Well now dear, what do you think about our Isabelle getting wed?" Mr. Pope began. "He's a steady chap and he's got a good job, but it always comes back to the same thing, our girl is just too young."

"Yes, but what a catch for her." His wife said thoughtfully. "She could so easily have fallen for some young lad down at the youth club. But Bernard wants her, and I feel quite proud, in a funny sort of way."

Mr. Pope gave her a small smile, "So you wouldn't mind then?"

"No, not really. They could get engaged in six months, maybe at Christmas, and possibly get married when Isabelle is twenty. That would give them plenty of time to change their minds if they were unsure. How do you feel about it dear?"

Mr. Pope patted her hand. "I agree completely. Lots of young ladies get married at nineteen or twenty. Yes, I think that sounds very satisfactory."

★★★

To Belle and Bernard, it seemed a long time to wait but finally Christmas arrived. A few weeks before, they had gone into the city and bought the ring. Belle chose a single solitaire which seemed to look best on her small slim fingers. She had no idea how much Bernard had paid for it, but it looked terribly expensive. Neither of them wanted to wait another year and a half to marry, but Belle said she would wait another few months and then talk to her parents. It was something she wasn't looking forward to. Mother was so prim and proper and Father not much better. However, she got the opportunity much sooner than she expected. On New Year's eve her parents went next door for a drink, but they didn't stay to see the New Year in and returned at ten o'clock, relaxed and mellow. Mr. Pope disappeared into the bathroom and his wife tapped lightly on Belle's bedroom door.

"Can I come in dear?"

"Yes, come in Mother. It's a pity Bernard has such a horrible cold. We were looking forward to seeing the New Year in together. Did you have a nice evening?"

"Very nice thank you. We are lucky to have such good neighbours. I thought I would just pop in for a chat before going to bed."

"I'm glad Mother, I wanted a chat too." She looked down at her hands clasped tightly in her lap. "Mother, this is so difficult for me to say, but Bernard and I don't want to wait until I'm twenty to marry. We love each other so much we want to marry and be together as soon as possible. Do you understand?"

Her mother was silent for a few moments. But rather than looking shocked, a smile appeared and a faraway look came into her eyes. Then she took Belle's hand and began to speak. "Of course I understand. You may find it hard to believe, but it was just the same for Father and me. Wait there, I'm just going to get the photo from my dressing table." She returned after a few seconds and sat beside Belle again, "I know this photo is very familiar to you. It's sat there on my dressing table all your life. But now you are in love, look at it again and tell me what you see."

Belle took the framed photo from her mother and looked at the young couple smiling adoringly into each other's eyes.

"Can you see how much in love we were? So in love Isabelle, that we anticipated our marriage."

Belle gasped and felt the heat sweep over her face. She looked at her mother but was shocked into silence.

Mrs. Pope looked at her. "I can see you find that difficult to believe dear, but it was only the once, and of course, we thought we might have to arrange a rushed wedding. You can become pregnant the first time, make no mistake, but we were lucky. As we were to find out, it took twenty years for you to come along. But that may not be the case for you Isabelle." She paused and looked sternly at her daughter, "You haven't ----?"

Belle found her tongue. "No, no Mother, don't worry. But it's been very difficult."

Her mother took her hand again, "Why don't you arrange the wedding for late July or early August. You'll be nineteen then. How does that sound?"

Belle hugged her, "Oh Mother, thank you for being so understanding. But what about Father? Will he agree?"

"Just leave your Father to me, I will talk to him."

She kissed Belle goodnight and left her to dream of her wedding day.

***

Bernard seemed quite happy to leave most of the wedding preparations to Belle. His sister Dorothea was to be Matron of Honour, and Bubs a bridesmaid. Bernard was not very fond of Bubs, but had agreed to this, knowing how close the two young ladies were. He had to admit he didn't care much for his sister either. They both hoped she wouldn't overstep the mark and try and take over the wedding arrangements. Belle's mother helped as much as she could, but too much shopping exhausted her, so Bubs was the one to help choose dresses and flowers etcetera.

Belle had discussed with Bernard what sort of house they would like to start their married life in. But in the end, they decided to rent while they looked around and found something they both really liked. But on a Sunday about six weeks before the wedding, Belle received a shock. They were walking beside the river when Bernard began to speak.

"By the way Isabelle dear, I've bought a house so you needn't worry about that any more. I'll be completing the sale in about six weeks' time. You will let me know if you want to see it, won't you? Although I am sure it will suit us."

Stunned, Belle looked at him. "You've bought a house? Without me seeing it? That's not very nice Bernard. What if I don't like it? I'm not very happy about this." She frowned up at him.

"Well that's too bad Isabelle, I paid for it after all. I don't recall you paying anything towards it." He glared back at her.

"Well how could I, I didn't know anything about it." She seldom got angry, but she was certainly angry now. "Who is going to be spending the most time there, tell me that? Who's going to be cleaning and cooking in the kitchen? Honestly Bernard, what a selfish thing to do." She strode off in front of him and when he caught up and took her arm she shrugged him off. "Take me home please, I need to be alone to think about this."

Bernard realised he had not done the right thing but was too proud to back down.

"Very well." was all he said.

They walked back to the car in silence and Bernard took her home. Belle climbed out of the car and with a cool goodbye, went indoors. To her relief her parents were out. She was too angry and hurt to cry, but as she paced up and down in her bedroom her anger slowly left her. When her parents came home she told them she had a headache. Though by the looks they exchanged she didn't think they believed her!

When Belle came down to breakfast the next morning there was a letter waiting for her. She recognised Bernard's writing and silently pushed it into her pocket. Her parents exchanged another look but said nothing. Belle ate her breakfast, then went upstairs to brush her teeth and get ready for work.

"Everything all right dear?" enquired her Mother.

"Yes, fine." Belle replied brightly. "See you later Mother." She kissed her parent's goodbye and shrugged into her jacket, picked up her bag and left for work. Once settled on the bus she took the envelope from her pocket and tore it open.

My darling Isabelle

I'm so sorry I have upset you, I realise now how high handed and thoughtless I was. I mistakenly thought it would be a lovely surprise for you. I can see now that I was wrong. I love you so much and I don't want to make you unhappy. May I suggest we go together to see the house as soon as possible. If it is not to your liking I will put it straight back on the market. Please will you meet me at lunchtime in the usual place, so that we can put things right between us.

Bernard.

Belle's lunchtime came, and she almost ran out of the building and down to the river. Bernard was waiting for her and she ran into his arms, crying with relief, uncaring of the people passing by.

That evening the estate agent took them to the house and waited in the lounge while Bernard took her round. It was a fairly modern two bedroomed, semi-detached house. The rooms were not large but were adequate. Belle noted the small downstairs cloakroom and the well-equipped kitchen. The lounge diner went from front to back, with the kitchen also overlooking the small, neat back garden. The house was perfect for them to begin their married life in, but Belle still felt a little resentful toward Bernard, so she didn't over enthuse. But after a while the concerned look on Bernard's face prodded her conscience and she admitted to him that she loved it.

As they left the house and drove towards a quiet spot by the river Bernard patted her knee and said. "You know what we haven't done yet dear?"

"No, what?" asked Belle.

"I haven't arranged for you to meet my cousin Rob and his fiancée Philippa. I meant to do it weeks ago and now it's only six weeks until he becomes my best man."

"I'm looking forward to meeting them Bernard, but a little nervous."

Bernard laughed. "There is absolutely nothing for you to be nervous about. They are a lovely couple. I've been close to Rob ever since we were boys and he's very easy to get along with, and Philippa is perfectly charming. You'll see. Shall I try and fix something up for this coming weekend?"

"Yes Bernard, the sooner the better I think."

Bernard was right, the four of them met at a pub half way between Oxford and Bristol where Rob lived with his parents. They were very soon at ease with each other and the afternoon flew by. Details of the wedding were discussed and approved. Rob constantly teased Bernard with tales from their childhood that he was intending to include in his speech on the day. Bernard didn't know whether to laugh or be cross! Although the men were first cousins they were completely different in looks and character. Rob was about six inches shorter than Bernard and fair haired. He had a round, open, friendly face and seemed to be permanently smiling- or about to! Philippa was a beautiful young woman. Also fair haired, she was almost as tall as Rob and very slim. Almost too slim, Belle thought. As they parted in the early evening, Belle felt she was saying goodbye to old friends.

CHAPTER 3

SEPTEMBER 1961

"Sit still Belle! How am I going to get your hair right if you keep fidgeting?"

"Sorry Bubs, I'm just so excited, and nervous. Can you hear my heart? I'm sure you must be able to, it's thumping like mad."

"Calm down Belle. Oh dear. Here comes the matron of honour." Bubs looked up with a wide, innocent smile on her face." Hello Dorothea. How lovely to see you. How are you?"

Bernard's sister, at twenty-seven years old and already married to George, flopped down on the bed.

"I'm very well Leonora, thank you. How is everything going? Are you nearly ready Isabelle?"

"Yes, thank you. I've just got to slip my dress on and then my makeup and I'll be ready. Your dress is hanging in the wardrobe. You're a bit late so you concentrate on getting yourself ready."

Dorothea gave her a sharp look. "Makeup, did you say. Bernard won't like that. He thinks girls who wear makeup look cheap."

Bubs butted in quickly, "Only if it's put on thick.

This is going to be very subtle Dorothea." She caught Belle's eye in the mirror and rolled her eyes towards the ceiling. Dorothea lifted her dress from the wardrobe and began to get ready. Bubs slipped Belle's dress over her head, being careful not to spoil her hair, then helped her to sit down again without creasing it.

"I'll do my makeup Bubs, you get ready. All of a sudden it's a quarter to eleven and we have got to leave in thirty minutes."

There was silence as the three young ladies completed their preparations.

There were gasps from Belle's parents and Bernard's Mother as they walked sedately down the stairs.

Belle's Mother wiped away a tear. "You all look quite beautiful." She declared. "If you're sure you're ready, I believe the car is waiting."

A nervous Bernard was waiting at the church and as the organ burst into life he turned and looked at his lovely bride, walking slowly down the aisle on her Father's arm. She did indeed look lovely in a long white dress, the bodice fitting her slight frame perfectly. With a sweetheart neckline and long lace sleeves, she couldn't have chosen better. She had borrowed her mother's pearl necklace and clip on earrings for luck and her headdress was also decorated with pearls. Her bouquet was made up of white and pink roses with a blue ribbon. Bubs and Dorothea were in pink and held small white posies. Bernard looked very smart in a navy-blue suit, white shirt and grey tie. The church was hushed as the bride and groom made their vows.

The minister said a few words, the last hymn was sung and the newly-weds were led into the vestry to sign the register. When they reappeared, the organ burst forth again with the triumphant Wedding March. The newly married couple stood outside in the glorious September sunshine while the photographs were taken, then everyone made their way to the local community hall where the reception was being held.

Bernard and Belle stood just inside the entrance and greeted the guests as they arrived. They were congratulated and Belle was told many times how beautiful she looked. Guests were handed a sherry or a soft drink and slowly moved towards the tables to find their allotted places. The meal was served and the babble of voices subsided as everyone enjoyed the food.

Belle tried to eat, but her usual healthy appetite seemed to have deserted her. She nibbled daintily on a small piece of meat and then a deliciously crispy piece of roast potato.

Bubs, sitting on her other side, touched her arm, "Are you alright Belle?"

"Yes, I'm fine, but a bit nervous and excited. I thought I would be alright after the ceremony, but my tummy is still knotted up."

"Have a few big slurps of wine, that should help." Bubs said, who could never be serious for long. As the meal drew to a close, the best man, Rob, tapped his glass with a spoon for silence.

"Ladies and Gentlemen, the bride's father."

Mr. Pope stood up and Belle looked at him anxiously. She could tell he was very nervous.

He cleared his throat. "Ladies and Gentlemen. Thank you all for coming today to see our beautiful daughter married to Bernard. We welcome him wholeheartedly into our small family. My wife and I feel confident they will have a good life together and we wish them every happiness." He sat down again rather hurriedly and with relief, while everybody clapped and smiled fondly at him.

Rob stood up again. "The groom will now say a few words."

Bernard stood up. 'Gosh', thought Belle. 'He looks as nervous as Father'.

Bernard began. "My wife and I- - - -." He got no further. The hall erupted with whistles and cheers. Bernard gave a huge smile and relaxed. He thanked everyone, but especially Belle's parents for allowing him to marry their lovely daughter. Mrs. Pope wiped a tear from her eyes – not the first of the day. Bernard spoke a little longer, then sat down amid cheers and applause.

Rob stood up again. "Bernard would have you believe he was always a good boy, but that was not always the case." Bernard's Mother gave him a look which he ignored. "Being four years younger, I was easily lead astray." There were hoots of laughter at this. "I did whatever Bernard asked me to, because he was my hero. Sometimes innocent things, other times mischief, which of course I got the blame for."

Everyone chuckled again. "But I forgive him." He turned to Bernard. "He's the best cousin I could wish for and apart from my lovely fiancée Philippa, I reckon he's picked the best girl in the world. Now I would like to thank Mr. and Mrs. Pope for all their hard work in making this such a successful day. Ladies and Gentlemen, please raise your glasses and drink to the bride's parents." Everyone sipped their champagne. "My thanks also to the bridesmaids, Leonora, also known as Bubs, and Dorothea for supporting and helping the bride on her special day. Raise your glasses once more Ladies and Gentlemen. To the bridesmaids." Here there were a few wolf whistles. "Finally, please, the Bride and Groom, Bernard and Isabelle, may they have a long and happy marriage." The guests responded with their glasses and applause. "Now the happy couple will cut the cake." Rob sat down and Bernard and Belle moved to a small table where the cake stood. The photographer was ready and the cake was cut.

Bernard and Belle spent the next hour or so mingling and trying to make sure no one was left out, they thanked everyone again for coming, and for their gifts.

At three o'clock Bernard caught Belle's eye and she gave a small nod. They said their goodbyes to Belle's parents and Bernard's Mother. Then to Rob, Philippa and the bridesmaids, and with a cheery wave they left to climb in a pre-arranged limousine which would take them back to Belle's home. Bernard gripped Belle's hand tightly and very soon the car drew up outside the small terraced house.

"Wait here please." Bernard instructed the driver. "We'll be about twenty minutes." He reached in his pocket for the house key and they let themselves in and closed the door. Then they were in each other's arms, kissing and smiling delightedly at each other, before reluctantly letting go.

"Come along darling." Bernard ushered her upstairs where their going away clothes were hanging in Belle's wardrobe and their suitcases already packed and ready to go in the car. Belle slipped off her lovely dress and hung it on a hanger and put on a pretty summer dress. Then a neat cream jacket to finish off the outfit. Bernard hung his suit and shirt up and put on casual trousers with a blue shirt. Belle felt a little shy but was surprised that Bernard seemed shy as well. Then they were ready.

"Come along wife, your car is waiting." Bernard pulled the front door closed and put the spare key through the letterbox, then they got back in the car.

"Right sir, it's The Beeches, Forest Road, isn't it?" The driver confirmed.

"Yes, that's right." Bernard replied. 'The Beeches' was Bernard's bosses house and their car was parked in his drive just out of sight. All they had to do was put their suitcases in and go. Their honeymoon was to be spent in South Wales, but they were spending their wedding night in a small hotel in the Cotswolds.

A friendly, middle aged lady greeted them, and they booked in. Belle signed her new name with a flourish. She was determined nobody would know they were just married so had practised her new signature at home.

"Would you like some refreshments?" Their hostess asked.

"A cup of tea would be lovely." Belle replied. "How about you Bernard? What would you like?"

"I'd like a whiskey and soda please, if that's possible."

"Of course, sir, would you like it in the lounge or in your room?"

"We'll take our suitcases up and then have our drinks in the lounge please. Is that alright with you Isabelle?"

An hour or so later Belle stepped from the bath and dried herself vigorously. She was trembling and her heart was beating a tattoo. She smiled shyly at Bernard as he took her place in the bathroom. As she waited Belle hung up her dress and jacket, climbed into bed and pulled the bedclothes up to her chin. Bernard was silent as he came out of the bathroom, a towel tucked round his waist. He turned off the light then walked to the window and drew back the curtains. The street lights cast a subtle glow over the room as he walked to the bed and pulled back the covers.

Belle woke and stretched. The sun was shining through the window and onto the empty space beside her. She could hear Bernard shaving in the bathroom and resisted the temptation to run in there and throw herself into his arms.

After a few moments of nervous hesitation last night, all the months of longing took over. The short, sharp pain was soon forgotten and the next hour Belle would always remember with a smile. Bernard had been an ardent lover and although not very experienced, he seemed to know just what to do to give Belle the most pleasure and satisfaction. In the end, they both fell asleep exhausted. Now they needed to get themselves ready, have breakfast and make their way to the cottage that awaited them in Wales.

After losing their way twice, they finally arrived at their honeymoon home mid-afternoon. They unloaded the car then looked around the cottage, it was old and rather quaint, but clean and well equipped.

"You'll have to watch your head dearest. The cottage wasn't built for a man over six feet tall." Belle laughingly told her new husband. Bernard took her in his arms.

"Yes, but aren't you glad we are in a cottage and not a hotel? There'll be no escape for you. I'll be able to drag you up to bed whenever I like."

Belle blushed prettily. "Can we unpack first please?"

The next week was spent walking and exploring the area. They ate heartily, sometimes in the cottage and sometimes at local restaurants and pubs. They found time for a swim in the sea on two exceptionally hot days, but all too soon the week was over.

CHAPTER 4

Bernard had spent most of his savings on the house deposit, but by pooling what they had left they had managed to get the basics for their home. Bernard wanted Belle to stop working and be a stay at home wife, but Belle certainly didn't. The fact that they were now short of cash meant Belle could persuade him that she must keep on working for a time.

Two weeks after returning from their honeymoon Belle thought she might be pregnant. She said nothing to Bernard in case it was just the excitement of being married which had sent things haywire. However, when a few weeks later she began to feel nauseous in the morning, it was clear that Bernard needed to know. The next day was a Saturday and he always brought them a cup of coffee to drink in bed before getting up for breakfast. Fortunately, he was always a happy morning person so Belle sipped her coffee and put her cup back in the saucer, then took a deep breath.

"Bernard darling, I have something to tell you and I'm not sure whether you will be pleased or not."

Bernard took her hand and said lovingly. "I think I can guess my dear. Are we going to have an addition to the family?"

"How----how did you know? Oh Bernard, are you cross?"

"No, I'm not cross. A bit surprised I must say, but also proud." He coloured slightly. "It shows how fertile we are, if you will forgive me saying so."

"Oh, Bernard dear, you can say whatever you like, we are married after all."

Bernard took her in his arms. "I'm so glad we are, little wife."

★★★

Belle put the ironing board away and left the iron on the draining board to cool down. She'd treat herself to a short rest with her feet up, then potter in the garden for a while. It was a month since she'd finished work but their always seemed to be something to do. There were still two months to go before the baby was due to arrive but she felt huge and uncomfortable already. She sipped some water and laid her head back, then the doorbell rang.

"Oh drat!" Belle said out loud, "Better see who it is." She opened the door to see Rob standing there. "Rob, come in, what are you doing in this part of the world?"

Rob gave her his usual big grin and stepped inside. "I had a couple of calls to make in the Oxford area but one chap has gone off to play golf, so I'm kicking my heels until he gets back."

Belle put the kettle on, "That's rather thoughtless of him. I presume he knew you were coming?"

"Oh yes, that's the sort of thing rep's have to put up with. His secretary said he'll be back in about an hour, so I thought, that's just time to pop in and see Isabelle and cadge a cup of tea. How are you?"

"I'm well thank you, but I feel rather like an elephant."

They sat down at the kitchen table and Belle offered him a biscuit. "How is Philippa?"

"She's fine thank you. Actually, I wanted to see you about something apart from a cup of tea." Rob grinned, "Philippa and I want to get married as soon as possible. We're fed up with waiting, I know it could be difficult for you, but we were thinking of August. The baby will be two months old by then. What do you think?"

"Oh Rob, just get married. Don't worry about me."

"But I want Bernard to be best man and it would be lovely if you could be there as well."

"Well I'll sit near the back of the church and slip outside if baby squeaks." Belle said with a laugh.

"We're trying to find somewhere to live and arrange the wedding. There seems to be so much to do. We've decided to postpone the honeymoon until September, children will be back at school then."

"Good idea, you could have trouble finding somewhere to stay in the school holidays. Oh Rob, I'm so excited for you. Do you want me to say something to Bernard?"

"No thanks Isabelle, let's make a date for a get together and I'll ask him then." He put his mug on the draining board and prepared to leave. "I'll ring tonight and we'll fix a date. Thanks for the tea." He kissed Belle's cheek and she walked with him to the door and waved him off.

They met two weeks later, halfway between their two homes. Rob knew of a pub with a good reputation. Bernard was thrilled to be asked to be best man and accepted straight away. Philippa gave them some dates in August, any of which would be fine, and promised to ring as soon as a date had been decided on.

★★★

Belle dragged her eyes away from her new daughter and looked down the ward to where the visitors were coming in. She saw Bernard stop and have a quick word with one of the nurses, then he walked down the ward, beaming.

"Darling, how are you? And this is our little girl. How tiny she is." He reached out and gently touched the babies' cheek. "I'm so proud of you dearest. The nurse said how brave you were, no fuss at all. I'm such a lucky man." He gave her some fruit in a pretty basket and a posy of rose buds. They kissed and smiled into each other's eyes.

"I can't wait to come home. I have to stay in a week, but I feel fine now."

"Well you mustn't rush and come home before you are ready. But I'm missing you already and I'll be glad when you're home as well."

They had decided to call the baby Christine, and Bernard had made it clear that it mustn't be shortened to Chris. Belle agreed. Christine was a long baby and destined to be tall when she grew up. She was also a good baby, but impatient when she was hungry. Belle was rather surprised when Bernard shared nappy changing duties, but he was turning out to be a loving, hands on father.

★★★

The day of Rob and Philippa's wedding dawned sunny and warm.

"I can't believe how much stuff a baby needs for the day." Bernard groaned as he lifted the pushchair into the boot. Christine slept for the whole journey, which took one and a quarter hours, and she was ready for a feed by the time they had parked. Once this was accomplished and the baby burped and changed, guests were beginning to arrive at the church. Because of the baby it had been decided it was simpler for the groom and best man to meet at the church. Bernard waited at the door and when a smartly suited and very nervous Rob arrived they shook hands and Bernard patted him on the back.

"I survived this old boy, and so will you."

Belle left it as long as possible before going into the church, Christine was awake but content as she walked slowly in with the baby in her arms. She found a seat at the back near the door and settled down to wait for the bride's arrival. As the majestic organ announced the arrival of Philippa, the baby jumped and her face crumpled. Belle hastily pushed her finger into Christine's mouth to calm her. It worked. Belle looked up as Philippa entered the church and gasped. The bride looked almost ethereal with her slim figure clad in a pale cream lacey dress. Lightly made up and with her blonde hair curling gently to her shoulders. The filmy veil was held in place by a circle of pale, wild flowers. She just looked like an angel. Belle could just see Rob as he turned to see his bride approaching and it was hard to find the words to describe the expression on his face. Awe, adoration, pride? All of these. Belle found herself crying and reached into her bag for a tissue. The service was very moving and yet joyous. The baby behaved and fell asleep half way through, much to Belle's relief.

CHAPTER 5

1965

Belle strapped Rose into the pushchair and took Christine's hand. "Come along, time for playschool. Let's go and find your friends."

"I want to go in the pushchair Mummy." Christine pushed her lips out.

"There's not room sweetheart and you are so good at walking. Rose is only one and not as good as you. It's only just around the corner, we'll soon be there."

Christine, at three and a half accepted this and walked along happily. Rose was fifteen months old and although walking, was inclined to tumble over frequently. Belle waved goodbye to Christine at the playschool, and set off for her parent's home. She usually called in several times a week, just to make sure they were both alright. She knocked, then let herself in with her own key. It seemed very quiet. Usually at this time they would be pottering around doing housework or maybe washing, but nothing seemed to be happening. Her father appeared at the sitting room door. He looked dazed and confused.

"What is it Father? Is something wrong?"

"It's your Mother. She hasn't finished her cup of tea and she has gone to sleep." His voice rose in a desperate wail, "I can't wake her. I can't wake her."

Belle's heart gave a lurch and she hurried through to the sitting room. Her mother sat in the armchair, her eyes half closed and her hands lying limply in her lap. Belle knelt down beside her and gently touched her hand.

"Mother?" There was no response. She felt for a pulse but she already knew that her Mother had gone. She got up and turned to her Father,

"Oh Daddy." Her childhood name for her father slipped out. She put her arms round him.

"Sit with her while I call an ambulance." She hurried to the phone and dialled 999. "It's my Mother, she's not breathing. I think it's too late, but please come as soon as you can."

Rose was still strapped in her pushchair and was grizzling to be let out. Belle hurried into the kitchen and found a biscuit for her, then set about making her father a hot, sweet, cup of tea because he was obviously in deep shock. She brushed the tears away and took the tea in to her father.

"Sit down Daddy and drink this while it's hot." She guided him gently to his chair. He looked up at her, weeping and distraught.

"She's gone hasn't she Isabelle? My darling Mary has gone. What am I going to do without her?" Belle didn't know how to answer him, she just knelt down and put her arms round him again. Then she heard the ambulance coming and hurried to open the door.

Belle and Bernard stood at the graveside. One either side of her father, supporting him as the coffin was lowered. It was a beautiful day and the birds were singing, but it seemed all wrong. She still couldn't quite grasp the fact that her mother was gone. A part of her had been prepared for it as her mother had become increasingly frail but now she wanted it to be a bad dream. Her father was heartbroken and could not be consoled and Belle was very concerned about him. Time would hopefully help him but it was early days yet. Belle glanced across the grave and her eyes met Bubs and then she looked at Rob and Philippa as they held hands and gazed down into the grave.

Neighbours and friends from her parent's church were all there to pay their respects and say goodbye to a gentle, sweet lady.

Belle's childhood home was small and people spilled out into the garden. Bernard had foreseen this and had brought round some of their own chairs. Mary Pope had been a much loved lady and many people had attended the funeral, and a large percentage of them were at the wake. Belle and Bernard, with help from Bubs, made sure everyone had a drink. The food they had prepared earlier was uncovered and people helped themselves. As often happens at funeral wakes, the sombre atmosphere of the burial lifted, people chatted and there was even the odd chuckle. Belle looked at her father. He seemed lost and she moved to stand beside him, slipping her hand through his arm.

"It's good to have so many friends Father, don't

you think?" He just nodded his head. "You must eat something," Belle said. "Come along, try and eat a little." She led him over to the food and put a few bits on a plate for him, then stayed by his side while he ate.

Although she felt relieved when people started to leave, she knew she would have to stay for a while and tidy up and keep him company. Then she would have to go home and collect the children from her neighbour Sylvia and put them to bed. The next few weeks were going to be very hard for them all, but especially for her father.

★★★

Belle rang the doorbell and let herself in. Three months had passed since her mother's death and she was still coming to see her father every day.

"Hello Father." She called out "It's only me. "Where are you?" But she already knew. Most times he would be in his chair in the sitting room, the newspaper on his lap, unread and staring into space.

"I'll put the kettle on." Belle said and went straight out into the kitchen. The remains of yesterdays' meal sat on the draining board, only half eaten. Belle sighed and tipped the food into the bin. She was relieved to see the toaster had been used and there were several dirty mugs, so that was something. But he was getting terribly thin and Belle was very worried. He didn't seem able to shake off his grief and take up his life again. Once he would have helped to keep the house clean and always did the washing up. But now he just sat in his chair. The television was seldom on and the garden neglected. Bernard kept the lawn tidy but everywhere else was covered in weeds. Belle had decided to leave them, hoping it would spur her father to get outside in the fresh air and regain his interest, but to no avail.

She took the tea into her father with a cheese and pickle sandwich for his lunch. He looked up at her. "You're a good daughter, looking after your poor old father. I'm sorry dear, you do so much and I'm no use to anyone. It'll be a good job when I'm gone."

"Now don't start talking like that again. Don't you think I still need you, and so do the girls. They don't understand why you are so miserable. You used to play with them and now you hardly speak to them at all. Father, you must try and get back into doing what you used to do. Working in the garden and doing the housework. And what about church? You haven't been for three months and they are so concerned about you. I'm sorry to nag Father, but you must eat. Look at you." Belle picked up his hand and pushed his shirt sleeve up, "See how thin you are getting. I don't think you care about how worried we all are about you."

Then to Belle's dismay her father began to weep. "I can't help it dear. I just don't want to go on without your Mother." He wailed. Belle wrapped her arms around him and held him until he calmed down.

"I think I would like you to see the doctor. He may be able to give you something to help."

"No, I don't want to see him and if he gives me tablets I'll throw them in the bin."

Belle looked at him and thought, 'Well at least that suggestion livened him up a bit.'

She took the cups out to the kitchen and ran some hot water into the bowl.

"Do you want to come and dry up?" She called out.

"No, just leave them on the draining board. They'll dry on their own."

Belle sighed again. She checked the fridge to make sure her father had milk and bread and took a ready prepared meal from the freezer. She had got into the habit of preparing enough for him whilst cooking the evening meal at home. She could do no more. Thank goodness she was seeing Bubs on Saturday. It would be good to unburden herself and Bubs could always cheer her up.

"Oh Belle, you are having a tough time." Bubs hugged her "Let's go around and see him. I might be able to cheer him up, I've always got on well with him."

It was Saturday morning and Bernard was playing golf and not likely to be home till mid-afternoon. They called the children in and tidied them up.

"We're going round to see Grandpa with Aunty B---. Leonora." Belle grinned at Bubs "Oops, nearly called you by the wrong name."

They set off and arrived at 10.45. Belle rang the bell and then let them in with her key.

"Cooey, it's only me Father."

"I'm in here dear." He replied from the sitting room. Belle rolled her eyes and indicated the dirty dishes in the kitchen with a nod of her head.

"Hello Father, how are you today? I hope you don't mind but Leonora wanted to see you."

Leonora bent and kissed his cheek. "It's ages since I saw you. Are you keeping well?"

"Yes, thank you, very well. And how are my two favourite granddaughters? He held out his arms for a hug. Christine ran to him, but Rose hung back, unsure. He had virtually been ignoring them for the last three months and this was the result. Belle hoped her words of a few days ago had made him realise how upsetting his attitude was. Bubs chatted to him in her cheerful way while Belle tidied up and checked for washing. She quickly made a sandwich for his lunch and covered it with cling while she waited for the kettle to boil. Putting three cups of coffee on a tray with some biscuits, she carried it through to the sitting room. Then returned with a drink for the children. Her Father did seem a little more animated. Bubs was managing to cheer him up. They stayed for an hour, then Belle washed up the mugs and they made their way home.

"Thanks Bubs. I really think you've helped. You know, he's quite cheerful with Bernard, but dreadful with me."

"Maybe you're being a little impatient Belle. After all they were together a long time and he obviously adored her. It's only been three months remember and they say the first year is the worst."

"I know. If only he would eat and do a few bits around the house, I'd feel better. But he's getting so thin." She unlocked her front door and they went in. "Let's have some lunch and you can tell me your plans for Christmas."

Belle's hopes were dashed when her father's short return to near normality only lasted a couple of days, then he seemed to sink even further into depression. Belle managed to have a chat to his doctor but it seemed there was nothing he could do.

"If he refuses to take medication or even come for a chat, I can't force him," he said. "Just keep trying to get him to eat and hopefully he will rally."

But he didn't and after becoming increasingly thin and frail, almost exactly one year after losing his wife, he too, passed away. Belle was distraught. She felt an overwhelming sense of failure. She should have been able to help him. What had she done wrong?

At the funeral Belle wept in Bernard's arms and could not be consoled. Later at her former home she managed to calm herself and help to take care of the mourners, but when Rob and Philippa said goodbye the tears started again. The three of them stood together, their arms around one another for several minutes, then Belle took a deep breath and blew her nose.

"Thank you for coming, have a safe journey home. I'll be in touch in a couple of weeks." She stood at the door, waved goodbye, then turned back into the house.

CHAPTER 6

Belle desperately missed her parents. Their calm, loving presence a short distance away had always been there – until a year ago. Now there was only Bernard, who could be quiet and introverted, and Bubs. Thank heavens for Bubs. Always cheerful and full of honest common sense. She and the children kept Belle going. But now Rose had started nursery school and Christine was at 'big' school and Belle would be alone for much of the day. But there was one bright event on the horizon. Bubs was going to marry her boyfriend Derek in a few weeks and the wedding was to take place in the local church. Knowing that Belle was in low spirits, Bubs tried to include her in choosing outfits and making arrangements. But of course, this was mainly at weekends when Belle had the children for company and Bernard, when he wasn't golfing.

"Oh Bubs. I'm so bored and fed up. There's got to be more to life than housework surely."

"Well now that the children are at school and nursery why don't you get a little job?" Bubs suggested.

Belle sighed, "What could I do? It would have to tie in with school hours and term time. Any way, the chances are Bernard wouldn't agree. You know what an old-fashioned stick in the mud he is. I would dearly love another baby but I don't think he will agree to that either. You know what he's like. What Bernard says is law and if I give an opinion he gets angry."

Bubs looked alarmed. "He doesn't get violent, does he?"

"Of course not. But he is quite scary when he's angry, so he doesn't need to hit me or anything. I'll wait till he's had a successful game of golf then I'll bring up the subject of babies."

Bubs gave her a hug. "It'll all come right, I'm sure."

Bernard glared at Belle. "I thought we had already decided Isabelle. Two children are enough. Why are you bringing this up again?"

"That was years ago dear. You are so good with the girls I thought you might like to try for a boy."

"No Isabelle and that is my last word on the subject."

"Please don't get angry Bernard. You see it's different for a woman. We long for a baby to hold in our arms. It's in our nature. Won't you think about it?"

"Isabelle, you make it hard for me not to get angry. You will insist on arguing with me. Now please, I want to hear no more on the matter."

Belle's shoulders slumped. She knew she'd lost the argument. She'd known even before she had asked the question, but felt she must at least try. Now it was best to forget about it and enjoy the last-minute preparations for Bub's and Derek's wedding. It was now autumn and the weather was changeable.

Bubs was marrying in white but there were to be no bridesmaids. There were lots of small girls in the family, but who to choose? To avoid offending anyone they decided not to have any. As Bubs had said, "It will be less fuss and less expense."

Derek worked on various pipelines all over the British Isles, but Belle wasn't exactly sure what he did. All she knew was that he moved around and he could be away for weeks at a time. Bubs seemed to accept this. She enjoyed her job and her family would be nearby. For the next few years they were renting a flat. Then later Derek hoped he would be given a desk job at the head office in Suffolk, then they could buy a house and think about starting a family. Belle didn't like to think about that. To have Bubs so far away didn't bear thinking about.

Belle had befriended the family next door, Sylvia and Roger and their two small children and often walked down to the school with them, but Bubs would always be special.

"So, what did Bernard say about another baby?" Bubs had popped round to see Belle while he was playing golf.

"What do you think? He got cross as always and I can tell you Bubs, he'll never change his mind. Oh I'm so fed up."

"Listen Belle, let's go into the city on the bus. The girls hardly ever go on a bus and they'll love it. A trip out and a look round the shops will cheer you up."

"Good idea Bubs. I've got some money saved, I might even buy myself something." She called the children, "Come along girls. Let me brush your hair. We're going for a ride on a bus."

An hour later found them on the top deck of a double-decker bus. The children could hardly sit still, they were so excited.

"Look Mummy, I can see in peoples' bedroom windows." Christine said.

"Mummy, Mummy we're so high up, but I'm not frightened." Rose squeaked.

"Shush girls, keep your voices down please, there's no need to shout." Belle admonished them.

However, the ride kept them amused and they were soon in the city.

Bubs and the girls waited outside the fitting room while Belle tried on some clothes in a cubicle. She had been persuaded by Bubs to try on an outfit displayed in the shop window. It was in denim blue, a colour which had always suited Belle with her fair hair. But there was a big problem. It included trousers and Bernard didn't like ladies in trousers. She looked at herself in the mirror. The trousers were classic straight leg and they fitted perfectly. The top was more a cardigan than a jacket, but very smart. Underneath, a pale floral, round necked top completed the ensemble. The mirror told her she looked good, if a little pale after an unhappy few weeks. As she stepped out of the cubicle, Bubs gasped.

"Belle, you look lovely. Oh, you must have it. Bernard can't fail to like you in it."

Belle snorted. "I wouldn't count on it Bubs." She couldn't say more with the children listening, but she wasn't hopeful. She paid at the till and the clothes were carefully folded and put in a carrier bag. Bubs bought herself some jeans and insisted on getting some tee shirts for the girls, ready for their summer holidays in Norfolk. They were quiet on the bus going home, being tired now, after all the excitement. Belle and Bubs chatted to them hoping to keep them awake.

"How about fish and chips tonight girls? Daddy likes them now and again and we do as well. Do you like them Aunty Leonora?"

They got off the bus and made a slight detour to pick up the food, which Bubs carried. Rose was very tired and Belle carried her. They were glad to get home. Bernard was home and sitting in the kitchen with a cup of tea and his newspaper. He looked up and smiled as they all trooped in. Belle had left him a note so he wouldn't worry about where they were. Rose immediately climbed on his lap and put her thumb in. "I'm tired Daddy."

"I bet you are dear. Have you had a nice day?"

"Yes Daddy, and Aunty Leonora bought us a tee shirt for our holiday and we've got fish and chips."

'Don't say anything about trousers.' Belle silently prayed. She would wait until Bubs had gone home and the children were in bed before she tried them on. She quickly warmed the plates with the water left in the kettle and dished up.

"Did you have a good game Bernard?"

"Yes, I beat George by quite a few shots. Poor George, I felt quite sorry for him. Then we had a bacon sandwich in the clubhouse. I've cut the grass as well."

Belle thought 'Good, he's in a happy mood'. She said out loud "Yes the lawn looks lovely dear, I noticed as we came in. I think we'll all sleep well tonight."

Belle and the children waved goodbye to Bubs an hour later, then the girls were bathed and tucked up in bed. Bernard read them a story while Belle washed up. She put the clean plates away, took a deep breath and pinned a smile on her face. Bernard came into the kitchen.

"They are asleep already. They must have been exhausted."

"I'll just make us a coffee dear, then I'll show you the children's tee-shirts and what I bought for myself. It's a little different but I'm sure you'll like it."

She slipped the new outfit on and combed her hair, then walked slowly and nervously back downstairs. There was complete silence as she walked into the lounge. For a split second she thought she saw admiration in Bernard's eyes, then his face hardened.

"Trousers? Why have you bought those? You know perfectly well my feelings about women in trousers." He glared at her "Take them off and return them on Monday."

"Yes dear, alright, I'm sorry. They are such a pretty colour I thought you wouldn't mind."

"It doesn't matter what colour they are." Bernard snapped. "Just do as I say and take them back on Monday."

"Can I keep the cardigan dear?"

"Yes, the cardigan is fine, but return that top as well. It's too gaudy."

Despite Belle's efforts not to argue, this was just too much. "Gaudy Bernard. It's pastel shades. How can it be gaudy?"

Then she instantly regretted speaking as she watched his face darken. She hastily said,

"All right dear, please don't get angry. I'll return the top as well." She ran back up the stairs and took them off, folded them carefully and put them back in the bag with the receipt. They were left on the top shelf of her wardrobe ready to be returned. All the time she was talking to herself

"Don't argue with him, it's not worth it. Just do everything he says and try and stay cheerful for the sake of the children. It's going to be a long, long time before you can walk away from him so just try and accept things."

She ran downstairs and into the lounge, and with a bright smile said,

"So how is George? Is he keeping well?"

***

It was a week before she managed to speak to Bubs. With Bernard playing golf again and the children watching TV, Belle dialled her number.

"So, what did Bernard think of your clothes then? I'm longing to know."

"Well he let me keep the cardigan, but I had to take the trousers and the top back on Monday."

"You're kidding! Having to return the trousers, that doesn't surprise me. But what was wrong with the top?"

"He said it was too gaudy Bubs."

"But that's ridiculous."

Belle sighed "Look, I've just got to do as he says or my life's not worth living. He gets so angry if I disobey him."

"I'm sorry to say this Belle, but what a horrible man you married."

"I know, but there's nothing I can do about it. But listen Bubs, when I first walked into the lounge with the outfit on, I was sure he liked me in it before he remembered he disapproved of trousers. I know I looked good. I actually think he's worried that other men might fancy me. I think he's more unsure of himself than he'd like us to believe. There's no doubt if he thought another man was looking at me he'd be as jealous as anything. It made me feel better in a funny sort of way. Can you understand Bubs?"

"Well not really, but if it makes you feel better then I'm glad."

She changed the subject by asking about the girls. Belle was able to tell her they were very well and loved their tee shirts. Even Bernard seemed to like them and said it was very kind of Bubs.

CHAPTER 7

Belle waited at the school gates with the other mothers, the school doors opened and the children erupted into the playground. As usual Christine was one of the first ones out. She hurtled across and flung herself at Belle.

"I got a star for my drawing Mummy."

"Let me see sweetheart. Oh that's very good. Well done." She waited for Christine to at least give a clue as to what it was. She could see it was an animal, but a sheep or a dog, she wasn't sure.

"We could draw any animal, so I drawed a cow. See Mummy, that's where the milk comes from."

Belle suppressed a laugh. "Yes, I can see. What else have you been doing today? Ah, here's Rose at last. Come on slowcoach. Why is Christine always first out and you are always last?"

"I've got lots of friends to say goodbye to." Rose informed her.

Belle took their hands and they walked home. She hung their coats up and gave them a biscuit and a drink and then put the kettle on for a cup of tea. Almost at once the doorbell rang.

"I wonder who that is at the front door?" Belle said.

But the girls had peeped through the front window and they knew.

"Uncle Rob, it's Uncle Rob." They chorused and ran to open the door.

"Let Uncle Rob get in the door, you two. Sorry Rob, they do like to see you." She kissed him lightly on the cheek.

"The kettles on, come on through."

Ten minutes later Rob was sipping a cup of tea with a little girl on each knee.

"Now sit still girls, this tea is hot and I don't want to scald you."

"So Rob, how's Philippa? She was a bit off colour the last time I saw you?"

Rob frowned, "She's still not right I'm afraid. But then she's never been robust and she still pines for a baby, but I somehow don't think that's going to happen now. We've been trying for four or five years with no luck so far."

Belle looked at him sympathetically.

"Poor Philippa. Has she been to the doctor about feeling unwell?"

"Yes, he's given her a tonic. But she's been taking it for nearly two weeks and doesn't seem any better. I'm really worried about her Belle."

"The tonic will soon begin to work Rob, I'm sure. Then when she's feeling better you must come over for the day. Bernard would like to see you I know."

Rob put down his empty mug, "Thanks Belle, I must be off home now and see how she's been today." He hugged the two little girls and kissed Belle, then made for the door.

"Take care Rob and don't forget to give me a ring."

She returned to the kitchen and began to prepare the evening meal while the children watched the TV. Try as she might she could not dispel worrying thoughts about Philippa. Rob was right. She had always looked fragile and delicate. Perhaps it was just as well that babies hadn't come along. It might have been too much for her. Belle gave herself a mental shake and told herself not to be gloomy. It was probably just a virus.

Later that evening when the children were in bed, Belle told Bernard about Rob's visit and his worries about Philippa. They decided to leave it a couple of weeks and then if Rob didn't ring they would ring him. And that is what happened. Belle listened and thought Bernard sounded rather serious and her heart sank. When he finally came off the phone he told Belle that Philippa was much the same and they had an appointment at the hospital. Rob would keep them informed. He said Philippa was off work but not taking phone calls and certainly not well enough to visit.

The weeks went by and Rob didn't call to let them know the result of the hospital tests, and seldom answered the phone when people rang him. He told Bernard on one rare occasion when he did respond that he no longer did the Oxford area for his company, but he was now covering Wiltshire and Gloucestershire. This was because Philippa was no better and he was able to be nearer. Then more weeks went by with no news and by now both Belle and Bernard were extremely worried.

Belle dropped the children off at school, picked up some bread from the corner shop and made her way home. The postman had been and she threw the letters onto the kitchen table while she hung her coat up. Three letters sat on the table. One was the electricity bill, another was a 'begging' letter and the third was addressed to them both. The handwriting looked familiar but she wasn't sure who's it was. She slit it open and took out the two sheets of paper, glancing at the bottom to see who it was from, then her hand went to her heart. It was from Rob.

Dear Bernard and Isabelle.

I am afraid I have some very sad news for you. I have lost my darling Philippa and I am devastated, as you can imagine. I cannot believe that I will never see her again. She was the love of my life and such a wonderful woman. We had known for some time that her illness was terminal, but it was her wish that nobody should be told. I have been at home with her for the last two months and with professional help her last few weeks were made as comfortable and peaceful as possible. I actually resigned from my job and didn't change areas as I told you. I just had to be with her. I'm sure you can understand that. The details of the funeral are enclosed and I hope to see you there.

Fondest regards
Rob.

"Oh no, poor Philippa." Belle put her hand over her mouth and struggled not to cry. Tears would come later when the children were in bed. Poor Rob, he would be heartbroken. Philippa had been so young, only thirty-one. 'Why is life so horrible'? Belle thought. First her mother, then a year later her father, now Philippa. Bernard would do his best to comfort her tonight, but he would be upset as well.

After the funeral Rob went home and for six weeks they heard nothing from him. Then a short letter arrived.

Dear Bernard and Isabelle

I'm sorry you haven't heard from me sooner, but I couldn't bear to be in the house alone, and just had to get away. I have rented a cottage in the Shetland Islands and I am trying to come to terms with losing my Philippa. I'm exploring the islands and doing lots of walking and the exercise and fresh air are helping me to sleep. But funds will not last forever and in a few weeks' I will be returning home. My old company may take me back, otherwise I will be looking for a job. I will contact you as soon as I am home.

Fondest regards
Rob.

Three weeks later Rob returned and they arranged to meet him one evening. Sylvia babysat and they drove to the pub where they had met on several occasions before. As they walked in they looked around for Rob but couldn't see him. It wasn't until a man sitting in the corner raised his hand that they recognised him. They were shocked and Belle gave an involuntary gasp. Gone was the round faced, smiley Rob. In his place, a thin gaunt man looking twenty years older. He stood up to greet them and Bernard shook his hand and hung on to it for a moment or two. Belle just had to hug him close and to her annoyance felt tears running down her cheeks. She brushed them away and took a deep breath. They all seemed at a loss and were unable to find the right words. Rob was the first to speak.

"I know I look dreadful but I've been off my food."

"But Rob, you must eat." Belle said, "Please don't do what my father did." Her voice wobbled and she couldn't continue.

"Come on old chap, Isabelle's right, you must take care of yourself."

Belle took Rob's hand "Would Philippa want you to neglect yourself like this?"

Rob looked down at his empty glass. "She made me promise to stay healthy." He gave a weak smile. "She said she would be looking down on me to make sure I kept my word, but it's been so hard."

"Well, we'll start right now." Bernard picked up the menu's and handed one to Rob. "The ham, egg and chips sounds nice. That's what I'm having. How about you Rob?"

Rob sighed. "I'll have the curry and I promise I'll try and eat it all."

When the food came, Belle chatted about the children, trying to raise Rob's spirits and to a degree it worked. He forgot for a while his grief and loneliness and listened to Belle and the children's antics and the curry disappeared. Belle didn't want a dessert but Bernard persuaded Rob to share a cheese board with him. Belle found herself relaxing as Rob finished the food and began to tell them about his cottage in the Shetlands and the places he had visited.

"It was just what I needed. Solitude and peace. Nobody bothered me and I could do whatever I wanted. If the weather was bad I would stay in the cottage and read or watch TV. But that didn't happen very often which was just as well, because I just got depressed. I needed to get out as much as possible."

Belle nodded slowly. "I understand Rob. I know what you mean." She ignored the look Bernard gave her and changed the subject. "Don't forget Rob, if you get your old job back, there's always a cup of tea when you do your Oxford calls."

Rob did get his job back and soon began calling in again. Belle would always have some of his favourite biscuits in the tin and would send him off with some homemade cakes in an effort to make him put some of the weight back on. He would also come over for the day every few weeks, usually on a Sunday and Belle would cook him food she knew he liked. Gradually he looked better and would smile more often, but Belle felt he would never really get over losing Philippa.

CHAPTER 8

"I think it's time you had a car Isabelle. I don't suppose you will argue about that will you? I've booked some lessons and you start next week."

Belle looked at him stunned. As usual there had been no discussion about it. What if she didn't want to drive? What if she was scared? This side of Bernard's character she was finding increasingly depressing and irritating. But she knew, unless she had a good reason, it was prudent not to disagree. Bernard looked at her expression and sighed.

"What's wrong now? Don't you want your own car? I can assure you that I can afford it otherwise I would not have gone ahead."

"I'm just rather surprised Bernard. You've never mentioned it before. But yes, I'm willing to try. It would be very useful for the grocery shopping. I could do it once a week instead of several times and I won't have to carry heavy bags home."

"Well that's alright then. That's settled." Bernard returned to his newspaper.

Belle dropped the children off at school, then walked the long way home so that she went past the local garage. She wandered up and down the second-hand cars until she saw a bright red Mini and knew that was what she wanted. She told the eager salesman that she could do nothing without her husband and made her way home. Suddenly, she was excited about having her own car.

Later Belle placed Bernard's after dinner coffee on the table beside him.

"I saw a lovely little car today dear. I fell in love with it. It's a Mini. Do you like them?"

Bernard rustled his paper impatiently. "There's no need for you to worry about that. I've put a deposit on a Ford Anglia and that will be much more suitable for you. I know how you women worry about colour so I can tell you it's a rather nice dark blue. I'm picking it up in a couple of weeks." He retreated behind the paper again.

Suddenly, Belle's patience ran out. "So yet again Bernard, you give no thought to what I might like. It doesn't matter what we're talking about does it? Food, holidays, clothes, houses and now my first car. I don't get a say in anything. I'm treated like a servant in Victorian times. Just do as your told and be grateful. That's it isn't it? Well I'm sick of it Bernard. I've had enough."

She stormed from the room and ran upstairs. The girls were asleep thankfully. She went into the bathroom and locked the door, flopping down on the edge of the bath and bursting into tears. She soon dried her eyes though. She must be strong and not let Bernard see her behave like a weak little woman. She sat there for an hour before she heard him come up the stairs. He tapped lightly on the door.

"Isabelle, are you alright?"

She remained perfectly still and silent. Let him stew for a bit. It might do him good.

"Isabelle dear, please answer me. Come along, unlock the door." He paused and waited a few moments. "Isabelle, if you don't let me know you are alright, I shall have to force the door and I don't want to frighten the children."

Belle unlocked and opened the door and walked past her husband, head held high and walked downstairs to the kitchen. She put the kettle on to make herself a fresh cup of coffee. Bernard watched her and seemed at a loss. She went through to the sitting room and retrieved her cold cup of coffee and threw it down the sink. Although she would rather have thrown it over Bernard! She washed the cup and made herself another coffee. She completely ignored Bernard, who seemed to be following her around. She took it through to the other room and sat in an armchair. Normally she would have sat beside him on the settee. A magazine was on the arm of the chair. Picking it up she flipped through the pages until she came to the comic strips. She gave quite a good performance of being amused, then turned to another page and started reading an article, sipping her coffee from time to time. She was aware that Bernard glanced at her occasionally but behaved as though he wasn't there.

Finally, Bernard cleared his throat nervously. "Err, I think we have to talk dear."

Belle jumped. "Gosh Bernard, I'd forgotten you were there." She hadn't of course. "What do you want to talk about? Have you organised some more of my life? Are you going to tell me what I must wear tomorrow? Or maybe what I should cook tomorrow evening? I await my orders."

Bernard reached out towards her, but his hand dropped as she flinched away from him.

"I know I probably overstep the mark dear, but it's just the way I am I'm afraid."

"There's no probably about it Bernard. You do overstep the mark, I must have some say in things. I refuse to be treated like a lackey any more. I don't want our marriage to deteriorate into a succession of arguments and cold silences. But I fear that that's the way it's going. You seem to have forgotten I'm on medication for depression. Don't you care at all?"

"Of course I care darling girl. It's just my way. I don't seem to be able to help myself. Come along dearest, let's go to bed. I need to show you how much I love you."

"If you think I'm in the mood for that, you are seriously mistaken Bernard." Belle snapped at him.

"Don't you love me anymore?" He asked.

It was strange to hear Bernard talking in that pathetic way, but at the same time, rather gratifying.

"I don't know how I feel any more Bernard, we'll just have to plod on and see how things work out."

CHAPTER 9

Belle adjusted Bub's headdress. "Is that alright, or do you want it more towards the back?"

"No, it's perfect where it is thanks."

Belle put two hairgrips in to hold it firmly in place, making sure they were hidden behind the flowers and lace.

"I don't think I have ever seen you look so lovely Bubs, and you're so calm. Aren't you nervous at all?"

"Well, a little, but I'm so looking forward to being married to my Derek."

Bubs had no idea how awful the last few weeks had been for Belle, it wouldn't have been right to unburden herself on Bub's special day. She found that acting cheerful and normal was becoming easier. The wedding was at half past three, followed by a reception at the community centre. Then in the evening the tables would be pushed back and there would be a disco and dancing. Belle's heart gave a lurch when she thought about what she had planned.

As ever, Bernard, despite his sweet talking, had insisted on her buying a dark grey suit for the wedding.

"But it looks as though I'm going to a funeral, not a wedding."

But of course, she was wasting her breath. He picked out a simple silk blouse to go underneath. Quite nice but not exactly exciting. Belle had gone back to the shops on her own and bought a deep pink lacy top. It had a scoop neck and three-quarter length sleeves. It looked lovely on. The colour suited her and it did wonders for the suit. Belle's plan was to change into it before the disco and hope Bernard wouldn't notice it under her suit jacket.

The wedding went off well and a happy bride and groom made their way to the hall where they would greet the guests. The tables had been covered with cloths and a small vase placed in the middle with three carnations in each. Trestle tables across one end were laid out in a buffet style, with a good selection of food, plates, cutlery and napkins. Each of the covered tables had place names, so everyone knew where to sit. After milling around for a few minutes, peace was restored. The food was delicious, the speeches went well, then everyone just mingled, chatting and laughing. Belle managed to forget about the pink top and the wrath of Bernard when he saw it, and relaxed and enjoyed herself. Although Bernard claimed not to like Bubs, he did like Derek and the two of them chatted for some time. The children were enjoying themselves too, running around with other children and looking very pretty in their new party dresses. Christine in blue and Rose in pink. But at seven o'clock it was time to take them home, get them ready for bed and calm them down with a story.

Sylvia had kindly agreed to come around and babysit so that Bernard and Belle could return for the disco later.

"Come along Christine, calm down, you're soaking the bathroom and Mummy. It's a good job I changed out of my best suit." Belle gave her daughter a stern look, then when this failed, lifted her out of the bath and wrapped a towel round her.

"Come along, you too Rose. Time to get dried and into bed for a story."

Rose, always the most obliging, allowed herself to be dealt with. Ten minutes later, teeth brushed and in their pyjamas, the girls were tucked up in bed. Belle glanced at her watch. They certainly wouldn't be there for eight o'clock when the disco started, but maybe eight thirty. As she read to the children she was aware that Bernard was tidying the bathroom before using it himself. Belle made a mental note to thank him several times to put him in a good humour. They kissed the girls' goodnight and pulled the door up. Bernard finished getting ready and went downstairs for a whiskey.

Heart thumping, Belle took off her everyday clothes and put on the suit skirt. Then put on the pink lace top with the pearls she had worn earlier. Lastly the suit jacket which, when fastened completely, hid the top. Then she opened her drawer in the dressing table and took out a pink lipstick, slipping it into her handbag. With a last peep at the children, who were already fast asleep, she ran downstairs.

"Just popping next door dear, to let Sylvia know we are ready."

Belle went into the ladies' cloakroom to leave her jacket and put a little lipstick on. She admired herself in the mirror, took a deep breath and headed for the main room, where already music was beginning to thump out. As she left the cloakroom she found herself walking alongside Bub's mother.

"Oh Mrs. Thomas, doesn't Leonora look gorgeous, and you look very nice too."

"Well Isabelle, I have to say dear, it's lovely to see you in something so pretty. We don't see you often enough in cheerful colours."

"No well, err—you see, Bernard doesn't like me in colours, only things like navy, beige and grey." Belle pointed to her skirt. "He chose my suit."

"But that doesn't seem right Isabelle."

"Oh, please don't say anything, Bernard would be so cross. Please come to the bar with me, I need some Dutch courage."

Belle had already seen Bernard looking in her direction and she didn't like what she saw on his face. She gave him a smile and a cheery wave across the room, then virtually dragged Mrs. Thomas to the bar.

"A glass of white wine for me please. What would you like?" She asked Bub's mother. The barmaid pushed a glass of wine towards Belle and stood waiting for Mrs. Thomas to make up her mind. Belle picked up her glass and swallowed several big gulps of wine. She realised her hands were shaking and she gave herself a mental reprimand. She was behaving like an alcoholic. Gulping down the wine? Shaky hands? Anyway, what could Bernard do or say here, in a room full of people? He was far too civilised to make a scene and hopefully by the time they got home he would have calmed down. They wandered over to Bernard and Belle took his arm and gave it a little squeeze.

"Have you got a drink dear?"

"Yes, I have, thank you." He looked at Bub's mother. "Everything is going well Mrs. Thomas. You must be pleased."

"Oh I am. I've enjoyed all the planning, but it is a bit of a worry. We've been so glad of a helping hand from your lovely wife. Don't you think she looks lovely today? I told her she should wear colours more often, but then one has to be more practical with children around. Now excuse me please. As mother of the bride I must mingle."

She disappeared amongst the guests and at that moment the band started to play a slow number.

"Shall we have a dance Bernard?"

"Well I suppose we'd better. Put your drink down Isabelle."

Belle turned towards a side table, but before putting the glass down, she emptied it. Bernard put an arm across her back and took her hand. They moved onto the dance floor sedately.

"You finished that wine rather quickly Isabelle. Not at all in a ladylike manner."

"Well you see Bernard, that's your fault I'm afraid."

"How can it be my fault? What are you talking about?"

"I'm frightened dear, if we were at home you would have lost your temper with me by now. I expect that will all come later. So, I drank the wine quickly to give me courage."

Emboldened by the wine and the people around, and her voice covered partly by the music, Belle continued. "It's a terrible thing, don't you think, to be frightened of one's husband. But don't worry, the pretty pink top that people have been admiring will be put in a bag and taken to the charity shop on Monday. How does that suit you?"

She looked up at Bernard defiantly. He seemed to be lost for words.

"Err, well—um, we'll discuss it when we get home."

'I bet we will'. thought Belle, then made up her mind she was going to enjoy the rest of the evening.

Bernard used his key to let themselves in. Sylvia came to the lounge door and said.

"Hello, have you had a good evening?"

"It's been great." Said Belle, "I haven't danced so much for years, but I'm very tired now. How have the girls been?"

"Not a peep out of them all evening. I've been up and checked them half a dozen times and they have hardly moved."

"Well I think they were exhausted from the wedding and running around at the reception, although they are usually good at night anyway. We're very grateful to you Sylvia. You must let me know when I can return the favour."

Bernard reached in his pocket and took out his wallet.

"Here Sylvia, buy something for your children." He handed Sylvia a five pound note.

"Thank you, Bernard. That's very kind but you needn't have bothered. We babysit for each other don't we?" However, she slipped the money in her pocket and with a smile, headed for the door. As soon as she had gone, Belle started to chat, hoping to delay the reprimand that was surely coming her way.

"I've got my second driving lesson on Monday dear. I'm really looking forward to it. I'm hoping I won't be so nervous this time."

But it was no good, Bernard was going to have his say. "So, Isabelle, you went behind my back and bought something you knew I wouldn't approve of. You come into the hall looking like a trollop and spend the evening behaving like one."

"What do you mean? This top is perfectly respectable. It covers all the bits that should be covered, and you can't see anything through it. And how dare you say I behaved like a trollop. You go too far Bernard."

His answer was to grip her arms painfully and thrust his face several inches from hers.

"And you have once again gone against my wishes. I am very angry with you." He shook her as he was speaking, and Belle was suddenly frightened. She thought he was actually going to hit her. For a few minutes she stared up at him, horrified. Then her head dropped, and her body slumped. What was the use. He wouldn't change. He couldn't change. Belle was a peaceable person. The thought of continuing arguments for the rest of her life was more than she could bear. She had tried that and it didn't work. She had tried gentle persuasion and that didn't work either. She just had to accept things and do as she was told. She must think about the positives of their marriage, Bernard was a hard worker and generous. He was a good father and usually found time to amuse their daughters, reading or playing with them. Belle longed for peace and knew she must learn to ignore the frustrations of being married to him.

She looked up at him. "I'm sorry Bernard. I'll try and be a better wife. Please dear, you're hurting me."

Abruptly Bernard let go of her arms. "I'm sorry too. I didn't want to hurt you. You just make me so angry. You will do as you said then, and take this garment into the charity shop."

"Yes, I'll do it on Monday morning after I take the children to school."

"Come along then, let's get to bed. I'm sure we are both tired. It's been a long day."

Belle pulled up neatly outside her home, put the brake on and switched off the engine.

"Very good Mrs, Johnson. You're coming along nicely. You have the makings of a good driver."

"Really. How can you tell after just four lessons?"

"It's your character, if you don't mind me saying so. You are calm, and you concentrate well. And I think you are beginning to enjoy it."

"Yes I am." Belle looked at her elderly instructor. "You remind me of my late father and I think that helps me."

"Well I'll see you again next week and we'll try a few more manoeuvres." Belle paid him and got out of the car, giving him a wave as he drove off.

"Mr. James is very pleased with me." Belle told Bernard later. "And I'm hardly nervous at all now."

"That's good dear. Put in for your test as soon as he thinks you're ready. Have a few more lessons, then perhaps Sylvia could have the children and we'll go out in your own car. What would you think to that?"

"Oh Bernard, that would be wonderful."

Over the last few weeks, bridges had been mended and they were getting on much better, although Belle wasn't sure that she still loved him. But she liked and respected him, so that was something.

★★★

A month later Belle applied for a driving test and three weeks after that, took her test and passed at the first attempt. Hardly able to believe it, she ran indoors, grabbed her keys and went for a drive. She had an hour before the girls came out of school. Plenty of time for a little drive around the quieter roads before taking the car back and parking it on the drive. Then she could walk with Sylvia to pick up the girls.

"Gosh, fancy passing first time. You are clever." Was Sylvia's reaction.

Belle had to agree with her. What she didn't tell her, or Bernard later, was the wonderful sense of freedom she felt. Just driving off, wherever she wished, felt so good. Her doctor had said 'When you feel down, go for a walk. It will help'. This proved to be the case and driving off in the car had the same effect. Belle felt that soon she would be able to come off all medication.

Bernard came in the front door and closed it behind him. Both girls immediately forgot about their television programme and hurtled out to greet him. Tired though he was, he always enjoyed these moments. Belle glanced out into the hall, a smile on her face. She put the saucepan of potatoes on the hob ready to cook a little later and went out to say hello to Bernard. He hung his coat up and went through to the lounge.

"Do you want tea dear, or are you going to have a drink?"

"I'll just have tea Isabelle please. I'll have a drink later. In fact, we'll both have a drink. I've had some good news today. I'll tell you about it later."

Belle had to be satisfied with that. Probably a rise and

she knew that would mean a little more housekeeping money for her. The girls were growing fast and eating more, so a rise would be handy.

It was eight o'clock, the girls were in bed and asleep, the washing up was done and now they were sitting down, each with a glass of wine in their hands.

"Do tell me your news Bernard. I'm longing to know what it is."

"Well dear, do you remember old Mr. Matthews, one of the founders of the company? Do you recall where we left the car before we went on our honeymoon? That's where he still lives, at the moment. Well he is retiring at last, on his 70th birthday in three months' time. I've been offered a junior partnership when he goes and obviously I've accepted."

"Well done Bernard. I'm so proud of you." Belle exclaimed.

"That will mean quite a big increase in my salary, so I thought we should move to a bigger house. I'm sure the girls would like a room of their own, don't you think?"

Belle put her hands up to her face. "Gosh I can hardly take this in. How exciting. The girls will be thrilled."

Bernard took her hand. "I want you to like our new home, so we must look together. Actually, they are building down Forest Road, I thought we could have a look at the weekend."

"Surely that's the road Mr. Matthews lives in, isn't it?"

"Yes, but he's downsizing and moving away to be near his son."

The weekend couldn't come fast enough for Belle. She loved their first home but it really wasn't big enough now. Forest Road was a quiet road, with countryside nearby, ideal for walks.

The weekend arrived, and they set off in Bernard's car to view the show house.

The first thing Belle said was. "Gosh, isn't it big?"

The site was just into Forest Road. There had always been a small field on the left, mainly unused, with a hedge at the rear and more fields beyond. All eight houses were detached with four bedrooms and a double garage on one side. There was a small garden at the front about fifteen feet deep and at the back the plot must have been about seventy feet. Belle and the girls fell silent as they stood and looked.

"Come on." Bernard said, "Let's look over the show house.

They greeted the gentleman in charge and he invited them to wander around at their leisure and then come back for a chat. The room he was sitting in was obviously the lounge and it was a good size. Leading off from it to the rear was a dining room. Also at the rear a generous kitchen. After a thorough look round they went back into the hall, which was also a good size and up the stairs. Three of the bedrooms were doubles and one had an en-suite. Then a smaller bedroom, which could be used as an office. Belle stood looking out over the rear garden. As yet, there were no dividing fences, but it was plain to see that it was three or four times the size of their present garden.

"Oh Bernard, it's all just wonderful, but it must be terribly expensive."

"I don't want you to worry about that. I may have to use some of my savings until I get my rise, but the house won't be ready before then anyway. Also, don't forget, we have to sell our house as well. Anyway, I have enough to give them a holding deposit. So dear, you like it don't you?"

"I love it." Belle turned to the girls, "What do you think? Do you like it too?"

Christine nodded enthusiastically but Rose seemed unsure. She didn't like change.

"You'll have your very own bedroom Rose and you'll still be going to the same school where your friends are."

★★★

As always Bernard dealt with everything in his usual efficient way. The house they had settled on was the third in from the main road. It would not be finished for several months so money was not an issue. Belle had been allowed to decide on the kitchen colours and cupboards. Half the rear garden was to be put down to lawn and most of the front too. Their home quickly sold and one lovely day in May, they moved in. Sylvia had been kind enough to collect the children from school, and so good progress with the move had been made.

The removal men put everything in the rooms where they belonged and roughly in the right positions, so there was very little heavy work to do. Belle asked them to sort the girls' bedrooms out first so that she could make up their beds and put as many of their familiar things around as possible. With their dolls and teddies on the beds it all looked good, if a little bare. Belle had previously suggested to Christine that it would be a good idea if Rose was in the bedroom closest to Mummy and Daddy because she might be a little bit frightened in a strange bedroom. Feeling very grown up, Christine had agreed. When Belle had made the men a cup of tea she drove round to Sylvia's and picked up the girls. It was 3.30 pm. and would give them a few hours to get used to the house before bedtime.

"Right, now girls, before we go in I must ask you to keep out of the removal men's way. They have almost finished, then you can have a good look round."

"Where shall we go then Mummy?" asked Christine.

"Your bedrooms are ready and some of your toys are there for you to play with."

The girls stepped into the house, wide-eyed and silent. Rose hung on to Belle's hand while her big sister ran up the stairs. Bernard was in the main bedroom putting the bed together.

"Hello Christine, come and give your daddy a hug."

Christine obliged but soon wriggled away to look at her bedroom. The first thing she saw was a sign hanging on the door. 'CHRISTINES BEDROOM' it said. She looked at it, gave an excited little squeak and then ran into her room. Belle was behind her and watched as she studied everything and then went to look out of the window.

"How do you like it darling?"

"It's lovely mummy, but where's my wardrobe?"

"We'll get you one soon. You must share with Rose for a few weeks, like you did before. The old wardrobe is in Rose's room. Shall we go and have a look now."

They walked next door where a sign on the door announced. 'ROSES BEDROOM'. Rose still had a tight hold of Belle's hand and was very quiet.

"Look sweetheart, your own bed and your teddies are waiting for you. You can see they love it already. Look how they are smiling."

Rose found her tongue. "They always smile Mummy, you are silly." She giggled, and to Belle's relief, let go of her hand and jumped on the bed. Then looking at Belle, she gave a huge smile and said." I like it Mummy."

At that moment Bernard came in looking very woeful. "Don't I get a hug then Rose?"

Rose rushed at him and leapt into his arms giving him a big kiss on the cheek.

"Now you two, Mummy and I are going to sort out our bedroom. It's just over there so play nicely, and we won't be long."

Bernard and Belle sat on the settee, a cup of coffee on the table beside them. The girls were in bed and asleep, their doors open a little way and a night light already glowing on the landing. Packing cases and cardboard boxes were still piled up in all the downstairs rooms, but the important things like food, were put away. Laying on the working top were the wrappings from fish and chips and four dirty plates and a bowlful of used mugs.

"Well I think that all went well, don't you Isabelle? But I'm tired now and I bet you are too. Thank goodness it's Friday and we've got the weekend." He finished his coffee and put the cup back in the saucer. Within a few minutes he had dropped off to sleep.

By the end of the weekend everything was sorted out apart from a few boxes in the spare room. There was no furniture in there and more was needed in the girls' rooms. Downstairs also needed more items. The tiny table they had used daily in their former home looked rather lost in the new dining room.

"We may as well have that table in the kitchen." Bernard said. "I don't know when we'll be able to get a proper dining room suite." He sighed. "Thank goodness my salary goes up next month."

Without thinking what his reaction might be, Belle said." Why don't I try and get a job dear? I know I can't earn much but it might help." Then she knew she'd said the wrong thing.

Bernard frowned "Certainly not. I'm not having my wife going out to work."

"But Bernard, lots of women work and I would make sure I am always here for you and the children."

"No Isabelle, it's not necessary and if you always want to be here for the children, what sort of job could you do? Playground supervisor? You would earn a pittance. If you want to get out of the house, go for a walk. Really Isabelle, I thought with a bigger house and a large garden to potter in, you would be satisfied. I had hoped you would stop complaining about being bored now we are here, but it seems not."

"Oh Bernard, that's not fair. I'm not complaining. I simply asked if I should get a job, but the answer is obviously no, so I won't mention it again."

CHAPTER 10

Belle missed Sylvia and Michael, but the neighbours on one side were friendly and although much older, Belle and Bernard got on well with them. James and Avril were in their fifties with three grown up children and two grandchildren. James was a doctor at the hospital in the city and Avril worked for a local charity three mornings a week. Belle would often have a cup of coffee with Avril when she wasn't working. Sometimes in one of their homes and sometimes out at the local café. Belle really enjoyed these outings. Just to get out of the house and enjoy adult conversation was good.

Bubs still came around to see her sometimes on a Saturday. But if Derek was home these visits were obviously curtailed. One Saturday Bubs announced that Derek had been given a desk job and would not be going away nearly so much.

"This means we will be able to buy our first home." Bubs said excitedly, "I'm so looking forward to it---except."

"Except what Bubs. It all sounds great to me."

"Yes, but I shall worry about you." Bubs took her hand "I know how down you feel sometimes and I won't be around to cheer you up."

"Don't worry about me." Belle tried to reassure her. "Things are not bad at the moment, and Avril is very nice. I wonder Bubs, if Bernard would let you come for the weekend now and again if Derek has to go away."

"I doubt it Belle. I know what he thinks of me."

"Well I'll leave it till you're settled in Suffolk then broach the subject. A good time to ask is when he's had a successful morning at golf and don't forget we've got a spare room now."

★★★

"What's the matter old girl? You seem rather down in the mouth today"

It was Saturday evening and Bernard had won at golf again and was affable. Belle took a deep breath. Oh, why was it so hard to ask Bernard anything? She could almost guarantee the answer would be NO, whatever the question.

"Bub—err, Leonora came around this morning, like she often does, and she had some news for me."

"Bad news was it dear?"

"Well good news for her but not for me. She's going to be moving to Suffolk in a few months." Belle's voice shook, "And I'm going to miss her so much."

"Does that mean Derek's got the promotion he was after?"

"Yes, it does and I'm pleased for them. They will have more time together and I think Leonora would like to start a family. She's so good with our girls and they adore her. I think she'll make a wonderful mother."

"Yes, I'm sure she will. I don't want to be unkind dear, but this could be a good time to let your friendship end. You know how I feel about her." Then he gasped as Belle leapt up and shouted.

"Never. Never. Never Bernard. Bubs will always be my friend no matter where she moves to. It could be Timbuktu, but she would still be my friend."

Then she burst into noisy weeping. Bernard got up and put his arms around her.

"Hush now, you'll wake the girls. Come on now, calm yourself. I can see I said the wrong thing."

He gave her a tissue, "Dry your eyes now and sit down. Let's talk about it and see if we can put things right."

Even in her distressed state Belle realised that Bernard was in an exceptionally good mood so decided to put her idea to him. She blew her nose and began.

"I'm sorry for making such a fuss Bernard dear." She wiped her eyes and crossed her fingers, "What would you say if Leonora were to visit now and again? I thought she could drive here on a Saturday morning, sleep in the spare room and go home Sunday. She wouldn't have that horrible journey both ways then. Well not on the same day anyway. Oh, please say yes Bernard."

She waited as Bernard gave it some thought. He glanced at her and took in the red eyes and the anxious expression. Then he patted her arm.

"I can see it means a lot to you my dear, so I will agree."

"Oh, thank you Bernard. That's so kind of you." She could hardly believe she had won a battle.

CHAPTER 11

Bernard kept his word and Bubs was allowed to visit after she had moved to Suffolk. That was two years ago, and Bubs had been a number of times. Derek still went away occasionally and usually for a couple of weeks, so Bubs would come then. She loved her new home and job and seemed content. Then she rang Belle one Saturday morning.

"Guess what Belle, I'm going to have a baby."

Belle squeaked with excitement. "Oh, I just wish you lived closer. I'm going to miss so much."

"You mean you want to share my morning sickness with me! In fact, you can have it all to yourself if you like! Oh Belle, I hope this doesn't last long."

"It won't Bubs, just a few weeks, then you'll be fine and you can come and visit."

Bubs gave birth to a son seven months later and Bernard agreed they could go and visit. It was August and a holiday had already been booked in Norfolk. Bernard said they could leave home early and visit Bubs and Derek on the way to their hotel.

Belle cuddled two week old Rowan.

"Oh, Bubs, he's gorgeous. Do you mind if I take him home with me?"

"Not at all. You can keep him till he goes through the night."

Belle giggled. "It's so good to see you, and Derek of course. And you have a lovely home."

"Well we like it but it's not as grand as yours."

"Don't be silly. It's very nice, and you have a park just across the road. That's a definite plus."

"Yes, it is, it's handy for pushing the pram around and Rowan will be able to play over there when he's older."

"Well Bernard and the girls are enjoying it, Rose is on the swing and Christine is on the climbing frame. She's always climbing. I think she should have been a boy." Belle sighed, "It's going to be difficult for you to come and see us now and I don't think it will be possible for me to come and see you. We must have lots of chats on the phone and I'll write as well."

"I know it will be difficult for a while Belle, but once Rowan is a year old it will be easier to travel with him."

Belle pulled a face, "You are joking Bubs. It just gets harder till they are school age, then things improve a bit. The girls are pretty good now, as long as they have something to do in the car."

"I can't believe they are seven and nine and Christine is so tall."

"Just think Bubs, another couple of years and she could be changing shape!"

"So, Belle, how are things?"

"Oh, not too bad. We seem to have a routine that works."

"Do you and Bernard ever--- you know?"

"Oh yes. If he didn't I'd think he was ill, or playing away."

"I bet you dread it though, don't you?"

"No actually, I don't mind. Although when he's been horrid I think, just get on with it. Generally speaking though, we have a peaceful life. Bernard tells me what to do and I do it." She rolled her eyes, then they both burst into laughter.

★★★

For the next few years things continued to run smoothly in the Johnston household. Belle almost never argued or questioned anything Bernard said or did. So, Bernard was kind and loving towards her. The children were usually good and enjoyed school and Bernard was loving and patient with them as well. Although Belle was fond of her husband she knew her love for him had died a long time ago. Bubs was now visiting occasionally and at Bernard's suggestion, Derek and Rowan sometimes came too. The two men had always got on well and the girls adored Rowan. Belle had made the garden her hobby and found enormous pleasure and comfort planning what she would do with it, then carrying those plans through. There was quite a large area of lawn for the girls to play on, with a slide and a swing. Belle had a vegetable garden at the back and a few fruit trees. Near the house was a rockery and a shrub border. In a corner near the back she had a seat with an arch over it and clematis were flourishing there. The seat was her haven. It was where she escaped to if the children were quarrelling or Bernard was bad tempered. Without saying a word, they seemed to understand. When Mummy sat on her seat they knew she was unhappy and must be left in peace.

Rob still dropped in for a cup of tea when he was in the area. Usually timing it when the girls were home from school. They did so love their Uncle Rob. Sometimes he would stay and eat with them. It gave him a chance to have a good chat with Bernard. He seemed almost his old self now, but was not interested in finding himself another wife, or even a girlfriend.

CHAPTER 12

1975

The peace of those years was shattered when Christine reached thirteen. She became sullen and argumentative. Not a good thing with a father like Bernard. She announced one day that now she was 'practically grown up' she wished to be called Chris. Everyone at school called her Chris and it was only at home that she had to put up with being called Christine. Belle held her breath and waited for Bernard to explode.

"While you live in this house my girl, you will be called by your proper name. You know perfectly well that I don't like shortened names. Now let's hear no more about it."

He returned to his paper, but Christine was not deterred. "I shan't answer to Christine, only to Chris."

Belle intervened. "That's enough Christine, don't argue with your father."

Christine looked disparagingly at her mother. "Well I knew you'd side with Dad. You're too scared to do otherwise."

Bernard leapt up and dragged Christine from the room.

'Who's scared now'? Belle thought, as she saw Christine's face.

Bernard sent Christine upstairs to her room and came and sat down again, his face like thunder.

Later that evening when Bernard was having a bath, Belle knocked on Christine's door.

"Who is it?" Came a grumpy voice.

"It's Mum. Can I come in dear?"

"I suppose so."

Belle opened the door, walked in and closed it quietly behind her.

"I expect you're going to nag me now." Christine glared at her Mum. Belle sat down on the bed beside her sulky daughter.

"Just listen to what I have to say. You know Dad will never, ever back down, no matter how much you argue. My friends call me Belle, but not when your father is around and I've had to accept it. In fact, it doesn't bother me now."

"Yes, but you're frightened to stand up for yourself."

"Christine, just listen. It wouldn't do any good. And yes, your father does frighten me sometimes, so it's easier just to agree and keep the peace. But do Rose and I have to put up with you two arguing all the time? It upsets both of us you know."

"Well I hate the name Christine."

"Well I'm afraid that's just too bad. Now, I think it's time that you and Rose had a quick bath and got to bed."

"Yes, alright Mum."

"And remember what I said, arguing will get you absolutely nowhere."

Christine didn't argue for a day or two but was slow to respond when Bernard spoke to her. It was at the weekend when it all blew up again.

"Have you done your homework Christine?" Bernard asked. Christine muttered something under her breath. "What's that, speak up girl."

Christine shrugged. "Nothing."

Bernard was not to be put off. He grabbed Christine's arm none too gently. "You muttered, my name's Chris, didn't you? You are a horrible, disobedient child."

Christine glared at him. "And you are a horrible father and I hate you." She wrenched her arm away, ran from the room and pounded up the stairs. Rose had been listening to this exchange wide eyed. Now she burst into tears and ran into her mother's arms. Bernard got up, went to his study and slammed the door shut.

"Oh Mum, what are we going to do?" Rose sniffed and blew her nose.

"I just don't know. I'm at my wits end." Was all Belle could say.

An uneasy silence hung over the house for the rest of the day. At lunchtime Belle made a sandwich and a pot of tea. She nervously knocked on the study door.

"I've made some tea dear. Would you like one?"

"Yes please, bring it in here if you wouldn't mind."

Belle did as she was asked and took a tray in with some sandwiches as well.

"Thank you dear. I'll eat in here. I can't bear to be in the same room as that girl."

"She's still in her room Bernard. And I'm certainly not taking food up to her. She can just stew for a while."

Bernard took Belle's hand. "I'm sorry you're upset dear, and Rose too. But Christine must learn to obey me. I will have a talk to her later, and don't worry, I will stay calm, but we've got to sort things out." He sighed. "We'll just have to see how it goes."

Christine had always been tall and skinny. Belle swore she could actually see her growing. Therefore, she was always hungry, consuming as much as Bernard. So Belle wasn't surprised when a pale girl came down the stairs at three o'clock.

"Mum, I'm very hungry."

"Are you? That's a shame." Said Belle, turning away and leaving the room.

"Mum, please. I really am. I feel all wobbly." Christine followed her from the room.

"Get yourself some bread and butter then. But nothing else, just bread and butter."

"Can't I have a cheese sandwich?"

"No, you cannot. It's bread and butter for the rest of the day----or nothing."

"You can't do this. It's cruelty to children."

"So, you admit you're still a child then, because you've certainly been acting like one."

Christine came up to her mother and began to cry.

"I'm sorry I upset you Mum, and Rose as well. I didn't think Dad would be so horrible about it."

Belle relented and put her arms around her. "Now don't get upset. Try and remember what I said a few days ago. You can't win Christine. Dad is the boss and we have to do as he says. When you are grown up and living in your own home you can call yourself anything, Cinderella if you want to."

Christine giggled. "OK Mum."

Belle put her hands on her daughter's shoulders and looked her in the eye.

"It really does upset me when you argue. It makes me want to run away and let you get on with it." She paused while Christine digested this. "But I don't suppose I will, so don't worry." She sighed. "Dad is going to talk to you later, he's promised to stay calm and I want you to make the same promise."

"Alright Mum. I promise."

Belle kissed her and made her way out to the garden. She sat on her seat and took some deep breaths, trying to dispel the depression that was settling over her.

Bernard called Christine into his study later and closed the door. Belle didn't know what was being said, but at least there were no raised voices. It seemed they were in there for a long time but in fact it was only half an hour. When they came out it was obvious that Christine had been crying but Bernard had his arm around her shoulders, so they were 'friends' again. Christine went into the lounge where Rose was watching the television.

"I'm really sorry I upset you Rose. Can we be friends again please?"

"Course we can." Said her peace loving little sister.

★★★

It was 1976 and Great Britain was sweltering in the hottest summer on record. Belle's beloved garden looked brown and half dead and everyone was praying for rain.

Bub's was coming to visit and Belle and the girls couldn't wait to see her. Rowan was now a lively five year old. Always cheerful like his Mummy. Both girls loved him, and they took him to the park while Bubs and Belle caught up on all the news. As usual, Bernard was golfing.

"How are Bernard and Christine getting on now?" Bubs asked.

"Oh, we have a few sulks but no big arguments, thank goodness. You don't look your usual cheerful self Bubs. Are you alright, or do you have a problem?"

"Actually Belle, I'm afraid I have some rather upsetting news for you."

"Oh dear, what's happened?" Belle's stomach turned over. Why was life so hard and so full of troubles.

"I'm glad your life is a little better now Belle, but I think you ought to know that things have not been right between Derek and me for some time now and we have decided to part. It's all quite amicable. We just don't love each other any more."

Belle sat with her hand up to her mouth, unable for some moments to say anything, then she stuttered. "I---I had no idea. What a shock. What's going to happen?"

"Well we want to keep things as normal as possible because of Rowan. Derek still goes away from time to time so he's quite used to him not being around. Anyway Derek's going to move close by so he can see him as much as possible."

"Can't you move back here and be near to your family?" Belle asked.

"Well I've thought of that, but to tell you the truth I love where I live now, and I really enjoy my job. Rowan is at school now of course and I finish in time to pick him up."

"But what about the school holidays?"

"That's all covered. There's a girl down the road with a son the same age and she has offered to have Rowan during the holidays. It will take a chunk out of my wages, but Derek is quite good about money, so he will help if necessary. Actually Belle, I think he may have someone else. I don't mind. I don't think I have been much of a wife to him. I'm not cut out for marriage Belle and that's the sad truth. I never should have married." She sighed. "But then I would never have had my Rowan."

CHAPTER 13

1983

Belle could hardly believe it. How time and the years flew by. Her life carried on as it always had, but the girls were grown up now. Rose was nineteen and about to marry and Christine at twenty one, was holding down a good job in Cheltenham and living in a flat with a girlfriend. Soon there would just be Bernard and herself living in this big house.

Five years ago, they had extended it and there was a large bedroom with an en-suite above the garage, which was their bedroom. Quite unnecessary, Belle thought, but Bernard said it would add value to the house. It was certainly a lovely room, with what the architect had called double aspect windows. One looking to the front and the other over the rear garden and the countryside. Bubs still came to visit when she could. Sometimes with Rowan, now a tall lad of twelve, or on her own if Rowan was with Derek. In the end everything had worked out quite well. Derek had re-married and Rowan had two half-brothers. Bubs said she got on well with his wife Ruth and she was happy with her life. She had boyfriends, but nothing serious.

As she told Belle, it was nice to have somebody to go to the theatre with or out for a meal. Rowan didn't want to come to Rose's wedding, he was at that age where he thought weddings were soppy! So, he stayed with his Dad and Bubs came alone, travelling down the night before and planning to stay till Sunday afternoon.

Belle was very fond of Dave, Rose's fiancé and the feeling was reciprocated. He was a plumber with his own company and he was very successful. And Bernard liked him, which was a relief. One could never be sure with Bernard. Everything went well, and the bride looked beautiful and blissfully happy. Then they drove away for a honeymoon in the Lake District.

The next morning Bernard went off to play golf. He had missed his Saturday game because of the wedding. Also, he always made himself scarce when Bubs was there. By doing so there was never an unpleasant atmosphere. The two friends strolled in the park and chatted as only best friends can.

"So how's his lordship been lately?" Bubs asked.

"Oh he's OK. You know how it is Bubs. I just accept everything he says or does and it keeps the peace. I've got used to it, but I dread the day he retires. Having him around all day will drive me mad. You know I have these little things to cheer myself up. He would be shocked if he knew. I have pop music on, quite loud." She giggled. "Even heavy metal would you believe? I put on a colourful tee shirt and dance round the lounge to it. Can you imagine what he would say if he could see me? Even the tee shirt would give him a heart attack. Then I take the music off the hi-fi and hide it with the tee shirt in your bedroom. Have you ever found it when you stay?"

"No, but I know there are some things on the top shelf of the wardrobe in a bag. But I've never looked inside."

"Well you have a look, it will make you laugh. And when I've had a dancing session I feel so much better and very daring."

"But surely Bernard won't be retiring yet. How old is he now?"

"Well he's only fifty-one so I've got nine years before I get taken away by men in white coats."

Bubs gave a shout of laughter and Belle began to laugh too. Oh, it was always a tonic to see Bubs.

It was the following Monday and Belle had spent all morning doing washing and housework. After a sandwich and a short break, she prepared some vegetables for their evening meal, then checked the washing on the line. It was all dry, so she folded it and brought it indoors. Then she put the ironing board up in the kitchen, plugged in the iron and gave a huge sigh.

'Is this all there is to life?' She thought. 'Gosh I'm so bored and fed up'. On an impulse she unplugged the iron and ran upstairs to Bub's room, retrieving the bag of 'secrets' from the wardrobe. Five minutes later she was back downstairs with the music on and she was dancing round the lounge in her colourful tee shirt. She only just heard the doorbell over the noise of the music. In a panic the music went off and she peeped out of the window to see who was at the door. Phew! It was Rob. She opened the door just enough to let him in, then hastily closed it.

"Hello Rob, come in. Excuse me a minute." She ran up the stairs with the cassette and put it back in Bub's wardrobe with the tee shirt. Then slipping back into her 'normal' clothes, she ran back downstairs.

"How are you Rob? Cup of tea?"

"I'm fine." Answered a puzzled Rob. "But what's going on?"

Belle looked at him pleadingly "Please Rob, don't say anything to Bernard about the music and the tee shirt. He'd go mad if he knew."

"I can't see what the problem is but I'll still say nothing, so don't worry."

"Thanks Rob, but promise me you'll keep it to yourself."

"I don't understand Belle, but I promise."

Belle handed him a cup of tea and sat across the table from him. She took a sip of tea and tried to calm herself. It was a relief when Rob started chatting about his day.

CHAPTER 14

1991

The last few years had been much better for Belle. When Rose had married and Christine's work took her to Cheltenham, loneliness had almost made her despair. But now there were two delightful grandchildren who she saw most days. Gary, confident and friendly and six years old. Megan, two years younger, quiet and shy and prone to tears. It was a great relief and consolation to Belle that the marriage between Rose and Dave was a happy one. Belle encouraged them to go out in the evenings, partly because she loved to look after the children and also it gave her an evening without Bernard.

Unfortunately, despite Belle's joy at being a Nanna there were lots of times when she felt like screaming with boredom and frustration. Suddenly she knew that things had to change. At forty nine years old it was now or never. The first thing she needed to do was lose some weight. The last time she had stepped on the scales the arrow had swung round and pointed to about one and a half stone more than when she had married. Then she decided it was about time she had a pair of trousers for gardening and a comfortable tee shirt. Something pretty but not too bright. The one in Bub's wardrobe had been thrown out. Belle was worried the grandchildren would find it when they played hide and seek. She smiled to herself. Now that was bright and no mistake.

The trousers would stop her laddering her tights and it would be easier clambering about on the rockery and digging. Also, she noticed how the back hedge badly needed attention. From time to time the brambles and nettles began to encroach and then it was time for a big tidy up. Bernard would do it if she asked him but he didn't enjoy it. Belle was grateful that at least he would take the bags of weeds to the local tip.

So Belle went on a shopping trip and bought herself her first pair of trousers. She decided jeans would be best for gardening, then a green tee shirt. Green seemed right somehow for gardening. Pleased with her purchases she drove home and put them, still in the bag, in Bub's room. She just wasn't brave enough to let Bernard see them.

In the mean time she had gone on a diet. Bernard didn't seem to notice that she only had one piece of potato instead of three. She still had a small portion of dessert, he would have noticed otherwise. But during the day when she was alone she cut right back. In two weeks she had lost five pounds and could already feel the difference round her waist. For several weeks Bernard noticed nothing, then one evening he saw

Belle hitching her skirt waistband back up to her waist where it should have been.

"You're looking rather thin Isabelle. Are you feeling quite well?"

Belle put on an innocent face. "Am I dear? I'm feeling quite well thank you. It's just the gardening I suppose. There's a lot to do at this time of year. But a few pounds less can only be good for my health, wouldn't you say?"

Bernard looked doubtful. "Well I wouldn't want you to lose any more."

"I'll try not to dear." Belle said, mentally chiding herself for allowing Bernard to notice.

The next afternoon Belle prepared a casserole and some vegetables for roasting and put them in the oven. Now she had an hour to get on with the partly weeded rockery. She changed into the new clothes and studied herself in the mirror. She looked so different, then in a moment of madness she pulled her hair back into two bunches. Three things for him to lose his temper over. She shrugged and ran downstairs. Pulling on her garden gloves she resumed her weeding and was soon absorbed in her favourite task. So absorbed in fact, that she lost all sense of time and when she heard Bernard's car in the drive she panicked. She knew only too well what his reaction would be to the clothes and the hair bunches. Pinning a bright smile on her face she greeted her husband.

"Hello Bernard, I was so busy in the garden I forgot the time. But don't worry, dinner will be ready in fifteen minutes. I'll just go and change."

She turned towards the back door, but Bernard gripped her arm in that painful way he was prone to, and swung her round.

"What do you think you are wearing? I can see you have been wasting my money again. You look dreadful. Return them tomorrow and don't argue."

Belle was about to say they had been worn, so couldn't be returned, but noting Bernard's face, she closed her mouth and silently ran upstairs to freshen up, change and brush her hair. She put the clothes back in Bub's wardrobe which was silly really, because he could soon find them if he wished and put them in the dustbin.

Bernard had upset her more than usual. He could depress her with just a few cross words. Perhaps because his complaints were so unnecessary. It seemed to Belle that he cared nothing for her feelings, he only wanted her total obedience.

Bernard glared at her all through dinner. Her appetite had disappeared, and she felt the food would choke her.

"Eat, Isabelle and stop sulking." Bernard snapped.

Belle put a piece of chicken in her mouth and managed to chew and swallow it, then put her knife and fork down.

"I can't eat any more Bernard. I'm sorry you will have to excuse me." She pushed back her chair and hurried from the room. Running upstairs and past her bedroom, she went into Bub's room and turned the key in the door. Lying on the bed she refused to cry although she felt like howling. All was silent downstairs as Bernard finished his meal. Belle must have fallen asleep on the bed because she was suddenly woken by a loud knocking.

"Open this door immediately Isabelle. Do you hear me?"

Belle swung her legs off the bed. "Bernard, I am at the end of my tether. You make me feel like throwing myself out of the window."

There was a stunned silence, then. "Don't be ridiculous woman. You're behaving like a spoilt child. Open this door at once."

"Is it any wonder I act like a child when I'm treated like one and spoken to like one." Her voice rose. "Now go away and let me think and stop bullying me. I'll come out later, maybe."

She heard Bernard mutter, then his footsteps going back down the stairs. After two hours had passed Belle plucked up courage and decided she must go down and talk to Bernard. But before she could open the door she heard him outside. "Isabelle, please come out now."

His voice was quiet and anxious. He had obviously calmed down.

"Come along now, we can have a talk and find out what's wrong. I'm sure we can sort everything out."

Belle unlocked the door and slowly opened it. Bernard looked at her frightened face.

"Don't worry, I'm not going to hit you, I never have, and I never will."

Belle took a deep breath. "You don't need to hit me Bernard. You frighten me just with your voice and your angry face." She followed him downstairs and they sat down in the lounge.

"Would you like a drink?" He asked gently.

"Yes please, I'll have a brandy and lemonade and not too small."

Without a word he prepared her drink and handed it to her. Belle thanked him and took several sips.

"Now what do you mean when you say I frighten you? You wouldn't really throw yourself out of the window, would you? Tell me exactly how you feel dear and I promise I will listen and not get angry."

So Belle did. "If I dare to question anything, you get very angry. You always seem to be cross and angry. Even though I usually accept everything you say. I'm not allowed to have an opinion. We can't just discuss things in a civilised manner, then come to an agreement like any normal married couple."

"What sort of things are you talking about?"

Belle flung her arms up. "Everything, just everything. Your decisions are always the right ones and I'm just ----stupid and should keep silent and just obey. What I think or what I like or dislike counts for nothing."

"I still don't understand what you are talking about Isabelle."

"Well just listen and I'll tell you. I'm not allowed to have a little job. My place is here, the little housewife at home, cooking and cleaning and lonely and bored,

bored, bored." Belle raised her hand to stop him interrupting. "I must go to Wales or Norfolk every year because that's where you want to go. And that's becoming more tedious as each year goes by. Oh, and then there's the food, week in week out, year after year until I'm sick of the same old thing. And my clothes, dull, old fashioned and frumpy. I have to wear what your mother wore. Well she's been gone fifteen years and she was forty years older than me and lived in another era. Then it's no Isabelle, you can't change your hairstyle either, you must always wear it exactly the same because I like it that way. Do you know Bernard, I feel like a nothing person. I feel I'm being ground underfoot, stifled----."

Belle stopped, then waited for Bernard to get angry with her, but it wasn't happening. In fact, he looked dreadfully shocked.

"Am I really such a bad husband?" He asked.

"In lots of ways dear, you are a good husband. You have given me a lovely home and security. You're a good father and generous and as far as I know, you have been faithful."

Now Bernard looked even more shocked. "Of course I've been faithful. Since the day I met you I've wanted nobody else. You may think you look dull and frumpy, but to me you are always lovely."

But Belle was determined to get everything out in the open. "It's just that you want to control me. I'm not allowed to be my natural self. We are all individuals with our own likes and dislikes. It doesn't mean we have to fall out. It's all about give and take Bernard, do you understand?"

He was silent for a few moments, then with a sigh he said. "Yes, I do. I'll try not to control you, if that's what you think I do. But it's going to be hard to change at my age. You see, I remember how my mother treated my father and I swore no woman would treat me like that." He paused, and a little of the old Bernard came back. "But, if you come home with some garish clothes, I shall find it hard to keep silent."

Belle rolled her eyes. "I'm not going to do that. Pretty clothes maybe, modern clothes possibly, but I will not be wearing fluorescent purple and scarlet or wear huge gypsy earrings. Nor will I be dying my hair red and wearing plunging necklines. Please don't insult my intelligence or my taste by suggesting such a thing." Belle glared at him as she finished her brandy and he had the grace to look ashamed. She looked at him and thought it was time to close the subject. He looked exhausted. The constant pressure at work and now this disagreement as well. She patted his hand.

"Let's forget it now dear and try and relax. Would you like a hot drink?"

Later as Bernard said goodnight he pulled her into his arms.

"I just want to look after you and care for you my dear, that's all."

"I know Bernard. But there's a fine line between caring and controlling and you crossed it many years ago. But we have agreed to try and improve things, so

I don't want you to worry about it any more. We'll be fine, I'm sure."

The following Saturday Bernard slept late, and Belle hoped it would do him good. He wouldn't be leaving for the golf club till 9.45 so if she woke him at nine he would have plenty of time to get ready and have some breakfast. But it was a beautiful morning and Belle was eager to work in the garden before it got too hot. So, slipping on the offending top and trousers she quietly closed the bedroom door and ran down the stairs.

At nine o'clock she peeped round the bedroom door and called softly. "Bernard, time to get up dear."

When she was sure he was awake she hurried back into the garden, making her way to the very back. She was on edge though, knowing that Bernard would be coming to say goodbye soon. She was determined to respond to his expected irritation with good humour but without backing down. Sure enough, as expected, he was annoyed.

"I see you've got those awful clothes on again."

Belle turned around with a smile. "Bernard, I'm clearing nettles and brambles from the back hedge. I'm not going to wear anything respectable, am I? And the trousers are protecting me from scratches and stings." She touched his arm. "Don't be an old grump dear. Remember our little chat the other day. Now go and enjoy your golf and don't worry over unimportant things."

Bernard tried to smile. "Alright dear. I'll see you later." He kissed her cheek and walked back down the garden to his car.

Belle gave a huge sigh of relief. She felt the short exchange had gone well.

Over the next few weeks Belle avoided any confrontations, delaying changing her lifestyle until things became less stressful for Bernard at work. At the same time, she continued to wear her 'outfit' whenever working in the garden, and he seemed to accept it and said no more.

CHAPTER 15

Belle unplugged the iron and put the pile of linen in the airing cupboard. As she folded up the ironing board the phone rang. Thinking it would be Rose, Belle answered with a cheerful "Hello."

"Mrs. Johnston?"

"Yes, speaking."

"It's Janice, from Brown and Robinson. I'm afraid your husband has been taken ill. We have sent for an ambulance, but we feel you should get here as soon as possible. Do you want me to send one of the staff to pick you up or will you be able to drive in?"

Belle's face paled. "Oh dear, I can drive. I'll come straight away. Is he very ill?"

"I'm sorry, I can't tell you any more at the moment Mrs. Johnston, but we think you should come immediately."

Belle put the phone down with a shaky hand. This was just what she hoped to avoid. If Bernard was suffering a breakdown, who could say how long it would take him to recover. He might even be forced to retire early. He would find that hard to accept. She dragged on a cardigan and picked up her handbag and car keys. It was just after three o'clock and the roads were busy with mothers driving to pick up children from school. Belle felt she would never get there, but it was actually only ten minutes later when she parked and ran into the offices of Brown and Robinson. She was greeted by a very pale Janice.

"Go into Mr. Browns room please Mrs. Johnston."

Belle did as she was told and found the kindly Mr. Brown waiting for her.

"Has the ambulance already taken him?" She asked, sitting in the chair indicated by Mr. Brown.

"Yes, they came very quickly." He was silent for a few moments and in that short time Belle knew what to expect. "I'm afraid this will be a terrible shock for you my dear but I'm so sorry, they couldn't save him. He collapsed with what they believe was a massive heart attack. He died instantly. He would not have suffered. I'm so terribly sorry."

Belle didn't seem to be able to answer. There was a rushing noise in her ears and her eyes refused to focus. She struggled not to faint, taking deep breaths and slowly, things righted. Janice came in with a cup of strong, sweet tea and placed it on the desk beside Belle.

"Would you like me to phone your daughter?"

Belle looked up at her gratefully. "Yes please, I'll give you her number."

Mr. Brown pushed a piece of paper and a pen towards her and Belle tried to steady her hand and write it down. As she took a few sips of tea Mr. Brown asked if Rose would be able to leave the children with someone. Belle assured him that she would be able to leave them with a neighbour.

"I think she should drive you to the hospital, you've had a terrible shock. You can leave your car here for the time being. In fact, I think a taxi would be better and if one is not available, Janice can take you."

When Rose arrived, and the news was broken to her, she completely went to pieces. There was no way she could drive so Janice willingly stepped in. Rose was heartbroken and wept uncontrollably. Belle held her in the back of the car, stroking her hair and trying to comfort her. Until then Belle had been dry eyed with shock, but now, with her sobbing daughter beside her, the tears came, and they cried together. The next few hours passed in a blur. The identification, which was an ordeal, then contacting Christine, who set off immediately to arrive an hour and a half later with Steve. They stayed the night and the following two days to help with the funeral arrangements.

PART 3

CHAPTER 16

It was the morning after the funeral and Bubs woke and looked at the clock. Seven thirty and all was quiet. Belle must still be asleep. But Bubs couldn't wait. Her throat was dry and she needed a cup of coffee. She slipped on her dressing gown and crept downstairs. After putting the kettle on she raised the blind and gazed out at the garden while waiting for it to boil. It was a beautiful June morning and as always, the garden looked lovely. Dave had been around the day before the funeral and cut the grass and the rest always looked immaculate. But it was big and now Bernard was gone the lawns and hedges would be Belle's responsibility and it was just too much. She was making the right decision. An apartment was a good idea. As Bubs took her empty cup over to the sink the door swung open and a sleepy-eyed Belle came in. Bubs hugged her, topped up the kettle and switched it on.

"How are you this morning Belle? How did you sleep?"

"Well it took me hours to get off. My brain wouldn't settle, then suddenly I went out like a light and I've only just woken up. How about you?"

"Oh, you know me, I could sleep on a clothes line. But once I'm awake I have to get up."

They made some toast and another cup of coffee, then sat at the table enjoying the quiet after the trauma of yesterday. Bubs finished her coffee and looked at Belle.

"So what thoughts kept you awake last night? Do you want to talk about it?"

"Oh Bubs, I was so young when I married. But I met Bernard, fell in love and that was that."

"I know." Replied Bubs. "I've often thought of all the fun you missed. It wouldn't have mattered so much if you had been happy, but that didn't last more than a few years, did it? Still, it happened, and it can't be changed now."

"Yes, I certainly was happy. We were very compatible regarding the intimate side of things and he turned out to be a good father. I was used to being an obedient daughter so being an obedient wife didn't bother me at first. But after my mother and father died, everything seemed to change. I started to feel trapped and frustrated and of course, depressed. It didn't take long to realise the lovemaking was all we had in common. But Bubs." Belle grinned. "Did I ever tell you about the curried mince?"

"Curried mince? No, you didn't."

"Well, you know how Bernard was. Plain English food, none of that foreign rubbish. I got so bored with it. So, one day I stirred in a teaspoon of curry powder and he said it was the best mince he had ever tasted. He asked me where I'd bought it and asked for a second helping. I longed to tell him the truth but thought it best to keep quiet."

The friends laughed together, then made their way upstairs to get dressed and make the beds.

Belle was first back downstairs. She pulled the vacuum cleaner from the hall cupboard and went quickly through the downstairs rooms, picking up the crumbs from the previous day. When Bubs came down she helped by doing the dusting. When all was done they sat down with a cup of coffee and a piece of chocolate cake left over from the day before.

"I shouldn't be eating this Bubs. I'm on a diet you know."

"I thought you looked thinner." Bubs replied. I put it down to the stress of the last couple of weeks."

"Oh no, it wasn't just that. I decided about six weeks ago that I was fed up with the way I looked. I was determined to change things no matter what Bernard said, so I started by trying to lose weight. Whether I would have been brave enough to change my clothes or hair style, we'll never know now."

Bubs sipped her coffee and finished off the cake. "So, what are your plans for the rest of the day Belle?"

"Well now the house is clean and tidy, I'll throw a few things in a suitcase and drive down to the South coast for a few days. I thought I'd leave about midday or a little after."

Bubs eyes opened wide. "What?"

"I said I'm going away for a few days--."

"Yes, yes, I heard you, but you've never been further than the supermarket. How do you think you will cope with a long journey like that?"

"Well I'll soon find out. Listen Bubs, I know it sounds fanciful, but I need to rediscover myself. Not to be just a wife and a mother. Do you know what I mean?"

"Yes, I do, but you just gave me an awful shock. And please Belle, promise me you will ring me when you get there." Then she put her hand to her mouth and gasped. "What about Rose? She's coming round after school with the kids. She'll find the place empty and all locked up."

"Don't worry. I've worked it all out. You know she helps out at the school during the lunch hour, well she'll be gone when I leave so I can pop a letter through her door. I don't want to talk to her. She does fuss so. In her own way she's as bad as Bernard. She'll say I can't do this and I mustn't do that, I know she's only trying to look after me but I just don't think I can bear it at the moment."

Bubs gave her a sympathetic smile. "Well you go and write your letter and I'll pack my bag. Would you like me to go soon or will we leave together?"

"Do you mind staying Bubs? I've still got some left over food in the fridge, you can help me use it up."

"How can you talk about food after that huge slice of chocolate cake? You must give me your diet details so I can do it as well."

Then they hung on to each other as laughter overtook them. Belle did feel a little bit guilty but couldn't help herself.

Both were ready to leave by midday and after a quick snack and with the house securely locked, first

Bubs, then Belle, pulled out of the drive. With a cheery wave, Bubs set off for home and Belle drove around the corner to put the letter through Rose's letter box.

Dear Rose

I am going away for a few days because I desperately need some time on my own. Please try and understand. I am going South, but not sure where yet. I will phone you when I arrive at my destination and during my time away you may even get a postcard.

It would be nice if you could all come to me for Sunday lunch next weekend if you are free.

I promise I will be careful so please don't worry.

Lots of love, Mum xx

CHAPTER 17

Belle had been driving for an hour. Her face was red with the effort of concentrating, just as she used to be when she was having driving lessons. It was years since she had driven on a motorway, and then only once. Everything seemed to be going so fast. She was desperate for a coffee and came off at the next service area, parked the car and joined the queue at the café. As she sat sipping her coffee, Belle couldn't help smiling. Gosh, Rose was going to be so frustrated. There was no way she could contact her mother. As far as Belle was concerned, it was a few days without Rose's fussing.

Twenty minutes later she left the service area, feeling much calmer now and ready to tackle anything the M25 might throw at her. At three thirty- five, with the M25 behind her, she pulled in again for another hot drink. As she sat and sipped her tea she mentally patted herself on the back. Instead of the driving becoming harder, the opposite had happened. Her confidence had grown and there were no concerns about finishing the journey. Brighton was her destination. It was somewhere she had always wanted to visit, and she was really looking forward to it. It was a Friday afternoon and the traffic was building up as people left work for the weekend. Progress was slow, and it was five forty-five before she reached the outskirts of Brighton. Almost immediately she saw a motel and pulled in to the car park, hoping there was a room available. The car park certainly wasn't full. The business men would have gone home, and the weekenders were still to arrive.

She picked up her handbag and walked into reception. An elderly couple were booking in and Belle looked through some leaflets of local places to visit while she waited. The receptionist was a lady, probably in her late thirties and very smart. She was dealing with the couple in a friendly and efficient manner. But it was her hair that drew Belle's attention. It was short and dark and had been skilfully styled. Highlights in several shades made it look individual and Belle was impressed and envious. The receptionist handed the couple their keys and pointed towards the lift, then she turned and smiled at Belle. "Good afternoon madam, how can I help you?"

"I'd like a room please."

"Just for one?" The receptionist enquired.

"Yes please."

"Let me see now. Yes, I have a room on the second floor, will that be alright?"

She put her hand to her hair and Belle realised that she was staring.

"Oh, yes that will be fine." Then she added, "I'm sorry I was staring at your hair. I do like it, it's lovely."

"Thank you, that's very kind."

They completed the booking in procedure, Belle was given her key and she left to get her case from the car and make her way upstairs. She had booked the room for four nights for now and could extend it later if she wanted. She unpacked and then went to find a phone booth. She decided the simplest way was to phone Chris and get her to pass the message on to Rose and Bubs. The phone rang a number of times and then a breathless Chris picked it up.

"Hello."

"Chris, it's Mum."

"Are you OK?"

"Yes, I'm fine. It's just that I've gone away for a few days and I need to let everyone know I've arrived safely."

"Gosh Mum, where are you?"

"I'm in Brighton. The problem is Chris, I don't have much change. Could you possibly let Rose and Bubs know that I'm OK?"

"Yes, of course. But Mum, how did you get there so quick? You must have left early to get the right connections."

"No, I left after lunch and I drove. Don't you think I'm brave?"

"Gosh Mum, I'm impressed."

Belle chuckled. "Well so am I actually! By the way, Rose does know I've gone away, but not where or how. I've no doubt when you tell her she'll have a fit."

"Yes, she will. You have a relaxing time Mum and we'll see you next weekend."

After a good night's sleep Belle made her way downstairs to the restaurant for breakfast. On the way she wanted to enquire about buses to the seafront. The same young lady was behind the desk and she could see by the badge on her jacket that her name was Clare.

"Good morning Mrs. Johnston. Did you sleep well?"

"Yes, very well thank you. I've had a very busy few weeks and I was exhausted."

Clare listened to her request for bus times and took a printed timetable from a drawer in her desk. Belle thanked her and turned towards the restaurant, then hesitated.

"Was there something else Mrs. Johnston?"

"I hope you don't mind me asking, but where do you get your hair done?"

"No, I don't mind at all, it's easy walking distance from here or you can park nearby. I'll give you the name of the salon and the phone number. Do you want to know which stylist does my hair?"

"Yes please, I was going to ask anyway."

Clare looked thoughtful, then said. I can make an appointment for you if you like. She's very popular so you may have to wait. When would be best for you?"

"Oh anytime. I'm on holiday so my times my own. Don't worry if you're too busy, there's no urgency." But inside Belle was screaming with impatience. By the end of these few days she wanted to look like a different person. And she knew when that was achieved she would feel like a different person as well.

"Well thank you Mrs. Johnston. It's always hectic on a Saturday with people booking in and out and enquiries on the phone. But I promise if I don't get time today, I'll do it first thing Monday morning."

Belle had to be content with that. Later she caught the bus to the seafront and walked along in the sunshine, feeling her body and mind relaxing. The shops here were mainly selling souvenirs or sweets, buckets and spades and postcards. Interspersed with cafes and restaurants and ice cream parlours. She crossed over the road and walked along the promenade for a while. After a coffee she made her way to the Royal Pavilion, somewhere she'd longed to visit for years. Already a queue was forming but before too long she was inside and enthralled. She moved slowly from room to room, spellbound with all the exotic décor and furnishings, until finally she was at the exit. Stepping back out into the sunshine she glanced at her watch. Gosh, it was just after two, no wonder she was hungry. She set off for The Lanes, where there would be more cafes and Belle decided to sit outside if possible and watch the world go by. Later, walking along The Lanes again she caught sight of her reflection in a shop window and as always, her heart plummeted. What a sight! A beige, slightly flared skirt was topped off with a white button up to the neck, blouse. On her feet, flat old -fashioned sandals. Her fair hair fell to just above her shoulders, the perm she'd had three months ago was now almost grown out. Her hair looked lank and uncared for. A pale, unsmiling face stared back at her and just about summed up the way she was feeling. Her pleasure at seeing the Royal Pavilion forgotten, she turned and walked towards the High Street, where there would be a Marks and Spencer's or a British Home Store's. Then she could enjoy an hour or two clothes shopping.

But just before leaving The Lanes she passed a small boutique, and in the window a flash of coral pink caught her eye. It was a pretty lacy top with a silver thread running through it. With a scoop neck and capped sleeves, it was perfect for this lovely weather. Belle stepped inside and a young lady came forward to help her.

As Belle stood in the fitting room and stared at her reflection, she couldn't believe how much better she looked. The coral pink seemed to bring a bloom to her cheeks and the off-white slacks she was trying on as well, complimented the top. She turned this way and that and could see how the weight loss had improved her figure. Taking a comb from her bag, she tidied her hair, then stepped out of the fitting room. The assistant was hovering nearby.

"I want you to be really honest with me. I've got no friend to tell me the truth. How does this look?"

The assistant looked her up and down. "I must say you look really lovely madam. The pink really suits you, but if you want me to be honest, I think the trousers are a little tight round the hips. Can you see madam, how the pockets are gaping a little?"

Belle smiled wryly. "Yes, I know, but I'm on a diet and I've already lost a stone and I intend to lose at least another half stone and I think that will take care of it."

"Yes, it will." The assistant replied. "Will there be anything else for you madam?"

"No thank you, I'll come and pay. Is it alright if I keep these on?"

"Of course, I'll put your other clothes in a bag for you."

'Or in the bin'! Belle thought.

As Belle had hoped, there were several large shops in the High Street and very soon she had purchased some pretty, strappy white sandals and a small white handbag. She paid and walked towards the door but noticed a rail of colourful tee shirts. She looked through them and a blue one stood out. Taking it from the rail she found a mirror, and holding the tee shirt up, she studied herself. The blue was the colour of a summer sky. Two white fluffy clouds adorned the front and peeping out from one of them was an orange sun.

"Oh, I like that." Belle said softly, But, she thought, Bernard would definitely not have approved of a sky blue tee shirt. But he's not here and from now on I decide what I want to wear! So, it was back to the till again, to pay and slip the tee shirt into the bag with the other items

By now Belle was feeling rather weary so she decided to get the bus back to the hotel and put her feet up for a while. As the bus trundled along she idly watched the houses, hotels and shops go by. Then they passed a Chinese restaurant, ornately decorated on the outside façade and looking inviting. Belle had never eaten Chinese food, but the aroma as she had walked by them near her home had always made her mouth water. Deciding to check with Clare that it was a good place to eat, she collected her bags together and prepared to get off the bus.

Clare was busy with paperwork behind her desk but looked up and smiled as Belle walked in. Then her eyes swept over Belle.

"You look nice, I don't remember you wearing those clothes when you went out."

"No, they are new, the top is pretty isn't it?"

"Yes, very pretty," Clare said, then added with a smile. "I just managed to speak to the hairdressers about ten minutes ago. They can fit you in at four thirty on Monday. How's that?"

"Oh, thank you so much Clare. I can't tell you how excited I am."

Clare handed her a piece of paper, "Here you are. I've written all the details down. I've managed to book you in with my stylist, Mel. Is that OK?"

Belle took the piece of paper and with a big smile, said a sincere thank you.

For the first time since arriving in Brighton, Belle wished she had a companion. Sitting in a restaurant alone seemed rather strange. Trying not to show her ignorance of Chinese food, she ordered her meal and sipped a glass of wine while she waited. A set meal for one had seemed far too much and so she had ordered from the menu. A waiter came over and placed a dish of prawn crackers on the table. Belle picked one up and took a delicate bite.

'Mm, delicious, these are really nice' she thought. A pretty young Chinese waitress approached after ten minutes and placed a number of dishes in front of Belle. It still looked an awful lot of food, but she took her time and ate it all. As far as Belle was concerned, Chinese food got a big tick!

Sunday was another bright and sunny day and Belle decided to walk off her big meal of the previous evening. She walked East along the promenade towards Rottingdean, passing the marina with its boats and yachts, large and small. Then after a while she turned and headed back towards the town. It was busy now, with couples and families enjoying the sunshine. She passed by an amusement arcade and in a moment of madness, went inside. This was yet another thing she had never been allowed to experience. With a tub of two pence pieces she wandered around looking at the machines and watching what other people were doing. She chose a machine and began to feed the coins in, laughing as the money rapidly disappeared.

"I hope you are looking down on me Bernard." She said softly. "I've driven all the way down here on my own, I've bought some pretty clothes and I'm having a new hairstyle. Last night I had a Chinese meal and before I go home I hope to have an Italian and an Indian meal. And right now, I'm playing the two pence machines and do you know what Bernard, I'm having fun!"

That evening Belle found an Italian restaurant and enjoyed a pasta meal, which was quite different but just as tasty as the Chinese food.

After another day of walking and exploring, an excited and very nervous Belle found herself sitting in a hairdresser's chair. She had to keep telling herself that Bernard wasn't around anymore. There was no need to be frightened, she could do whatever she liked. Mel ran her hands through Belle's hair and they began to discuss what could be done. They talked about Clare's hair and the shape of her face compared with Belle's. They agreed there wasn't much difference but Mel suggested not quite so short and more wispy ends. Belle wanted highlights and because she was fair, auburn highlights were decided on.

"Right." Mel said, "Let's make a start."

Clare looked up from the paperwork on her desk. "Good evening madam. What can I do for you---- Good gracious, it's Mrs. Johnston. I didn't recognise you, you look fabulous!"

"Well thank you Clare, and I do have to thank you, for pointing me in Mel's direction."

"Turn around." Clare instructed, and Belle gave a twirl. "I like the way she's done the back, it's softer." She smiled broadly at Belle. "Well you certainly must eat out tonight. Somewhere posh I think."

Belle laughed "Well actually I'm going to eat next door tonight, and probably soon. I've had a busy day and I'm rather tired and hungry."

After her meal Belle sauntered up the road to a phone box. She rang Rose first who had plenty to say but Belle cut her short, asking her to phone Chris and Bubs and let them know she was alright.

On Tuesday Belle decided to drive inland away from the coast. She visited a stately home and later walked round an open garden. That evening, on Clare's recommendation, she ate at an Indian restaurant. The meal was a shock to her palate, but she enjoyed it none the less.

She had already booked one extra night, but was now eager to get home to her family. But there was one more thing she needed to do before she left Brighton. She was down prompt for breakfast the next morning and then quickly packed. She told Clare how much she had enjoyed her stay and that she felt like a new woman. Clare agreed that she looked like one. Belle settled the bill and Clare said it was alright to leave the car there for a couple of hours.

Belle caught a bus down to the front and found her way back to the High Street again. She bought gifts for the family and a box of chocolates for Clare, then looked for the make-up department in one of the big stores. Soon she was seated on a stool and a heavily made up young lady was studying her closely.

"I only want very subtle make up." Belle said, "I've never worn any before and I need to get used to it."

The young lady gave a small chuckle. "I know I wear too much, but you have lovely skin so we needn't bother with foundation or powder, but I would advise a little blusher because you are rather pale, and a touch of eye make-up. Shall we try some?"

Belle was uneasy. Had she made the right decision or was she simply too old to start? But she just nodded.

"And probably a pale coral lipstick, similar to your top." The girl continued, "Now just relax madam."

Belle placed the box of chocolates on the desk and smiled at Clare. "I just wanted to give you a little something because you have been so kind to me."

"Oh Mrs. Johnston, you are naughty, but thank you. I must say you look quite different to when you arrived a few days ago. Your family won't recognise you! I hope you will visit us again sometime in the future."

CHAPTER 18

Belle pulled into her drive, wearily climbed out of her car and unlocked the garage door. She glanced at her watch, it was just after four o'clock. After putting the car away, she took the back-door key from its hidey-hole above Bernard's tool rack and let herself into the house. Dumping the suitcase at the foot of the stairs, she went around the house opening the windows to let some fresh air in.

Then she rang Rose. "I'm home Rose, have you got time to come around for a cuppa?"

"Oh Mum, I'm so glad you're home. I'll be round in ten minutes."

Belle put the kettle on, then went upstairs with the suitcase and opened the bedroom windows. She caught sight of herself in the full-length mirror. Even though she was aware of her new appearance, it was still a shock to see herself. It was almost a stranger staring back at her. Quickly touching up her lipstick and tweaking her hair, she took a few deep breaths and ran down the stairs, suddenly nervous of granddaughter Megan's reaction to her. She was a shy and sensitive child and liable to burst into tears if anything was different. Gary at seven and two years older, was quite the opposite. Bright and outgoing and full of confidence, but at the same time, a caring little boy. She took the mugs out and heart thumping, waited for Rose's reaction.

Rose took the children's hands for the short walk to her mothers. "Now Megan, Nanna Is going to be nice and brown from the seaside and I bet she's bought some new clothes. But it's still the same Nanna who loves you, so I don't want any tears. Do you understand?"

Megan nodded.

"I bet she'll make a fuss." Gary looked at his sister.

"No, I won't, so there." Megan retorted, sticking her tongue out.

Rose gave the two hands clasped in hers, a shake. "That's enough you two, if you quarrel as soon as you see Nanna, she'll go away again. Is that what you want? Right, here we are." They walked around the side of the garage, rapped on the back door and went in.

"Nanna, we're here." Called out Gary.

They walked into the kitchen and stopped in stunned silence. Then three things happened. As predicted, Megan began crying.

Gary said. "Wow Nanna."

And Rose's mouth dropped open. Then, impatient with her daughter, she pushed the clinging child away and walked over to Belle.

"Gosh Mum, I hardly recognised you. You look err--- you look--- so young!"

Belle couldn't help laughing. "What do you think of your 'new look' Mum then?" Turning to Megan she said sharply. "Be quiet Megan, what an awful noise."

Megan was so surprised by her Nanna's tone she calmed down and allowed Rose to wipe her eyes.

"You promised me you wouldn't cry Megan. I'm disappointed in you." Then turning to Belle, she said. "You look amazing Mum, doesn't she Gary?"

"Mm, you look like a film star Nanna." Which made Belle laugh again. She poured boiling water on the tea bags and pulled a fresh bottle of milk from the carrier bag on the table.

"Come on Rose, sit down and drink your tea. Do you want some juice children?"

It was six o'clock and Chris had just got in from work. No sooner had she hung her coat up than the phone rang.

"Hello."

"Chris, it's Rose, Mums home and you won't believe what she's done to herself."

"What do you mean? Has she had an accident?"

"No, nothing like that. You'll be stunned when you see her on Sunday. You are coming to Mums, aren't you?"

"Yes I am. What's Mum done then?"

"She's gone all trendy. I'm not going to say any more, but you wait till you see her."

"Well that sounds very positive. How does she seem otherwise?"

"She seems very well, but Chris, she seems too happy if you know what I mean. Dad's only been gone a few weeks. I expected her to be a bit sad still, and subdued, but no, she's on top of the world."

"Well I don't think she's exactly heartbroken over Dad. I don't think you realised how much he dominated her and it was easier for her to just comply. I tell you Rose, I wouldn't let anyone treat me like that."

Rose sighed." Well she's certainly breaking out now. But I have to say Chris, she looks amazing. It's taken years off her."

"I can't wait to see her on Sunday." Chris said.

"Hello Bubs, it's Belle, I'm home and I wondered if you are free this weekend?"

"Hello Belle. Yes, I'm free. How are you? Did you have a nice time? When did you get home?"

Belle laughed." Questions, questions! Yes, I'm well, I had a lovely time and I got home about four o'clock. Now can you come over on Saturday? I know it's only a week since you were here but I'm longing to see you."

"Yes, I can, but I'm going to the hairdresser in the morning. I could get to you late afternoon. How would that be?"

"Great. Oh, Bubs I've got so much to tell you."

The next morning Belle put some washing in the machine, then sat down for some tea and toast. Half an hour later the wardrobe door stood open and a big sigh escaped her lips. All her lovely new clothes were in the wash and she was left with the drab ones from her past life. Beige, grey and navy blue. Then she remembered her gardening top, which was clean and hanging in Bub's wardrobe. She fetched it and put it on with a navy skirt and cardigan--- and it looked quite good. After tidying her hair and putting some make up on she made a shopping list and left for the shops. She backed her car out and noticed her neighbours were out the front of their house. James was cutting the hedge and Avril was sweeping up the trimmings. Belle moved forward and stopped, winding down the window.

"Good morning you two. You look busy."

Avril moved over to the car. "Yes, we thought we'd make an early start, it's going to rain later. I say, what have you done to yourself?"

"I've been to Brighton for a few days and had my hair done. Do you like it?"

"Yes, it's lovely. Quite a change. I thought I hadn't seen you. Did you drive there?"

"Yes, aren't I brave. I said to my friend Bubs and my girls, I had to get away. They quite understood. Now I have to get some food. Do you need anything while I'm there?"

Belle parked at the supermarket and took a trolley. She just needed enough to see her through until Friday. It didn't take long, and she was soon in the queue at the checkout of her favourite assistant.

"Hello. I haven't got much today."

"Good morning. You look nice today. I like your hair."

"Thank you." Belle smiled to herself. All these compliments, she would be getting conceited.

The rest of the day Belle pottered about doing jobs around the house and tidying the garden. The next morning, she was up bright and early, drove to the new 'Park and Ride' and caught a bus into the city. She shopped and had some lunch and then shopped some more. At three o'clock she arrived back home again, exhausted but satisfied. After making a cup of tea she took her drink and her purchases upstairs and laid everything out on the bed. She had two more pairs of trousers, two fleeces, a pretty blouse and another tee shirt, plus a denim skirt and a summer jacket. The last purchase was another pair of black sandals, with an inch and a half heel.

There was a shout from downstairs. Rose had arrived with the children. Belle leaned over the bannister.

"The kettle boiled a few minutes ago. Make yourself a cuppa and come up and see what I've been up to."

***

Belle had been busy all morning on Saturday, cleaning and baking. Now it was mid-afternoon, Bubs would be here soon, and she needed to freshen up and change. It was very important that her friend should approve of her new look and of course, Chris, tomorrow. It was almost four when the front door bell rang. She hurried to the door excited and nervous. A big smile spread over Bub's face when Belle opened the door. For a few moments she was stunned into silence, then she gave a happy laugh and stepped inside.

"Belle, gosh. I can't believe it! You look wonderful. At least ten years younger than last week."

"Thank you. I'm so relieved you like it, because this is the new me."

The previous day Belle had taken most of her old clothes to the charity shop. Now she had a new life as well as new clothes and she was going to make the most of it.

Tomorrow would be her forty ninth birthday and she had made herself a birthday cake. But she must respect her daughters' feelings and tone down the celebrations as they remembered their father.

Bubs took her bags upstairs, then came back down for a cup of tea. She stood in the kitchen doorway and looked at Belle preparing the drink and suddenly realised she was quietly weeping.

"Whatever's the matter, Bubs dear?"

"I'm so happy for you, that's all. All the years of doing what Bernard demanded and now, well it's the old you from thirty years ago and it's made me feel quite emotional." Bubs wiped her eyes and sat down. "Sorry Belle, I know it's sounds silly but it means a lot to me to know you're going to have a better life now. I can't say anything tomorrow when the family are here. I know they thought a lot of Bernard, especially Rose."

"Yes, you're right, and I know Rose is rather puzzled by the way I'm behaving. Chris will understand though." Belle took the lamb from the oven and left it at the back of the hob to 'rest'. The vegetables were either in the oven or simmering on the hob and the table was laid. The wine was open, and she was enjoying a glass while she prepared the meal.

There was a knock at the back door and Chris and Steve came in with a cheery "Hello". Chris dropped her coat and bag on a chair.

"Where's this glam Mum I've been hearing about?" She looked Belle up and down, a huge smile on her face, then hugged her. "You look great Mum. Good for you. What do you think Steve?"

"What a transformation. How old are you? Twenty-nine?"

They all laughed, then Chris disappeared to hang her coat up and Belle began to carve.

"Here, let me do that." Steve took the knife from her and attacked the joint.

At that moment Rose, Dave and the children arrived and Bubs came downstairs to greet everyone.

There were lots of hugs and kisses and Dave refused to release Belle. "Cor, I don't half fancy you Ma-in-Law. How about a date?"

Belle dissolved into giggles and struggled to regain her composure. "Behave, you naughty boy and get everyone a drink while I dish up."

After they had eaten, everyone helped to clear the dining room and load the dishwasher. Belle made coffee and they all retired to the lounge. Although wary at first, Megan climbed on to Belle's lap as she always used to and snuggled up for a cuddle.

"Will you please all stop staring at me and talking about me?" Belle said. But it was spoken with a big smile. She told them all about her holiday and her initial nerves in the car.

"Oh, and the food. For the first time in my life I ate Chinese, Italian and Indian food and it was lovely."

Everyone looked stunned. "You mean you've never had an Italian meal?" Rose asked.

"No, never, and I don't have to tell you why, do I?"

Everyone was quiet for a few moments, then Rose spoke again.

"I never realised Mum, I'm sorry."

"Don't worry, things will be different now. It did me good to get away and think about the future. I need to let you know I'm putting the house on the market in a few weeks' time."

Rose looked shocked." You can't do that Mum. It's our home, where we grew up."

Belle and Chris both glared at her.

"I beg your pardon Rose. What did you say? Are you telling me what to do now?"

"Sorry Mum. I didn't mean to boss you about. Forget I said it please." Rose looked contrite.

"Why do I need a five bedroomed house? Why do I need a huge garden? Well the answer is, I don't, so I shall sell it. My plan is to buy a modern apartment in a nice area." She put up a hand to silence Rose again.

"Just hear me out please. Then I'm going to travel. It's something I've always wanted to do, and now I can. When the money comes through from the house, I will be giving some to you two girls. I will still have more than enough for my needs. We had no mortgage on this house and your father had a life insurance as well as savings, so I have no money worries."

There was silence in the room while her family and Bubs digested this news. It was broken by Gary.

"If you have lots of money Nanna, please can I have some?"

CHAPTER 19

Every spare moment Belle had was used for packing up items she wanted to keep and filling bags and boxes with stuff for the charity shop. Chris and Rose had told her which things they would like and had already taken some. There had been a lot of interest in the house and one couple were very keen and had made an offer. It was now late August and seven weeks since Bernard had passed away, although it seemed much longer. It was hard not to look in Estate agent's windows and Belle had weakened. The result was, she had seen exactly what she wanted. A small, exclusive development, too small to call an estate, of several blocks of apartments. Six to a block and in well-kept grounds. She didn't hesitate and put a deposit on a vacant one. It was on the first floor and consisted of two double bedrooms, with en-suite to both, and a huge kitchen diner and lounge. She loved the open plan design, where guests would be close by while she made drinks or prepared food. As so often happened, her thoughts turned to Bernard. Would he think she was doing the right thing? He would probably say she was lowering herself by moving to an apartment. He would add with a sneer, it was only a flat. Belle sighed and resumed her packing.

Just then there was a familiar rat-tat-tat at the door.

"Rob." she said out loud. Belle let him in with a smile and they hugged.

"How are you Rob?"

Rob's eyes swept over her admiringly. "I'm fine, but, how are you? I must say that you look great."

"Thanks. I'm OK, but I'm glad to see you. I was thinking about things and getting a bit fed up."

Rob looked at her sympathetically. "I understand. It takes a long time to get over losing someone. I should know. I thought I would never get over losing my Philippa. In fact, even now, I have my moments, if you know what I mean?"

Belle nodded but was silent for a few moments while she made the tea. Should she tell Rob the truth about her marriage. Chris and Rose had some idea now, so maybe Rob ought to know as well.

"Well actually Rob, we were never that happy really. Not after the first five or six years anyway. It all started to go wrong after my parents died."

Rob looked shocked. "So, was Bernard not very understanding during that time?"

"Oh don't get me wrong. He was very good then. He dealt with a lot of the details and he was marvellous with the girls. I suppose I have to take some of the blame for the way things were. I desperately wanted another baby, I felt it would help me get over it you see, I was so depressed when they both died and I couldn't seem to snap out of it."

Rob rubbed her arm. "Not surprising, losing them

both within the year. So, what happened, couldn't you conceive?"

"Bernard said no and that was that. I tried to explain but he just got angry like he always did if I queried anything. I thought a little job might have helped, but he got angry about that as well."

"Poor Belle. I know Bernard could be a bit humourless, but I always thought you seemed content."

Belle put her mug down with rather a thump. "Content, that's the last word I would use in describing my marriage." She paused, not wanting to criticise Bernard too much as she knew the cousins had been fond of each other.

But Rob was already worried by their conversation. "When he got angry, he didn't hurt you, did he?"

"No, not really. But he used to grip my arms so hard he bruised me on a number of occasions. To tell the truth Rob, he frightened me. I often wondered if I'd argued too much, whether he would have hit me."

"But why did he get so angry? Surely you have the right to express an opinion."

Belle shook her head." I'm afraid not. He expected instant obedience. I wasn't allowed to question any of his decisions or say what I thought. So, I mainly just kept quiet and did as I was told. It was easier that way."

"Poor Belle" Rob said again, "I had no idea."

"Well why would you Rob? You probably just thought it's the normal me, rather quiet and old-fashioned."

Rob looked thoughtful. "So how did Bernard seem? Do you think he was happy with the way things were?"

"It seems a dreadful thing to say but I really don't know if he was happy or not. Oh, dear Rob, let's change the subject. I'm beginning to feel quite depressed." She stood up and took the mugs over to the sink.

"Oh Belle, what a waste of your life."

"I'm learning not to think like that. Why ruin the rest of my life by being bitter about the past. It was partly my fault anyway. I should have stood up to him right from the beginning, but I was too scared."

She sat down again opposite Rob.

"Still, it's in the past now and I'm going to make the most of the rest of my life. Doing all the things I wasn't allowed to do before, like this." She touched her hair. "And these." She smoothed her hands down her clothes. "And travel."

Rob grinned, "Well you do look gorgeous as I said before. Where are you going to visit next?"

"Well I rather fancy France. I've never been abroad. But it will have to wait until the house is sold and I am settled in the apartment. Did I tell you about that?"

The next half hour sped by as Belle described the apartment and soon Rob had to leave to get home and do some paperwork. But before he left he said to Belle.

"You know Belle, all my life I've looked up to Bernard. I guess I had him on a pedestal, my hero. But he's just fallen off."

"I'm sorry Rob."

"No, no, I'm glad I know the truth, but it will take time to sink in."

The next day as Belle was doing her chores and thinking about her chat with Rob, a thought occurred to her. If Rose got to hear about her plans to travel abroad on her own she would start to fuss. Belle rang Rob's home phone and left a message.

"Rob. Please don't say anything to my girls about me going abroad. That's just between me and you."

A few minutes later there was a tap on the back door and Rose walked in. She sometimes popped in during the morning, so they could have a more relaxing chat without the children.

"I'm glad you've come this morning Rose. Do you think Dave could help me to sort out the loft?"

"Course, Mum, I'm sure he won't mind."

"That's good. He'd better come in the van though, I think it's going to be mainly rubbish." The phone interrupted them.

"Hello, Belle speaking."

"Don't you mean Isabelle?"

'Oh blast'! Belle thought 'It's Dorothea'. Then aloud. "No Dorothea. You are the only person who calls me that, I prefer Belle if you don't mind." She rolled her eyes at Rose. "What can I do for you Dorothea?"

"I thought I'd better ring you as you haven't bothered to ring me. It's your turn you know."

Rose saw her mother beginning to get annoyed,

"It doesn't matter whose turn it is. I'm afraid I haven't given it a thought."

"Well you should then. I am your only sister-in-law after all and it's your duty."

Belle snapped. "I have no duty to you Dorothea. Kindly don't start telling me what to do."

"Well it seems to me you need someone to do that, now Bernard can't do it any more."

"Dorothea, just listen to me and don't interrupt. I was bossed and bullied by your brother for thirty years. And you are just like him, as was your mother. I don't need that, thank you very much. I am breaking all contact with you from this moment on. I never want to hear from you again. Give my love to George, and my sympathy." With that she slammed the phone down.

"That's telling the old battle axe." She said to an astonished Rose.

"I can't believe you did that Mum."

"Well I can't stand the woman. You don't like her surely?"

"No, but I don't like you to talk about Dad in that way."

"I'm sorry Rose, but that's the way it was for me. You're an adult and you must accept it. I'm not telling you to feel differently about your Dad. It's good that you remember him with affection. But it's not the same for me. Try and understand."

★★★

It was November and at last Belle was in her apartment and loving it. In her large open plan living area there was a window over the sink in the kitchen which looked out over the gardens. On the same side at the other end, French windows opened out onto a small balcony, just big enough for two chairs and a table. Another window overlooked a small car parking area and beyond, to the countryside. Although it was winter the gardens still looked quite colourful. The garden designers had included some evergreen shrubs and the different greens and golden tones worked well. Two days had passed since moving in and it was now a Monday. The removal men had put the furniture in the rooms as asked and were very helpful but there had still been so much to do. Her daughters and their husbands had been with her over the weekend and everything was now tidy. But Belle was rearranging things more to her liking in the kitchen.

It hadn't taken her long to realise that she was going to have lots of spare time. James and Avril were coming for a coffee on Wednesday and Rose and Dave for a roast dinner on Sunday, but apart from that she had nothing planned. Then with a jolt she realised she could get a job. She didn't need the money but she desperately needed something useful to do, and the company of other people. Then she remembered all her travel plans, so a paid job was out of the question. Maybe voluntary or seasonal work would be better. Would they accept frequent absences? Well there was only one way to find out!

What did she want to do? Shop work, or maybe a café? Or perhaps helping people in hospital or at home. Belle decided to have an early lunch, then go into the main shopping area and make enquiries.

She wandered down the street, still unsure what she wanted to do. She'd been in the Oxfam shop and looked around, picked up and paid for a book, but wasn't inspired. An employment agency had been no help. Now she had decided to try some card shops and toy shops for work up to Christmas. She went into the arcade of small shops that were popular with local people. There were eleven businesses there, five down each side and one across the back. Some succeeding and some not doing very well. The larger shop at the back sold cards and small gifts and Belle made her way there. It was six weeks to Christmas and the shop was doing a brisk trade. She picked up some cards and glanced around. She could only see two assistants and they were both at the till, one taking the money and the other one putting the items in bags. The cards all looked rather untidy and a small cuddly toy was on the floor. She felt she stood a chance. Taking the cards over to the till, she joined the queue. As she paid she said to the lady on the till.

"I can see you are very busy right now, but when it's quieter do you think I might be able to have a word with you?"

The assistant gave her the receipt and change and said. "If you call back when we close at six o'clock I can give you a few minutes."

Belle smiled and said. "Thank you." She felt ridiculously excited over something so mundane as working in a card shop. But it was thirty years since she had last worked, and she so hoped something would come of this. She drove home and tried to relax and read while she waited.

Six o'clock found her back in the shop. The door was locked a few minutes after she arrived and the younger lady was stationed there letting the last few customers out. She glanced at Belle.

"I'm sorry, we're closed now."

"I know." Belle replied. "I was asked to come back at six and see the other lady."

It was another ten minutes before the last customer left. The two ladies looked at each other with a tired smile, then around the shop at all the tidying up to do. The older one came over to Belle.

"Right madam, sorry to keep you waiting. What can I do for you?"

"I wondered if you could do with some help over these busy weeks? I am available, and I would really enjoy working here."

"Well, it would certainly help. We haven't been able to tidy up or fill the shelves all day, we've been so busy. Tell me a bit about yourself." She sighed. "Come out the back so that I can take the weight off my feet."

Without making any comment, she put the kettle on and made three mugs of tea.

"Now, what hours could you do?"

"I can do any." Replied Belle. "I live alone so I'm free to do as I please." (Oh, how good that sounded to her).

"What experience do you have?"

"None I'm afraid, but I'm sure I could pick it up." She gave a little laugh. "I'm itching to help your colleague tidy up."

"Well I'm willing to give you a trial. It would be mainly tidying up, filling up, and generally helping the customers. If you get on alright I'll train you on the till. The wages are just basic shop rates I'm afraid. It's all I can afford."

"Oh, that doesn't matter. I just need to work and meet people. Since my husband died I get rather bored and a bit lonely. To tell the truth, I've wanted to get a job for years but my husband wouldn't allow it."

"Well you can start as soon as you like. The hours would be 10.30 until closing, Tuesday to Saturday. Will that be alright?"

"That will be fine. When would you like me to start?"

"Is tomorrow too soon? If you could come in at nine I can give you some instructions before we get busy, then the next day you can start at 10.30."

Belle soon got into the swing of things and by the end of that first week she really felt she was being of some use. The older woman, Nancy, was the owner and Di was her niece. Belle got on well with both of them, although there was little time to chat. Breaks were short and hurried and they were lucky to leave the shop before six thirty. By the time she got home she was exhausted and too tired to cook.

So, the first chance she got, she made several big casseroles and froze them in small portions so she only had to pop them in the microwave. But she was loving it and even Rose understood why she wanted to do it. She'd had to delay the coffee date with James and Avril indefinitely.

At the end of that first week Belle was invited out for a drink.

"It's just to the local pub. We go every Saturday for about an hour or so. Some of the people from the other shops in the arcade come as well. It's a good way to finish the week and swap news. How about it? Would you like to join us?"

Belle hesitated.

"Don't come if you'd rather not." Nancy added.

"Yes, I would like to come please. You just took me by surprise. I've never been to a pub before just for a drink. Only for an occasional meal."

Nancy and Di both gaped at her. "You mean you've never been out for a drink?"

"No never."

"Gosh, was that your husband stopping you, or did you never fancy it?"

"It was Bernard. He was so old-fashioned. He should have been born in Victorian times." She sighed. "I shouldn't keep running him down. He had his good points."

"Come on then, let's go and have a drink. I know we have to stop at one, because of driving, but it still helps."

As they sat round a large table in the pub, Belle got to know a few more of the people who worked near to them. There were eight people in the group, six women and two men. There was a lot of teasing and flirting, but nothing serious and Belle enjoyed it. She sat close to Nancy and was surprised when her boss opened up and confessed to being divorced.

"Believe me Belle, I know what some men can be like. My ex just couldn't be faithful, and in the end, I'd just had enough and told him to move out. That was ten years ago and I've never got seriously involved with anyone since."

"I don't think I will." Belle replied. "I've got my family and friends, who needs men?" They laughed.

"Mind you." Nancy said. "I like a little bit of you know what from time to time, but I've got a friend who's willing to oblige."

Belle felt herself colour up and was too embarrassed to make any comment.

The weeks leading up to Christmas flew by and soon it was Christmas eve. Nancy handed Belle her final wage packet.

"There's a little bonus in there. It's been great having you here. We'll miss you, won't we Di?"

"We certainly will. Pop in and see us won't you?"

Belle said she would.

"How would you like to do the two weeks leading up to Valentines' Day?" Nancy asked. "Just 10.30 to 2.30 as many days as you can manage."

"Oh yes please, I'd like that." Belle said enthusiastically.

Rose had suggested some weeks before Christmas that Belle should go to them for the day. She was aware that her Mother had not worked for years and knew she would be exhausted. Belle didn't argue and when she awoke Christmas morning she still felt weary. But after a leisurely morning in the quiet of her apartment, she was recovered enough to enjoy the rest of the day. On the twenty seventh Bubs came to stay for three nights. Rowan was grown up now and would spend those days with his father or friends. She arrived early afternoon having bought a sandwich on the way, but was ready for a cup of tea and a chat.

"So how was the job? Busy I bet, the last few days."

"Very busy. I don't think I've ever worked so hard. I'm going back for a couple of weeks leading up to Valentines' Day, but not such long days. More and more Bubs, I feel like I've joined the Human race. I even went out for a drink on Saturday nights!"

"What did you drink?" Bubs asked.

"Brandy and lemonade usually, sometimes a glass of wine."

"Gosh, I'm surprised and delighted. They sound like nice people."

"Oh, they are Bubs, really nice."

"I've been thinking about a holiday soon." Belle said thoughtfully. "Somewhere warm and sunny, like Cyprus. Would you be able to come with me? Have you any holiday quota to use up?"

"Yes, I've still got a week to be used by the end of March. But Belle, you don't have a passport, do you?"

"Oh blast. How stupid am I? How long will it take to get one?"

"Ages. I can't see us getting away before the end of February or even March. What a shame."

"Yes, it's jolly annoying. And a lot of offices will be closed till the new year. But I'll be there as soon as they are open and I'll let you know how I get on."

"Why Cyprus Belle?"

"Well a customer was telling me about it. Apparently, it's very pleasant in the early part of the year. You know, not too hot. We're not very good if it's hot, are we? But there's still snow up on the Troodos Mountains and it's supposed to be lovely up there. Also, most Cypriots speak English, which will be handy, and there's lots to see and do."

"Just think Belle, it will be the first time you've been abroad and the first time you've flown." She leaned over and hugged Belle. "I'm just so happy for you, and so proud of how you are changing your life. It would have been easy to have just plodded on as you were."

Getting a passport proved to be frustratingly slow. Nothing could be booked until she had it in her hand. But by going to the main passport office she managed to have it sorted out by the end of January. Belle immediately went to the travel agent and was able to reserve a holiday for two until she could speak to Bubs. It was all arranged over the next few days and she had been able to get the first week of March. Now she was filled with excitement and nervousness, but she tried to stay calm. Working the first two weeks of February helped.

★★★

Belle and Bubs climbed into Dave's car while he loaded the suitcases in the boot.

"This is very good of you Dave." Bubs said. "It's going to make it so much easier for us."

The journey to Gatwick went smoothly and they arrived in plenty of time. Belle gazed around her. She'd seen airports on television of course, but to actually be there, amongst the noise and the crowds was quite different and confusing. But Bubs was a seasoned traveller and headed straight towards the correct queue and later, after booking in, suggested they have a coffee until it was time to go through to the departure lounge. A short time later they boarded the plane.

"You sit by the window Belle. It's interesting to look out and watch how quickly we leave the ground behind. I always try and work out where we are by picking out the towns and the rivers, but it's not easy. How are you feeling? Not too nervous I hope."

"No, I'm just a teeny bit nervous and very excited. Oh Bubs, why couldn't Bernard have done this? I'm sure he would have enjoyed it."

"I don't know if he would have." Bubs replied. "He was a funny old thing about anything foreign, wasn't he?"

"Yes, you know Bubs, I think he was scared, although he would never have admitted it. Scared of a language he couldn't understand and scared of different cultures, and different foods. He had to be an expert or he didn't want to do it, whatever it was."

She grabbed the seat arms as the plane started to move out to the end of the runway. She felt the surge of power as it hurtled along and then took off. She was silent as she gazed out of the window, watching the ground becoming more and more distant. Then with a big grin she turned to Bubs.

"Wow! That was amazing."

After a while the drinks trolley came around and they both had a glass of wine and were given a small packet of nuts to go with it. Bubs had explained that sometimes, planes went through turbulence, but it was nothing to worry about, but knowing what to expect helped. They were served a meal and later a trolley came around again. The hostesses were charming and Belle couldn't resist telling them that it was her first flight. The hostess looked surprised and wished her an enjoyable journey.

It was late afternoon when they landed at Paphos airport. They collected their suitcases and were directed to a waiting coach. Although it was a short journey from the airport to the hotel, there were so many drop-offs, it was nearly an hour before it was their turn and the coach was nearly empty.

A man stepped forward to help them with their suitcases and they followed him into the hotel. Bubs glanced at her friend. "Gosh Belle, it's ever so posh. Did you fib to me about the price?"

"No, I certainly did not. It's winter Bubs and a last minute booking, that's why it was so cheap. I looked in the travel agents window last week and it was even cheaper."

A young lady walked up to them, confirmed their names and introduced herself as their courier.

"I'm Ruth, let's get you booked in and Christos will help you with the suitcases up to your room. I'll leave this itinerary with you and you can let me know if any of the trips interest you. Dinner is at seven o'clock and I'll see you there."

Their room number was 310.

"That's good, said Bubs. Four is my lucky number and three and one makes four."

Belle gave her a look. "You're mad, did you know?"

Once in the room, which was lovely and overlooked the sea, the friends soon had everything unpacked.

"Which bed do you want Bubs?"

"You have the one near the window as it's your first trip." Bubs said. Then, "Oh blast, a button has come off my cardigan. I've got a small mending kit with me but my sewing is awful."

"So's mine." Said Belle.

"I thought you were good at all house wifely things."

"No, I'm like you, hopeless at sewing. But I'll have a go." She sat on the edge of the bed and frowning, threaded a needle and sewed the button back on.

"There you are, all done." Belle handed the cardigan over.

"Thanks ever so—" Bubs broke off and started laughing. She couldn't speak and held her stomach and mopped her eyes.

All the time Belle was asking. "What? What have I done?"

Finally, Bubs was able to tell her that the stitches had gone right through to the back of the cardigan and it would be impossible to wear.

That evening, once more, Belle's taste buds were given a treat. Some of the food was traditional Greek and some English for people who preferred it. Belle ate the Greek, whenever possible and they both agreed it was delicious. Ruth gathered the newcomers together after the meal and explained each trip and what they could expect to see. Some would take them away from the resort for most of the day, but others were in and around Paphos and would only take up half the day. They booked two all day trips and one of just half a day, saving the rest of the holiday to enjoy the beach area and do their own thing.

The next day, a Sunday, was free and they explored Paphos and walked along the beach. But a paddle in the sea was abruptly halted. It was very cold, and it seemed unlikely that their swimming costumes would be used. Although the hotel had a pool, it was also unheated. A few hardy souls used it during the week, but most visitors gave it a miss.

On Monday they took a trip into the Troodos Mountains. A small twenty-seater coach was used for this. The drive up was very scenic and fascinating.

"Oh, look at that dear little house." Belle pointed out the window. "And the church, isn't it lovely? You can see how much they love it. It's so well looked after.

Do you think they paint it every year to keep it looking so good?"

"I should think so." Bubs responded. "And the little cafés look so inviting, I wish we'd hired a car, then we could have stopped for a coffee at all of them."

Belle laughed. "The coffee's so strong. You would be flying back down to Paphos."

Slowly the scenery changed, and snow began to appear. Rather dirty by the roadside, but still pristine under the trees. Finally, the coach pulled into a car park and everyone piled out.

"Brr. I know why Ruth said bring a coat now." Belle wrapped her coat around her tightly. Some of the people from the coach started to throw snowballs and soon they all joined in. Ruth led them to a café where they bought hot drinks and some delicious local pastries. The plan was to look at a famous church and then have some lunch.

The church was beautiful. It seemed as though the whole interior had been painted with 22 carat gold leaf. Once again, they could see how cherished the holy places were. After a simple hot meal, they climbed aboard the coach and headed back down towards Paphos. The driver stopped several times for people to get out and take photos of the views, the pretty villages and the orange and lemon groves.

Later, as they freshened up in their room, ready for dinner, Bubs said. "What a lovely day. I really enjoyed it. How about you Belle?"

"It was magical." Was the answer.

On Tuesday they wandered along the sea front, then, as the day warmed up, they made their way into the town and found the Botanical Gardens where they spent a couple of hours wandering and resting on the seats provided.

"Gosh, it's nearly two o'clock and I'm starving." Bubs patted her tummy.

They soon found a café and ordered some local snacks to keep them going till the evening. A handsome waiter brought their food and Belle was amused as he began to flirt with them and watched Bubs respond.

After he had gone she pretended to be shocked by Bub's behaviour.

"Why would he flirt with two middle aged ladies?" She wanted to know.

"We are on our own and you would be surprised how many women of our age, and older, come here looking for romance. But you needn't worry about me, I just like to flirt but nothing more. Do you mind if we go back to the beach for a while when we've finished eating?"

"Of course we can. It should be very pleasant."

Bubs leaned back against the sea wall and closed her eyes. "This is the life."

But after forty-five minutes, Belle was bored. She gave an involuntary sigh.

"I bet you want to explore. Am I right?" Bubs opened one eye and looked at her with a grin.

"Yes, sorry, I know I'm fidgety. It's just that I don't want to miss anything. There are so many places in the world that I want to go to. I may never come back here again so I want to make the most of it."

"Tomorrow should take care of that." Bubs replied.

The Land Rover bumped over the uneven ground and Belle and Bubs hung on. They could have taken another trip in a coach, but this sounded much more fun. The driver could take them down smaller roads and narrow tracks where coaches couldn't go. Even at times, leaving the tracks and seemingly going cross country. But there were so many interesting things to see. Some natural and some man made, many years ago. Just after one o'clock he pulled off onto a green area with trees creating a shady place to sit.

"Right. Everybody out." He reached under the seats and pulled out some rugs and fishing stools.

"Make yourselves comfortable. There's shade over there if you prefer it. I'll get some food on the go."

He reached under the seats again and took out a small barbecue and some fuel and found a level area to stand it. As the heat began to build up he lifted a cool box from the front passenger seat and took out meat and placed it on the barbecue. Then from another box he produced plastic cups, plates and cutlery. As the wonderful aromas of cooking meat began to make everyone's mouth water, the driver, an English man called Tom, took a bottle of white wine from the cool bag and a bottle of red from the box and offered everyone a drink.

Bubs and Belle leaned their backs against a tree and sipped their wine. "This is heaven." Bubs said.

The barbecued meat was very good and so tender, it melted in the mouth. There were bread rolls and salad to accompany it. Once they had finished eating, everything was packed away and they all got back in the Land Rover to continue the adventure. Tom took them to a rugged area of coastline where he parked again. They walked across a rocky cliff top, about thirty feet above sea level. Tom stopped and pointed a few feet ahead.

"See that hole in front of us? We can climb down there and get to the beach. Is anyone up for it?"

Everyone said. "Yes!"

They all scrambled down through the hole and onto a steep path leading into a cave. The floor of the cave was also rocky, so Belle and Bubs hung on to each other. Then they were out on the sea shore in brilliant sunshine again. Tom didn't hurry them back. They sat on the rocks, chatting and watching the waves gently breaking on the shore.

But then he called. "Come on everyone. Back to the Land Rover now please."

It was quite a hard climb back up to the top, but they were all soon seated in the vehicle and bumping back on to the road.

Tom stopped once more at a small café for a drink and a cake, then onwards back to the hotel.

That evening they sat in the hotel lounge and talked about the day. Both felt tired and not hungry enough for a full-scale meal.

"Let's just have a coffee and a light snack." Belle said.

A waiter came over and they told him what they wanted. He asked them for their room number and Belle signed along the bottom of his pad. As always, the coffee and pastry were delicious. It was the third time they had done this, and it saved bothering with money. Everything about the hotel was first class, the room, the food and the service. They couldn't fault it.

"I'll tell you something Belle. My Rowan would have loved today."

It was Thursday already, and they could hardly believe it. How the time was flying by. They had decided to visit the Baths of Aphrodite today, where people of all ages were bathing. The water was very cold, so they opted not to go in. It was reputed to restore fertility, but neither of them wanted, or needed to risk that happening! On the way back, they were given a tour of the Tombs of the Kings, which were dated from the fourth century B.C. Ruth had suggested the previous day that they might like to visit the Paphos Mosaics, so they took a taxi to get them there and spent some time looking at them and reading all the information. But then it was Bubs turn to get bored.

"Come on Belle. Let's see if we can get a bus back. I saw several on the way here." They spent some time buying gifts and mementos, then got the bus back to the hotel, tired out after a full and busy day.

The next morning Ruth came up to them at breakfast and asked if they would like to go to a real Greek restaurant for lunch.

"You don't want to hang around the hotel on your last day, do you? I've got half a dozen other people interested and we can go in two taxis. Would you like to do that?"

There was no hesitation and they were pleased they did. The food was more authentic than in the hotel, and they both enjoyed it very much. That evening they just had a snack and then went up to their room and packed as much as they could because the coach taking them to the airport would be picking them up at 9.00a.m.

As the coach headed for the airport they silently looked out the window for a last glimpse of places they had visited.

"I was a bit shocked when you were paying just now Belle. Those little snacks we kept signing for, and the trips, nearly doubled the price of the holiday."

"Yes, I know, but I don't want you to worry about it. I've still got some money left over from selling the house and I can pay most of it."

Bubs argued, as Belle knew she would, so they decided to leave it and sort it out when they got home. In actual fact, Belle was comfortably off but she didn't want to sound as though she was boasting. She was confident they would come to some agreement.

CHAPTER 20

It was the end of April and Belle had been helping out at the card shop over Easter. Now she was sitting in her lounge with the television on and a meal on a tray. She was watching a programme about vineyards in Provence, in the South of France. The fork of food stopped half way to her mouth. It looked so beautiful there. The scenery, the coastline and the immaculate vineyards. Suddenly Spain, where she had been planning to go next, was forgotten. That night, as she lay in bed, all she could think of was Provence. And, crazily, driving there. To have the chance to stop and look whenever she pleased was irresistible. But what an adventure. She would have to deceive her daughters because they would certainly try and stop her, even Chris. She couldn't sleep but tossed and turned until the early hours. The first thing that came to her mind on waking the next morning was France, and she began to make plans. Four or five days to get there, a fortnight there and four or five days to get home. Three and a half to four weeks, perfect. She had breakfast and tidied the kitchen, then put the washing in the drier. She jumped as the door buzzer sounded. She hurried over to the window and saw Rob's car, and Rob himself, grinning and gesturing for her to release the door. She watched him coming up the stairs and gave him a hug.

"I thought for a minute you were away again. I had to cadge a cup of tea from Rose in March."

Belle laughed. "Well you're lucky to catch me. I shall be going away again soon."

"Where to this time?"

"I haven't decided yet, but I'll give you a ring before I go. The world's a big place Rob and it's all out there waiting for me. I'll be fifty this year and I've got a lot of catching up to do."

"I'm delighted for you Belle. Good luck to you. Thanks." He took his mug of tea and sipped, and Belle sat down beside him.

They chatted about his work and Belle told him about Cyprus and showed him the photos.

"How was the flying? Did you enjoy it?"

"It was fine, although I couldn't honestly say that I enjoyed it?"

They talked on for another half an hour then Rob left to make a call on a customer.

The next morning, she drove to the shops, parked and made her way to the travel agents.

"I just wanted to pop in and tell you how lovely our holiday in Cyprus was." She said to the young lady.

"That's good, I'm glad you enjoyed it."

"I'm going to be a bit cheeky actually. I may want you to book the ferry to Calais soon, but I need some information on Motels in France. I'm thinking of driving there and I don't know how far I'll get each day so I can't book in advance."

"That's no problem. I'll give you the names of several of the hotel groups. There are different levels, obviously. Some are very basic, then they go up to really nice ones. You'll want the motels at the actual services I expect. You may have to go off the motorway sometimes, usually only a short distance though."

She wrote some names down and pointed out one in particular. "This one is 'middle of the road ' and very nice. There are hundreds all over France. What I would advise you to do is to stop at the first one you see and pick up a book of all their motels. That will give you prices and locations and directions for getting there. I believe there is at least one in Calais, so it might be a good idea to get a book there as soon as you get off the ferry."

"Thank you very much. When I've decided on my dates, I'll call in and book the ferry."

As Belle drove home, she began to feel quite anxious about driving on and off the ferry, and then having to drive on the 'wrong' side of the road in France. And at the same time looking for the motel in a busy city street. But surely someone on the ferry would know where it was. There were sure to be staff around who did the crossing on a regular basis, they would know. She was glad she could remember a little French from school, but a phrase book would be very useful.

Belle parked on the car deck and made her way up the stairs, following the other passengers. She was surprised how big the ferry was and for a moment, panicked at what she had taken on. Taking a door to the outside deck she stood in the cool sea breeze and took a few deep breaths to calm herself. Once back inside, it didn't take long to find an information desk.

"Do you happen to know where the Flamingo Motel is in Calais, please?"

"Yes madam, there are two. Which one do you want?"

"The easiest one to get to by car. I've never driven in France before and I'm extremely nervous."

The young man was very reassuring. "You'll be fine. Just remember to drive on the wrong side of the road and go around the roundabouts the wrong way." He chuckled. "After an hour or so, you'll wonder why you were anxious. Anyway, just follow everyone else when you leave the ferry until you come to a roundabout, then take the first exit. That will take you down the coast road. Follow that for a couple of miles and you will see the motel on your left. You can't miss it, it's very large."

"Thank you so much." Belle said, and walked off to find a restaurant. It was one o'clock and she was very hungry after an early start and very little breakfast. Joining the queue, she looked around her at the large dining area and beyond, through the windows, to the blue sea. To her surprise, France could be clearly seen on the horizon. She hadn't expected to see it so soon.

The announcer reminded everyone to adjust their watches and Belle did so. She played safe with her meal and chose scampi and chips, then sat down as near to a window as possible. When she had finished eating she got up for a cup of tea, then sat at a table near the front. The French coast suddenly seemed very close. Surely, they would be called back to the car deck very soon. But everyone was still sitting around, looking perfectly relaxed. She glanced at her watch, still half an hour to go. They appeared to be sailing alongside the coast. Belle could only presume this was the course the ferry had to take. She sat back and tried to relax while she could, thinking about her adventure. Naturally, Rose and Chris had wanted to know where she was going.

"I'm just going South." She had told them truthfully. "And I'll have to see where I end up."

Apart from the lady in the travel agents, nobody knew of her plans, not even Bubs. Tomorrow she would phone them and tell them where she was. Hopefully the motels would have a phone.

Then, all drivers were called back to their vehicles.

Belle sat in her car and waited for the car deck doors to open. Her heart was thumping and once again she had to ask herself why she was doing this. The doors began to open and after a few minutes, the cars at the front started to move. Then it was her turn. She bit her lip and edged forward, out through the gaping mouth of the ferry and over the ramp. Then she was driving through the port and out to the road beyond. Her knuckles were white as she gripped the steering wheel and turned the air-con towards her face. She was behind another English car and it was going quite slowly, so that helped. In no time at all she was at the roundabout. The English car went straight on, as did most of the vehicles, but Belle turned right. Very soon she saw the motel come into view. She signalled left and pulled into the centre of the road, where one could wait till the road was clear. Then she was in the hotel car park. She switched the engine off and took a few deep breaths. So far, so good. But she was damp with nerves, shaking and her mouth felt dry. After a few minutes she popped a peppermint in her mouth, picked up her handbag and walked into reception.

"Bonjour, good afternoon. Please could I have one of these?" She took a booklet from the counter and held it out for the young man to see.

"Yes madam, help yourself." He said with a smile.

Belle sat in her car and studied the book and checked the route and road number she wanted to take. She didn't expect to get very far today. It was already three thirty and she was exhausted. "Come on woman". She said aloud to herself. "All you've done is a bit of driving and sat on a ferry. "You can do a few more miles yet".

She soon found herself back at the roundabout and took the first exit again which would take her to one of the main motorways in France, the E-15/ A26. The next half hour was nerve racking, but eventually she found herself on the motorway and heading South towards Bethune, where she would be able to find a Flamingo Motel. Compared to English roads the traffic was light and at one point there was nobody in sight to the front and only one lorry a good distance behind. So, Belle relaxed, and the miles sped by. It was about eighty miles to Bethune and she was there and in the motel car park before six o'clock. She discovered that the receptionist here spoke good English, as had the one in Calais, so she was soon booked in, and in her room on the second floor. Her window looked out over the car park and beyond to some industrial buildings. Then as she looked she spotted the motorway just beyond that. She had bought a pack of sandwiches on the ferry and as soon as she had unpacked she ate them and made a hot drink with the facilities provided. Then she headed back down to reception to use the phone.

"Hello Chris, it's Mum."

"Where have you ended up then?"

"I'm in France."

"What? There's just no stopping you."

"It was a bit scary at first, but I soon got used to it. Can I do what I did last time? Take it in turns to ring you, Rose and Bubs and then you can pass it on."

"Yes of course Mum, good idea."

"I'll make the calls short Chris, then I can write with more details."

"OK, enjoy yourself and take care."

Belle went back up to her room and studied the atlas again, trying to tie things in with the motels. She began to fall asleep, so got off the bed and had a quick shower. As she snuggled down her last thought was 'I bet I'll have trouble getting to sleep now'. Then she slept.

She stopped the next night just North of Lyon, then on the third night she reached Aix-en-Provence, each night using a Flamingo Motel. The next morning, she picked up some leaflets from reception and headed into the heart of the vineyard area. Now she could take her time, stopping frequently and taking photographs. She picked up a detailed map from a tourist office and tried to decide the best place to look for a hotel. She finally decided to take the main road along the coast to Toulon, then inland to Cuers. By the time she had enjoyed lunch overlooking the Mediterranean Sea and found her way to Cuers, it was after three o'clock. Once more she made her way to a tourist office. As she struggled to explain to the young assistant what she was looking for an elderly lady came up to them.

"Excuse me for interrupting, but I may be able to help."

She spoke a few words in rapid French to the tourist lady, then drew Belle to one side.

"I hope you don't mind me sticking my nose in, but I think I know what you're looking for. Shall we go and have a cup of coffee and a chat or would you rather I left you to sort it out on your own?" The lady was obviously British, and from her accent Belle guessed she was from Wales.

"I'd be grateful for some help." She said. "I haven't used my French since school."

She followed the lady to a nearby café and they ordered coffee.

"My name is Elsie and I come here twice a year, so I know the area well. I always stay at a small hotel on the outskirts of the town. It's quiet and a very pretty area, the lady who runs it is rather sweet and I think she has a vacant room at the moment. I'm sorry dear, what's your name?"

"I'm Belle Johnston. It's very good of you to help."

"Not at all. Would you like to look at the hotel?"

"Yes, I would, it sounds nice."

"The problem is, my car is at the hotel and I came into town on the bus. Do you have a car?"

"Yes, it's just around the corner. I'm ready when you are." She said with a smile. They paid for their coffees and left to walk the short distance to the car. Fifteen minutes later Belle pulled up in front of a small hotel. It was an old building, but the style was rather grand. As they walked into the hotel a lady came through from the rear. Elsie greeted her and explained in her excellent French that Belle was looking for a room.

The lady smiled at Belle and said. "Come with me please."

Belle and Elsie followed her through the hallway and up the stairs and along to the end of a corridor.

"My name is Louise." She said over her shoulder. "The room is small, perhaps too small for you."

She unlocked the door and they stepped inside. The room certainly was small, but very pretty and a long window looked out over a garden.

"It's lovely, I'd like to have it please." Belle was delighted with it.

Louise said there would be a meal at seven and both ladies said that would be fine.

"I will leave you to unpack, then you can rest in the lounge if you wish, until seven o'clock."

Louise's English was remarkably good and as they sat in the lounge later, Elsie told her that she had spent some years living in England, so that explained why.

"So, have you any plans while you are here?" Elsie asked.

"I'd like to drive around and look at the scenery and spend some time on the coast. And if it's possible, I'd like to look over a vineyard. It must be very interesting."

"Well I won't make a nuisance of myself, but I'm here if you need any help. I know where there is a vineyard that is run by an Englishman called Frank. He's always happy to show people round and his wine is very good."

"Oh, really, as soon as you are free, I'd like to do that."

"How about the day after tomorrow?"

"That would be great. Thank you, Elsie."

Belle settled down straight away. She had a tiny en-suite and the bed was very comfortable. Louise was a good cook and, as Elsie had said, a very nice lady. The next morning, with the map on the seat beside her, Belle set off to explore. The camera was taken out of her bag and used many times. And she enjoyed driving round the small country roads after three days on motorways. When she got back to the hotel that evening Elsie told her that she had rung Frank and he said to go around in the morning about 11.30.

"I'll come with you and introduce you, then I have to see a friend in Toulon and say goodbye, so I'll come in my car. I have some wine to pick up from Frank and say goodbye to him as well. I usually take some home."

"Oh, when are you going?" Belle really liked Elsie and although they had only known each other for a short time, she knew she was going to miss her.

"The day after tomorrow. I'd like to stay but I've been here for a month already. I usually have a month in the spring, then again in the autumn. It's a second home for me really."

The next morning Belle followed Elsie's little red car round the small roads for about three miles, then they pulled into a wide gateway. Immediately, Belle's eyes were drawn to the view. Thousands of vines grew in straight lines down the slope, and in the distance, was a tiny sparkle of sea. Just inside the gate was a house and further over were the buildings for equipment to maintain the vines and produce the wine. They parked and walked a few yards towards the vines.

"He'll be out there somewhere." Elsie said, then she looked to her left as a man came out of one of the buildings. "Ah, there he is."

Belle looked up. He was walking towards them, a smile on his face. A strange sensation swept over Belle, one she hadn't felt for many years. Frank was tall and slim, but with wide shoulders. His arms and face brown from working outdoors. He had dark wavy hair and startlingly blue eyes.

"Wow." Belle didn't realise she had spoken out loud.

"Yes. Gorgeous, isn't he? If only I was twenty years younger." Elsie sighed, then she grinned at Belle. "He's fancy free." She added softly.

"Hello, Elsie me darling. Is this your friend Belle then?" He shook Belle's hand and kissed Elsie's cheek. "I've sorted your wine out. Just four bottles of your favourite red, is that right?"

"Yes, it will have to do. It's too heavy to take more. If I had driven here like Belle, I would take four dozen! I must be off now, I'll see you in September Frank. They hugged fondly, then Frank kissed her on both cheeks, French style. Then she hugged Belle.

"Enjoy the rest of your holiday dear."

"I will, please can I have your address back home? I'll drop you a line when I return."

They exchanged addresses and then Elsie was off. Belle and Frank waved till she was out of sight. Then Frank turned those amazing eyes in Belle's direction.

"We'll walk among the vines first, then we'll have a coffee before I take you into the barns."

Belle followed him down the slope, her eyes taking in his slim hips. His hair was just long enough to be partially covering the back of his neck, the black mixed with a small amount of grey. He turned to wait for her, smiling as he did so. Belle felt herself blush. She couldn't believe how she was feeling, rather like a teenager, not a woman approaching fifty. He began to tell her about the history of the vineyard and the different grapes.

"I came here with my wife fifteen years ago. It was very neglected, but we worked hard to bring it back to this condition. I think I've read every book about wine production there is." He smiled at her. "And I've had help and advice from my neighbour, Pierre. My wife went back to England ten years ago, she couldn't settle."

Belle couldn't think of anything to say to this, so she remained silent. After about half an hour they made their way back to the house and Frank ushered her in.

"Please, sit down by the French windows, it's very pleasant there."

He made coffee and brought it over, sitting down beside her. Reaching behind, he picked up an album and showed her photographs of how the vineyard looked when he first took it over. He pointed to one photo.

"See how small the house was then, and it was rather primitive."

They continued to look at the photographs of the improving state of the vines and the house over the years. When Belle had finished her coffee, Frank put the album away and they went outside and strolled down to where the vines began. He explained about irrigation and pruning and told her more about the different types of grapes, then lead her back up the slope to the first barn. Belle tried to concentrate as he explained what the various pieces of machinery were used for, but her emotions were not behaving. As they walked to the other barn Frank said.

"You're on your own Belle, does that mean you are single?"

"Yes, I was widowed last year, but I didn't have a happy marriage."

"That's a shame. It's always sad when things don't work out." He pushed a door open and lead her into the other barn. "It's strange really, when I see my wife now, we get on really well, but she's got somebody else now and I'm really pleased for her."

"How about you Frank? Have you got anybody?"

"Not at the moment, I've had a couple of girlfriends, but nothing serious." He swept his arm around the barn. "This is where I process the wine. But to be honest, most of the grapes go to a co-operative. That's what a lot of the smaller vineyards do."

He went to a barrel and poured a little wine into a glass. "Try that, it's probably my best white."

"Mm, that's lovely." Belle said with a smile.

"Would you like to try a red now?"

"No, I'd better not, I'm driving. Perhaps I can come back another day and try it?"

"That's an excellent idea. How would you like to come back Sunday evening and I'll cook you a meal and we can sample another of my wines?"

"I'd like that." Belle said.

"I can't do tomorrow evening." Frank said regretfully. "I've got a winemakers meeting."

He explained a little more about the process of bottling the wine and selling to various outlets, some in the local town and other places further afield. Then they made their way back to Belle's car. Frank put his hands on her shoulders and kissed her cheeks.

"Until Sunday evening then, about seven?"

"Yes, that will be fine. Bye Frank."

She drove down the road for a short way, then pulled into a layby and switched off the engine. Looking out over the view, her heartbeat steadied. Although she was pleased to be seeing him again, she was also nervous. She'd only ever known Bernard. Only ever dated Bernard. Just rather an innocent really, in the world of romance.

Dear Bubs

I have arrived safely in Provence and have found a lovely little hotel where I will probably stay for the duration of my holiday. I'm enjoying myself but I don't know whether I would do it again on my own. Still, never say never. I just had to write and tell you that I have met the most gorgeous man. He owns a local vineyard and he showed me around today. He's English and single and we've got a date for Sunday. Oh Bubs, this dating thing is all new to me and I'm excited and scared. I have a feeling that things are going to move pretty quickly! Tomorrow I'm going down to the coast to explore. The weather is perfect, and the scenery is as stunning as I had hoped. I will write again after Sunday!!

Love Belle

The dining room was busy when Belle went down the next morning, but she was relieved to see Elsie sitting alone and saving a place for her near the window. She beckoned her over.

"I'm so glad you haven't left yet." Belle said warmly. "I wanted to say goodbye and thank you for all your help."

"Did you find the vineyard interesting?"

"Yes, very, and I sampled some of the wine. I'll definitely be taking some back with me."

"He's dishy, isn't he?" Elsie said. It made Belle laugh because Elsie was at least seventy.

"Yes, he is. I'm seeing him Sunday evening. He's going to cook me a meal."

"Oh, you lucky thing. Have a lovely time and behave---- on second thoughts, why should you."

They both laughed and went back to their breakfasts.

After Elsie had left, Belle went back to her room and took out her map. She was seeing Frank tomorrow evening, so today was hers to do as she wished, and she had the whole day. Plenty of time to drive to the coast and explore there. Whilst there she could buy postcards and stamps and send one each to Chris and Rose, which she did.

Hi from Provence. Having a lovely time. Everything is good. Hotel, weather, food and scenery.
   Love, Mum xx

On the way down to the coast she saw other vineyards and when she noticed one with a restaurant she turned in to have a coffee. After a drink and a pastry, a small shop took her interest and she wandered around, picking up a bottle of wine and a punnet of grapes, then it was on to the coast. Once there she parked and stood looking at the sea and breathing in the sea air. Once again, she wished she wasn't alone. Everywhere she looked, people had companions. They walked past her, chatting and laughing. Giving herself a mental shake she moved along to find a tourist office, determined to make the most of her time there.

She arrived back at the hotel just after five o'clock. Louise came out of her private rooms at the back of the building.

"Have you had a nice day Belle?"

"Wonderful, but I think I'll have a rest before dinner."

"If you prefer, there is shade in the garden." Louise suggested. Then added "Frank phoned, he will ring again later."

"Oh, thank you. I will go in the garden, there may be a nice cool breeze out there."

It was after nine when Frank rang again.

"I don't know why I didn't think of it before, but as tomorrow is Sunday and I'm free all day, would you like to go out for a drive around the area?"

"Oh Frank, I would really love that. I've had a nice day, but it's not the same on your own."

"Alright Belle. That's good. You can tell me all about your day when I see you in the morning. Is nine thirty too early?"

"No, that's fine." They said goodbye and rung off. Belle almost danced back into the guest's lounge. She couldn't think of anything more perfect than spending the day exploring with Frank.

When she came downstairs on Sunday morning, Frank was already there, chatting to Louise in French, far too fast for Belle to pick up anything they were saying. He turned and said.

"Good morning." Then he kissed her on the cheek.

"Good morning". Said Belle.

"Have a good day." Louise said. "Frank says you won't want a meal tonight. Is that correct?"

Belle said it was, they said 'au revoir' and went out to the car. Belle wasn't sure what the make of the car was, but she would describe it, if any one asked, as big and chunky! Very much the sort of vehicle one would expect Frank to have.

"As you went down to the coast yesterday, I thought we would stay inland today. Is that alright?"

"I really don't mind where we go." Belle said "I'm so looking forward to the day."

Frank smiled at her. "What I'm planning is to drive East to a town called Grasse. I'm taking a scenic route, then when we get there we'll have a look around and then have some lunch. There's a lovely cathedral and other interesting things to see. Then on the way home I know a nice restaurant where we can eat. But we'll have a night cap at my place if that's OK with you?"

"That all sounds lovely Frank. It's so good of you to give up your Sunday for me."

"I'm looking forward to it as well." said Frank, "It's a long time since I had the company of a lovely lady for a whole day."

Belle relaxed and gazed from the window at the views and the vineyards and sometimes lush woodlands with a carpet of bluebells. As the car was French, Frank was sitting on the left, which gave Belle the best views. They stopped for a coffee and then continued on their way. As they approached Grasse, Belle could see it was a fascinating town. Built on different levels and with varied architecture, there was obviously going to be lots to take in.

"It's too early for lunch." Frank said "Let's have a drink and decide in what order we want to see things."

"I'd really like to see the cathedral." Belle sat down at one of the pavement tables and Frank sat opposite. Soon they were sipping a delicious coffee. Frank grinned at her across the table.

"So, Belle, have you noticed anything about Grasse?"

"Yes, it smells." Then she burst out laughing. "Perhaps I should say, it seems to have a pleasant aroma."

"Mm, that sounds better." Frank chuckled "The reason it has a 'pleasant aroma' is because perfume is made here. I understand there are three manufacturers.

We'll have to see if they do guided tours. There's lots more as well." He put down his empty coffee cup, "As soon as you are ready we'll go and look at the cathedral."

As they left the café, he took her hand and it seemed quite natural to do so. Frank seemed to know the way, but Belle was glad to see a sign pointing to 'Cathedrale De Grasse'. They were already quite close, Frank told her and five minutes later the building came into view.

"Amazing isn't it?" Frank gazed up at the tower reaching into the sky. "I'm pretty sure we can go in and hopefully, up some way as well." But they couldn't go up the tower.

However, the interior of the cathedral was magnificent, and it took them an hour to look round. As they stepped back out into the bright sunshine, Belle said.

"I'm very hungry, could we have something to eat please?"

"Of course, I know just the place."

He led her just around the corner to a small café, and into the cool interior. He greeted the waiter who stepped forward and asked him something in French.

"Oui, monsieur."

He led the way to the rear of the building and out in to a garden with half a dozen tables. Belle gasped, they were up very high, and they could see for miles. The waiter took them to a table in the shade of a tree and pulled the chair out for Belle to sit down.

"Merci." Belle thanked him with a smile and turned to take in the view while Frank ordered a glass of wine for them. They were looking out over what appeared to be a prosperous suburb of Grasse. Beautiful villas, in generous grounds, covered a large area. They all seemed to be surrounded by trees and many of the villas were white.

"Gosh." Was all she could say. Taking out her camera, she took some photos, then swung the camera round and took one of Frank with the tower of the cathedral behind him. Then Frank took a couple of her with the view behind her. The waiter came back with their wine and took a picture of both of them, which pleased Belle.

After they had eaten a light lunch, Frank suggested they go to the 'Musee Fragenard'. They wandered along leisurely, enjoying each other's company. Sometimes silent, sometimes chatting and finding out about each other's lives. Finally, they came to the Perfume Museum and stepped into the coolness of the building. The museum was not large though, and soon they were back out into the heat of the afternoon.

"I know where there are some lovely gardens." Frank said. "Let's go and sit there for a while, then we'll make our way back to the car."

They sat in the gardens for an hour or so, then returned to the car and began the journey back.

"If you don't mind, I think I would like to eat back at the vineyard." Frank said. "I do a mean stir fry, what do you think?"

"That sounds lovely." Belle replied. "And nice and light. I don't think I can manage a big meal."

Frank parked the car and unlocked the door into the house.

"Go in Belle and make yourself comfortable. I just need to check round and make sure everything is OK."

"I think I'll stay outside Frank. It's cooling down now and it's a lovely evening, I'm going to walk through the vines for a while."

"Alright, when I've checked round I'll start on the meal. I'll pour a glass of my red wine for you. Don't get lost."

He turned towards the barns with a smile and Belle watched him walk away, then sauntered down to the vines. Twenty minutes later, as she walked back up, wonderful aromas wafted her way. She stepped inside the house and Frank put down his spatula and walked towards her.

"It will be about ten minutes. Are you feeling hungry?" He held her shoulders lightly as he looked down at her.

"Yes, I am, and it smells lovely."

He kissed her lightly on the lips. "And so do you." He said. Then he put his arms around her and kissed her again, his lips lingering longer. Then he abruptly released her and with a laugh, hurried back to the hob. "I'd better concentrate on the food, I think."

The food was delicious, although Belle hardly knew what she was eating. She was very glad it was a light meal, but even so, she couldn't eat the crusty bread Frank had put on the table. When they had finished he loaded everything in the dishwasher and started it. The house seemed to be just one huge room downstairs, but Frank took her on a quick tour. The room they had eaten in was an open plan kitchen, dining and living room area. A door lead through to a square hallway and leading off from that, there was an office and a shower room. Upstairs, Frank told her that he had three double bedrooms and a family bathroom. They returned to the living room and Frank asked her to sit on the settee while he made coffee.

"So, Frank, the young people in that photo. Are they your children?"

"Yes, they are, but that was taken some years ago. Phillip is now twenty-five and Helen is twenty-three. Do you have children?"

"Yes, I've got two daughters. I was married very young, so they are older than your two. Chris is thirty and Rose is twenty-eight. And I'm a grandmother to two delightful children, Gary and Megan. I really miss them when I'm away, but I was determined to travel."

Frank put down his cup and then took Belle's and put that on the table too. Then he took her in his arms and kissed her.

"You are a lovely woman. Did you know that?" He kissed her again and Belle felt herself respond. "I want to make love to you Belle, and I think you feel the same. Am I right?"

Belle could only nod.

It was eleven o'clock and all was quiet as Belle let herself into the hotel. Louise had loaned her a key and she locked the door on the inside, left the key on the hall table and made her way upstairs. As she snuggled down in bed, she was glowing. The evening had been wonderful. The delicious food and then the excitement of making love. Frank had told her that it had been a long time since he'd 'had a cuddle', which made her smile. And of course, it was the same for her. Frank had apologised for rushing things, but as Belle pointed out, she had kept up with him. It seemed only natural that they should make love again at a more leisurely pace. For Belle, making love twice in an hour was something she had never done before. To Frank's surprise, as they lay entwined afterwards, Belle had burst out laughing.

"What's so funny then?" He sounded quite hurt.

"Sorry, it's not you. I could just imagine Bernard saying. 'If it's done properly you shouldn't have to do it again'. It's just the sort of thing he would have said." She took a deep breath. "I shouldn't be horrible about him, but he was such a stuffed shirt."

Now Belle just felt content and very sleepy. She rolled over on to her side and was soon asleep.

Dear Bubs

Your goody-goody friend is not so good any more. Yes, Frank and I are lovers. Gosh, it feels so wicked just writing it down. Don't tell the girls for goodness sake. I don't mind them knowing I have a gentleman friend, but they will think I'm far too old to have a lover. I expect I shall see Frank most evenings although he does have meetings and other friends to see, so I mustn't take up all his time. He needs to deliver some wine to some shops on the coast in a couple of days time, and has asked me to go with him. It will be so much more enjoyable than when I went on my own. In the meantime, I shall explore the local town tomorrow and maybe get some gifts for everyone.

Please write back soon. I miss you—honestly.

Love Belle xx

Belle had been in Provence a week, and now it was Thursday and Louise had given her a letter which had arrived in the post that morning. Belle ripped it open eagerly.

Dear Belle

You see what happens the minute I let you out of my sight! Ha ha! I'm happy for you dear, but please be careful. You must make sure you have some photos of him. I shall want to know everything about France and your hotel etc. and of course everything about Frank, well, almost everything anyway. It sounds like you are having a wonderful time. Rose phoned me and wanted to know everything! I told her you had a friend, but as requested, I didn't tell her you had dragged him off to bed. Have you had nice weather so far? What's your hotel like? When do you plan to come home? Please write back soon. It's like an exciting serial on TV and I just can't wait for the next episode.

Your loving and jealous friend

Bubs xx

Belle had become good friends with Louise, as Elsie had. Sometimes, if Louise had shopping to do in the town, Belle would go with her. She even kept her own room clean and tidy and helped in the garden. She was going to see Frank again on Friday evening and they would spend Sunday together, when he planned to drive into a more mountainous region. He was going to take food and drink, as he had a car fridge to keep things cool and a small gas stove for making hot drinks. 'Best to be prepared'. He said.

Sunday turned out to be another beautiful day. Frank called for Belle at eight o'clock and she was ready and looking forward to the day. She climbed into the car and gave Frank a kiss, then secured her seat belt. Frank handed her an atlas.

"Right, this is where we are going." He pointed to a mountain which was over three thousand metres high. "Not right to the top." He laughed, "But as near as we can get. You probably know, when the road is highlighted in green, it's a scenic route. I thought we would take this road."

He traced it with his finger. "Then cut up through the smaller roads, do a left here and a right here and then just follow this road."

"OK, I've got that. It looks a long way."

"It is." He grinned at her wickedly, "But I've got sleeping bags, just in case."

They had a wonderful day, stopping for a coffee, which Frank made, and a delicious French pastry from a village patisserie. Then they pressed on until they got to their destination. Up here there were ski villages, although there was no snow at this time of year. Many of the chalets and shops were closed for the Summer and there were only a few people about. Frank parked the car and they walked up deserted footpaths, pausing from time to time to take in the amazing views and to catch their breath. They came to a group of tall conifer trees and Frank suggested they rest and have a sandwich. He took his waterproof jacket out of his backpack and laid it on the ground. Belle sat down.

"Phew, that was quite a climb." She took off her fleece and undid a couple of buttons on her blouse.

"Don't stop." Frank said with a cheeky grin as he peeled off his tee-shirt. The sun warmed his bare skin and he leaned back against the tree. Then his glance lingered on Belle.

"There's not a soul about." He said, "And you look about nineteen with roses in your cheeks and I want you."

Belle looked around, she was as eager as Frank. "Let's go under these trees." She said.

Frank picked up the coat and they walked in among the trees.

"There's nothing like a bit of lovemaking to liven up your appetite." Frank said later with a chuckle as he bit into a sandwich. They finished off the food and drank some water.

"Better make our way down to the car." He said. "Then we'll take a different route home. It's a bit longer, but you'll be able to see the Italian border. Would you like that?"

"Oh, yes. Especially if I can put a foot into Italy. I can say I've been to Italy then, can't I? Oh, look. Is that the Med. I can see?" Belle pointed excitedly out through the windscreen.

"Yes, it is, and actually, if you look at the atlas, you'll see we are in Italy." He grinned as Belle gave a squeal of excitement. "I'm going to drive down to the coast, then we'll turn West and drive through Monaco."

"Monaco. Wow!" Belle gazed at him, hardly believing what he was saying.

"Look at the atlas and you'll see. As soon as we are on the other side of Monaco we'll see if we can find somewhere to eat. It's five thirty now, so it will be an hour or so before we get to Nice or just beyond."

"Coo. We're not posh enough to eat in Nice."

"We'll find somewhere that's not too posh, don't worry. In fact, I think I know somewhere, as long as it's still in business."

Belle never thought she would find herself eating in a small bistro between Nice and Cannes. They had both freshened up their faces and hands in the car with tissues and cold water. Then combed their hair and brushed down their clothing.

"How do I look?" Said Belle.

Frank gave her a long look. "You look like someone who's been recently ravished." He said.

The meal was simple, but tasty and the ride back along the coast was very enjoyable. The sun began to go down and it became cooler. They fell silent, Frank concentrating on his driving and Belle fighting sleep. She didn't want to miss a thing. It had been an amazing day, but now she felt very tired. They arrived back at the hotel and Frank kissed her goodnight.

"You look exhausted Belle." He grinned at her. "I think you'll sleep well tonight."

Belle gave a sigh and tidied her bed. She was having a lovely holiday, but she was missing her family so much. She had sent cards to everyone and the children had written back.

'We miss you Nanna. Wen are you cumming back'? Belle smiled at their spelling.

She had been here now for three weeks. It didn't seem possible. She felt very torn. Her longing to be home was vying with her affection with Provence, Louise and of course, Frank. She was aware that her feelings for him were mainly sexual, although they did get on well together. However, they were dining out tonight, and in style. It was Franks' fifty third birthday and Belle was treating him to a meal at his favourite restaurant. She had been into town the previous day and had bought a new blouse. It was in a silky material and in a peach colour, which she knew suited her. But she had been very daring because it had a rather deep neckline. Not like the film stars wore, she said to herself, but showing off more cleavage than she ever had before. It came with a chiffon scarf which could be draped round the neck if the evening was cool.

She picked up Frank so that he could have a few drinks and wouldn't have to worry about driving. She hoped he would allow her to pay as it was his birthday, but knew that was unlikely to happen. His masculine pride would never accept it. As they headed for the restaurant, she was aware of Franks' eyes on her.

She smiled to herself and thought. 'I bet he's enjoying the neck line'. But as she turned and gave him a quick smile, it was obvious he was thinking quite the opposite, although he said nothing. His face was unsmiling, and he was unusually quiet. They arrived at the restaurant and Frank asked for a table in a quiet corner. They ordered a bottle of wine and began to study the menu. Suddenly, Belle turned her head away and sneezed behind her hand.

"Oh, excuse me Frank." She reached down for her handbag which was on the floor and found a tissue. As she tucked it into her pocket, Frank leaned over the table and said in a fierce whisper.

"For goodness sake Belle, cover yourself up. Have you got a cardigan or something?"

Belle stared at him in astonishment. "W-what's the matter? I'm not cold."

"You may not be cold, but that blouse is not decent, especially for a woman of your age." He glared at her, his face hard. Suddenly it was a pair of dark brown eyes Belle could see and she began to tremble.

"I'm sorry Frank. I've got a scarf in my bag." She clutched her blouse together and reached down for her bag again.

"Here we are. I have the scarf." She draped the scarf around her neck. "Is that better? I'm very sorry dear. Please don't be angry with me."

She reached for her glass, but her hand was shaking so much she nearly knocked it over. She took several sips of her wine and tried to calm herself. How silly she was behaving. It was only Frank, not Bernard, but for a moment---.

Frank spoke, "No, it's me who should be sorry. I was too harsh. I just don't like to see a woman showing too much---you know." Belle remained silent, "Please Belle, say you forgive me." He held out his hand, palm upwards, "Put your hand there please."

Belle did as he asked and gave him a shaky smile, "Of course I forgive you, but you know now what my husband was like. I had to obey him at all times or he would make my life hell. But you are not my husband, Frank. You can ask me nicely if there is something you don't like, but you cannot order me."

"No, you are right." He looked contrite, "I was out of order."

They were suddenly aware that the waiter was hovering nearby and waiting for them to order food. Once that was done, both chatted comfortably until it arrived. Belle had only ordered a light meal, but even so she struggled to eat it. The disagreement with Frank had upset her and taken her appetite away. Her head was beginning to ache and she would rather have been in her little room, back at the hotel. She knew Frank was aware of her lack of enthusiasm for her food, but he just got on with his meal and said nothing. When it was time to leave Belle said.

"I would really like to pay for this Frank. For your birthday treat from me." But as she had guessed, he refused to let her, and she had to accept it.

"Will you come back to me for a nightcap?" He said as they climbed into Belle's car.

"I don't think so Frank, not tonight. I've got a thumping headache. I'll just drop you off, then go home and take a paracetamol and go to bed. I'm sorry. Maybe another time."

Frank accepted this and sat quietly for the journey back to the vineyard. Belle pulled up outside his house and Frank leaned over and held her for a few minutes, then kissed her before climbing out. Belle gave him a wave and drove back to the hotel.

"You are back early tonight." Louise said.

Belle explained about her bad head. "I'm going to take a tablet straight away. I'll soon be fine. But before you go Louise I must tell you I have decided to leave tomorrow morning. I miss my family very much and it's time to go home. I'm going up to my room for half an hour or so, then I must pop out for five minutes. When I come back I would like to pay you because I shall leave early in the morning and I may not see you."

"Oh, I shall be sorry to see you go." Louise said, "I have so enjoyed having you here."

Belle went up to her and gave her a hug, "And I've enjoyed being here. I've had a wonderful holiday."

"Off you go then and take a tablet for your headache. I'll see you later."

Belle had known as she had tried to eat her meal in the restaurant that it was time to go home. Knowing Frank had been exciting and fun, but he had shown another side to his character, and it was one Belle didn't like. Now she had made the decision she was eager to start the journey home. She sat on the edge of her bed waiting for her headache to ease. She had her writing pad in her hand and started to write a letter.

Dear Frank

By the time you read this, I will be well on the way towards home. I have had a fantastic holiday and that is mainly down to you. I must thank you for that, but it's now time for me to see my family and friends back home. Please take care of yourself and I wish you all the best with the vineyard.

With fondest regards.

Belle xx

She folded the letter and put it in an envelope, then wrote 'Frank' on the front. Feeling slightly better, she ran downstairs and out of the front door to her car. She drove to within about fifty yards of Franks house, then parked and walked quietly along the lane to his property. He had an outside post box and Belle pushed the letter through the slot, took a long last look at the house and then hurried back to her car.

Louise came through when she heard Belle and the bill was settled quickly, then Belle went back to her room and packed as much as she could. She had told Louise she wouldn't be needing breakfast and had already said goodbye. However, when Belle went downstairs at six o'clock in the morning, Louise appeared in her dressing gown.

"I had to say goodbye cherie." She gave Belle a container with sandwiches and cake in it. "For the journey. Please drive carefully, you have a long way to go."

Belle left as quickly as she could. Not only was she keen to begin the journey, but she was also very sad to be leaving.

CHAPTER 21

It was exactly two thirty when Belle let herself in to her apartment. It had taken several trips from the car before everything was upstairs. She clicked open her two large suitcases and lifted out her bags of laundry. Very soon a pale load was swishing about in the machine. Now she lifted the phone from its cradle and dialled Rose's number before flopping down on the settee.

"Hello, Rose speaking."

"Hello darling, it's Mum."

"Mum, where are you?"

"I'm home, I wanted to catch you before you picked up the children. Can you come around for a cuppa?"

"You bet. Try and keep me away. I'm dying to hear all about your holiday. I'll be there in about half an hour."

At three thirty, the buzzer sounded, and Belle pressed the button to open the main door. She stood at the top of the stairs and watched with a big smile as Rose and the children ran up to her. Gary was first as she knew he would be. He flung himself at Belle and gave her a big hug. Then Rose, equally pleased to see her. As always, a solemn Megan, shy after a month apart from Belle was last.

"Come on you silly girl, give Nanna a hug."

Megan did as she was asked, with a smile.

"Come in, come in. Oh it's so good to see you." Belle said, "There's only tea or water kids, until I get to the shops."

"I'll have tea please Nanna. I like it now, don't I Mum?"

"Yes Gary, you're getting quite grown up, aren't you?"

Belle looked at Megan, "Water or tea sweetheart?"

"Nothing, thank you." Whispered Megan.

"Oh, just give her some water Mum. She can drink it or be thirsty." Rose rolled her eyes at Belle and they both laughed.

"Well come on then, tell me all about your holiday and about this man you met."

"The holiday was fab. Oh Rose, it's so beautiful there, just as I thought it would be. The weather was lovely 99% of the time and the hotel was perfect."

Rose grinned at her. "And was the man perfect as well?"

"Almost. Very good looking. In fact, very, very good looking."

Rose chuckled, "And?"

Belle turned to the children, "Have you finished your drinks?" She winked at Rose, "Would you like the TV on kids?"

"Yes please Nanna."

"Well you know how to put it on Gary and change channels, don't you? Off you go."

The children moved to the other end of the large room and put the TV on.

"When you see the photos." Belle said, rummaging in a bag, "You'll know why I couldn't resist him. Here they are."

She took the photos out of their envelope and handed her the one of Frank in Grasse. Rose looked at it, then looked at Belle and then back down at the photograph, "Wow."

"That's exactly what I said the first time I saw him." Belle said with a chuckle. "He had the most gorgeous eyes. In fact, he was just gorgeous."

"Did you go out much with him Mum?"

"Yes, four or five times a week. Sundays, we went out for the day and then I'd see him in the evenings. He would cook a nice meal and then we'd—well, you know—I'd get out my knitting and he would do a crossword."

"Oh yes, and you expect me to believe that."

"Well Rose, what we did, I will leave to your imagination."

"You surely didn't sleep with him, Mum." Rose looked shocked.

"Of course I did." Belle said matter-of-factly, "Why not?"

"I just can't imagine it, that's all." Rose said, biting her lip.

"Well, don't try Rose, just accept it, OK?"

"Yes, OK." She picked up the photos and slowly looked through them, commenting as she went and asking questions. Belle had four envelopes with pictures in and Rose looked at them all. Then Gary got bored with the TV and he looked at them as well.

"Who's this man Nanna?"

"That's Frank. I met him in France. He grows grapes." She picked up another photo, "See, this is the vineyard where he grows the grapes. Then he uses them to make wine."

"Doesn't he eat any of them?"

"Yes, some of them, look, these over near the barn, they are nice to eat, but most of the others are rather sour."

Rose interrupted then, "Mum, not only did you make a friend, but I just can't believe how far you drove, and on the 'wrong' side of the road. A year ago, you were just going down the road to the supermarket. I'm full of admiration."

Gary's eyes were going from one to the other, "How far did you go Nanna? Was it a hundred miles?"

"Fetch my road atlas darling, and I'll show you." First Belle showed him a map of Oxford, "See, I live here and that's where I shop. That's about a mile away. Now look at this page, this is Oxford. It looks small doesn't it? And you can't see the road where I live any more. So, I drove along this road called the M25 and then down this motorway to Dover. From here to Dover is about a hundred and twenty miles."

Gary gasped, "That's a long way."

Belle continued, "Then I got on a big boat which is called a ferry. All the cars are on the bottom deck, hundreds of them, and lots of big lorries as well. Then everyone goes upstairs where there are places to sit down and restaurants and shops."

"Gosh, it must be a huge boat."

"It is quite big, but there are lots of ships which are bigger."

"How long were you on the boat for Nanna?"

"One and a half hours, then we had to drive off. And the next bit was the hardest. Your Nanna was really scared."

"Why Nanna, what did you have to do?"

"Well Gary, what side of the road do we drive on in England? Do you know?"

Gary thought, "Yes, on the left."

"That's right, but in most other countries people drive on the right and that's what I had to do. It felt very strange, I can tell you."

"Mm, I bet it did. But Nanna, how many miles did you drive in France?"

"Oh gosh, Gary I think it was about seven hundred miles."

Gary's eyes were nearly popping out of his head, "Seven hundred miles! You must have been so tired."

"Well I stopped at motels for the night, several times."

Satisfied, Gary jumped up and ran back to the TV and Rose and Belle exchanged a smile.

"I want everyone to come for Sunday lunch. Chris and Steve, Uncle Rob and Aunty Bubs. Are you and Dave free?"

"Yes, we are."

"That's good. I'll be in touch with everyone else tonight."

She just caught Chris between coming in from work and going out again with friends.

"Glad you're back Mum. No, we aren't doing anything on Sunday so we'll see you then."

Belle was on the phone to Bubs for fifty-five minutes! There was a lot to talk about. She was also free on Sunday so that was good. There was no reply from Rob's phone, so she left a message and hoped he would remember to check his answer machine.

The next day Belle got the bus into the city to buy some bits and pieces, which included a short length of lace to stitch into the offending blouse to make it more 'respectable'. She was back home by lunchtime and after a quick snack, tackled the pile of ironing. She was just putting the ironing board away when the intercom buzzed. She glanced out of the window. It was Rob. She let him in and watched as he walked up the stairs.

"Rob, how lovely to see you. Come in."

Rob gave her a hug and followed her into the lounge. He pulled out a chair and sat at the table while Belle made tea, then she sat opposite him and started to tell him about France.

"I've been worried about you, going off to a foreign country on your own, I wish you hadn't, but I'm relieved you're home safe and sound."

"I was perfectly safe Rob. I met a nice lady as soon as I got to Provence and I stayed in the same hotel as her. Then I met an Englishman who owns a vineyard and I felt quite safe with him as well."

A small frown appeared on Rob's forehead, "An Englishman you say!" He paused, took a deep breath and smiled, "And did you date him?"

"Yes, I did and Oh Rob, he was really dishy. I thought I'd died and gone to heaven."

The frown came and went again, "Yes, well, what else did you do?"

Belle proceeded to tell him, omitting all the things of a personal nature. Sticking to places she had visited on the coast and inland. He stayed for an hour, then left to make a call after reassuring her that he would be there on Sunday. Belle was very thoughtful as she took the cups over to the sink. Rob had seemed rather serious and a bit disapproving. Surely, he couldn't be jealous, they were only friends after all. There had never been anything else between them. Perhaps he'd just been worried.

Bubs arrived at lunchtime on Saturday and they spent the afternoon chatting, laughing and making plans.

"You never actually told me why you came home so suddenly when you seemed to be having such a lovely time." Bubs queried.

"It was Frank." Belle told her about the blouse and Franks reaction to it. "It was really weird, Bubs. For a few minutes it was like sitting across the table from Bernard.

The way Frank glared at me and the way he spoke. I started to apologise, and I felt myself shrivel up, does that make sense? How I used to be with Bernard when he was angry. Then I realised how I was behaving and got annoyed with myself and him. If we had been alone and not in public I would have told him, nobody tells me what to do. But I didn't want to make a scene, so I just covered up with a scarf. Then, after we had eaten I made an excuse—I had a headache anyway—and dropped him off and went straight back to the hotel."

"You did the right thing Belle. Do you think he guessed?"

"Probably. But I didn't see him again. I just put a letter in his mail box and came home."

"Aren't you sad though? You seemed to be getting on so well."

"Yes, I'm a bit sad. But our relationship was a bit like when I first knew Bernard. You know, I was in lust, not in love."

Bubs gave a shout of laughter, "My, how you've changed."

Belle got up and took her road atlas from the bookshelf. "Anyway Bubs, you remember me telling you about Elsie. Well, I thought I might go and see her. She lives in St. David's in Wales. Two or three nights should be enough. Please, Bubs, say you'll come with me."

"I don't see why not. My holiday year started in April and I haven't had any days off yet. But if we could include a weekend it will only use a couple of days from my allowance."

"Yes, of course we can. Oh, Bubs it will be so much nicer to have someone with me. How do you feel about going in early July?"

"I'll just have to check at work. I'll let you know." Bubs answered.

Belle had brought her dining room furniture with her when she moved to the apartment. The table sat in the middle of the kitchen with an oil cloth on it for protection. When she had guests, it was easy to pull out the two leaves to make a large table which would sit eight people comfortably and ten at a pinch.

She loved her Sunday lunches, with her family around her, and Bubs and Rob if they were free. With a nice table cloth on and her best dinner service, you could forget you were sitting in the kitchen.

After they had eaten, and the dishes were in the dishwasher, everyone apart from Belle and Rob went out for a walk. Rob sat in a comfortable chair in the lounge and soon nodded off. Belle smiled fondly at him and then prepared a salad as quietly as possible, then she filled a sponge with cream and jam. When all was done she sat down and read a magazine until everyone returned from their walk. The children put the TV on and everyone sat around chatting while Belle and Rose made a cup of tea. Rose leaned close to Belle, "Did he propose Mum?"

Belle looked at her with a puzzled expression on her face. "Did who propose what?"

"Did Uncle Rob ask you to marry him of course?"

Belle was still mystified, "No, why would he do that? I don't know what you're talking about Rose."

"Oh, Mum, anyone can see he's crazy about you."

"Absolute nonsense Rose. We're like brother and sister. This is not the first time you've tried to fix us up, but I hope it will be the last. For your information, Rob was asleep the whole time you were out."

Belle picked up two cups of tea and took them through to the lounge, shaking her head and her lips pressed together in annoyance. Chris took her tea and glanced at her mother's face, but said nothing. But later on, when Rose and Dave had taken the children home to get ready for bed, she caught her mother in the hallway.

"Did my dear sister upset you earlier Mum?"

"Yes, she did rather. She seems to think that Uncle Rob and I are romantically involved, but it's simply not true. If we were, would I have gone off to France and had a passionate affair with Frank? Honestly, she does talk rubbish at times."

Chris nodded, "Yes, she does, she needs to put her brain into gear before she opens her mouth. Although, Rob is fond of you, there's no doubt."

"Well I'm fond of him, but not in that way. I just wish she wouldn't interfere."

Chris gave her Mother a smile. "So, Mum, changing the subject, Steve and I have decided it's time for us to try for a baby before we get too old, but I'm not expecting it to happen straight away."

Belle gave her a hug, "Good luck my love. More

grandchildren would please me no end."

That evening, Belle wrote to Louise to thank her for a lovely stay in her hotel and to let her know she was home safely and all was well. But she didn't give her address, there was no need. That chapter of her life was over.

One bright Friday morning in early July, Belle and Bubs left Oxford and set off for South Wales. Because it was quite a long journey to St. David's, they decided to spend the first night in Llanelli. The following morning they had time to wander along the front, before setting off to their final destination. Belle had contacted Elsie and she was expecting them early afternoon. She had insisted that they must stay with her, in her cottage just outside St. David's, so Belle had readily agreed. When they pulled up outside, Elsie was in the front garden, dead-heading the roses.

"Oh, isn't it pretty?" Bubs said. " Look Belle, the cottage and the garden, just picture perfect, isn't it?"

Elsie walked over to the car with a big smile on her face. "How lovely to see you again Belle." She kissed her on both cheeks. "And this must be Bubs. How do you do? Have you had a good journey?"

"Yes, fine thanks. We were just admiring your cottage and garden Elsie. You are lucky to live here."

"Yes, I am in one way, but old places cost a lot of money to keep in good condition. It's a listed building you know, which means I can't do anything without permission and that can be really irritating. Anyway, give me one of your bags and come in. We'll have a cup of tea and you can tell me all the news."

She led them into the tiny hallway and up a steep flight of stairs to their room. It had twin beds and a small dressing table. There was just room for a single wardrobe in one corner. The window overlooked a small rear garden, which was just as neat and tidy as the front.

"Unpack, my dears, then come down. I'm dying for a chat."

She left them and it didn't take long for them to put away their few things. Elsie took the tray of tea through to the back garden where she had a small patio. She had made some Welsh cakes and they were delicious. They chatted about Llanelli and drank their tea, then Bubs excused herself to use the bathroom. As soon as she had disappeared, Elsie leaned close to Belle and said.

"Is it alright to talk about Frank in front of Bubs, dear? I don't want to put my foot in it."

"Yes, it's OK. Bubs knows more about me than anyone else, even my daughters. We don't have any secrets from each other."

"That's good. Ah, here she is. Do either of you want more tea?" They both declined.

"Right Belle, so what happened after I left? Did you see much of Frank? Tell me all."

"Oh, Elsie you do make me laugh. Yes, we saw a lot of each other and we really hit it off. He took me around and he showed me loads of places. Have you ever been to Grasse?"

"Oh yes, it's lovely isn't it? Where else did you go?"

"We went up into the mountains to the ski resort and down to the coast. I had a lovely time."

"But you decided to come home?"

"Yes, and quite suddenly. Frank and I had a disagreement which was a shame. But you know Elsie, I was falling in love with him and it wouldn't have worked. There's no way I could have lived out there, lovely though it is, I would miss my family and friends too much, so perhaps it was all for the best."

"Yes, I agree. That's what happened to his wife of course."

"Mm, I know. So, Elsie, that's why I haven't got a boot full of your favourite red wine, I'm sorry, I fully intended to bring some back for you."

"Don't worry about that Belle, I'll be going out again in the Autumn."

"Please can I look round your garden?" Bubs asked.

"Of course you can my dears."

They all stood up and began the short walk around Elsie's rear garden. Apart from a patio and a small lawn, it consisted of herbaceous borders down both sides. There was an old brick wall across the bottom which was nearly obscured by several creepers. Against the house were three pots, each with a tomato plant in. These were heavy with tomatoes but, as yet, were showing no red.

They wandered back to the patio and took the mugs indoors.

"Mm, something smells good." Belle said.

"Yes, I know it's summer, but I popped a chicken

casserole in the oven. It's easy and we can leave it to cook slowly.

Bubs was first to wake next morning and although she moved about quietly, Belle stirred and opened one eye.

"Good morning sleepy head." Bubs said with a grin, "I can hear Elsie in the kitchen, so I'm going down to cadge a coffee. Shall I get one for you?"

"That would be lovely thanks."

Ten minutes later they were sitting on the edge of their beds, sipping coffee and planning their day.

"I really want to look at St. David's Cathedral. That's the most important thing for me. What about you Bubs? Where do you want to go?" She reached over to her suitcase, where the road atlas had lain since yesterday. They looked at it together.

"Do you know Belle, I don't mind where I go. It's all new to me anyway. But I must see the sea at some point. Let's ask Elsie the best place to go."

Elsie suggested St. Brides bay.

"There are some nice beaches there. The first beach you come to can get quite busy, especially in the school holidays and weekends. There are a couple of smaller beaches further on. I should try those. Do you want any more toast?"

As Elsie had prepared a full English breakfast, they both said firmly that they couldn't eat another crumb.

"Do you want me to pack you up a picnic my dears? It won't take me long."

"No thank you Elsie, I don't think we'll be wanting

anything else to eat until tonight." Bubs said with a smile at their hostess.

"OK. How would you like to eat out tonight at our local pub? I could book it for seven, if that's alright with you?"

They all agreed that was a nice idea.

They decided to go to the beach first, and to St. David's in the afternoon. As they sat on some rocks later, Bubs turned to Belle. "How much does Elsie know about you and Frank?"

"I just told her that we'd had a romance. She was dying to know more but that is just between you and me Bubs. She tried to find out, but I just wagged my finger at her and told her not to be naughty."

"She's great Belle, I really like her. Do you think you will stay in touch?"

"I would like to, but you never know what's around the corner."

"That's true, you've proved that over the last year."

"Bubs," Belle hesitated, "I've been thinking about my next trip."

"Yes, carry on."

"Well, I've never been to Spain as you know, and I would like to go in September."

"Good idea, it's not too hot then."

"Yes, but I want to drive. I really enjoy it."

"Not all the way to Spain Belle, that's much further than you went last time."

"I know, just hear me out. I was lonely in Provence

till I met Frank. How would you like to drive down with me? You really seemed to enjoy the holiday in Cyprus. It will give you a chance to see France and then we could stop at the Costa Brava. That's not so far as the other Costas. I thought we could leave on a Saturday morning. Take four or five days to drive down, stay a week on the Costa Brava and then you could fly home."

Bubs gazed at her, silent for a few moments. "You've got it all worked out haven't you? I'm going to have to think about this Belle. It's a big ask."

"Just say no if you don't want to. I'll still go, but it will be more fun with you."

Bubs suddenly turned towards Belle, a huge grin on her face. "Who said anything about not wanting to go. I was just teasing. I think it's a great idea."

She ducked as Belle threatened to box her ears, then they both burst out laughing.

"Come on, we must have a paddle." Bubs said.

They took their sandals off and ran down to the sea.

"Remind me how old we are." Giggled Belle.

"About eight and a half I think."

Belle rolled her eyes, then added, "I know I shouldn't say this, but I'm a bit hungry. How about a sticky bun and a hot drink to keep us going?"

They sat on the rocks again and dried their feet as best as they could on a few tissues. Then slipped their sandals on and headed back to the car. They drove back up to St. David's, parked and walked into the city centre. There were several cafes to choose from and they were soon sitting at an outside table with a cake and a cup of tea. They looked in several of the shops and Belle bought a small gift for each of her grandchildren. It was just a short walk to the cathedral and the ruins of the Bishop's Palace. There were lots of tourists about, but inside the cathedral it was cool and peaceful.

"Belle, is it my eyes, or is this building on a slope?"

Belle stood still and looked down the length of the cathedral.

"It does seem that way, let's ask that man over there. He looks as though he's here to help. The man was indeed an expert on the history of the cathedral and was able to answer their questions.

"Yes indeed, there is a slope. This end is three metres higher than the other end."

"Goodness, three metres, that is amazing." Said Bubs.

They thanked the man and continued to walk around until they had seen everything. At five thirty they were back at Elsie's and sitting in the garden with a cold drink. The pub they were dining at was only a few hundred yards down the road, so they were able to walk there. They had a delicious meal and once back in the cottage, they chatted in the cosy sitting room until late.

It was sad to say goodbye in the morning, but they needed to leave promptly because of the long journey home. There were hugs and promises to come again and then they were on the road. By the time they got home it was just after four o'clock, Bubs had shared the driving which had helped. They unloaded the car, then sat down with a hot drink.

"I think we'll have a take away tonight. Is that OK with you Bubs?"

"Yes that's fine. I don't mind what I eat, as long as it's food."

Belle looked at her and shook her head, "You're mad." She informed her.

It seemed rather strange that neither Bubs nor Belle had mentioned the big birthday coming up. It was Belle's fiftieth and she had an idea that Rose had made plans. There were cards on her birthday and Rose had suggested that maybe they could go out for a meal on Saturday. Belle agreed and promised to keep that evening free.

"We'll pick you up at six Mum, then you can have a drink."

Saturday arrived, and Belle stood in front of her opened wardrobe. She reprimanded herself for feeling guilty. Why shouldn't she have lots of clothes? She could afford them. Nothing remained of her old life, not even an item of underwear. Her wardrobe was full of modern, colourful garments and not one single item in grey or beige. But what should she wear tonight? It was her evening and she wanted to stand out. She finally chose a dress in dusky pink with a round neck and three-quarter length sleeves. The bodice was fitted, and the skirt was full, ending at mid-calf. It was finished off with a wide belt of the same colour, with a silver buckle. Belle had bought it in the spring, but she had never worn it. With a pair of heeled sandals in off white, (also unworn) and a matching handbag, the ensemble was complete.

She showered and washed her hair and then completed her preparations. As she put her make up away and applied some perfume, she heard the door buzzer go. Doing a quick check in the full-length mirror, she hurried over to the intercom to let Rose in.

"Mum, you look absolutely gorgeous, and this must surely be your thirtieth birthday!"

Belle laughed, "So I look Ok then?"

"You certainly do. I want to give you a big hug, but I might crease your dress."

Belle responded by giving Rose a hug.

"Your chariot awaits madam." Rose said, and they made their way downstairs.

Knowing how her mother loved Chinese food, Rose had booked a popular restaurant just ten minutes' drive away and now they were on their way. Dave had also been stunned by Belle's appearance and as he drove towards their venue, his eyes kept going to the inside mirror for another peep at her.

Unknown to Belle, the restaurant had closed off a section of seating for the evening, and as she stepped past the screen, there were cheers, and everyone sang happy birthday to her. She felt herself blush and she gazed around in astonishment. She had an idea that Chris and Steve would be here, and maybe Bubs, but not this many. The guests did include Chris, Steve and Bubs, but also her neighbours from her first home, Sylvia and Michael, and from her second house, Avril and James. Also, Di and Nancy from the card shop and of course, Rob. Belle gazed at them all in delight and then sat down.

Dave tapped his glass and stood up. "On behalf of Belle, I want to thank everyone for coming tonight to help celebrate her thirtieth birthday, it is thirty, isn't it? I think you will all agree that she looks absolutely amazing. Belle, enjoy your evening."

Everyone clapped and cheered as he sat down.

Belle stood up. "Thank you, Dave and Rose, who I think arranged all this. It is lovely to see you all and I hope you all enjoy the evening as well."

This was followed by more cheers and clapping, then several waiters appeared and began to load the table with dishes of steaming food.

It was ten minutes past ten by the time people started to leave. Rob was sleeping at Rose's and Bubs was staying with Belle. Chris and Steve were booked into a hotel, while all the others were local enough to get home.

As Belle and Bubs let themselves into the apartment, Belle said. "What a fabulous evening."

"Yes, it was." Bubs agreed.

CHAPTER 22

Belle had suggested that it would be a good idea for Bubs to take out insurance, so that she could help with the driving in Europe. Although Belle was happy to do most of the driving, her friend might like to take a turn. Bubs said she would drive down to Dover, then Belle could take over once they got off the ferry. So here they were, the car parked on the car deck and making their way up the steep stairs to the passenger deck. Bubs was rather surprised by how big it was and by how many people were already queuing at cafes and restaurants, or hovering around the shop doors, waiting for them to open. They joined the queue for some hot food, it seemed a long time since breakfast and they were both hungry. They sat down with a plate of chicken curry and rice each and tucked into the food, delaying any chat until they were finished. Bubs finished first and walked back to the servery for two coffees. As she sat down again, she glanced at Belle.

"Do you wish you could see Frank again?"

"No, not really. It was a pleasant interlude but nothing more." She took a sip of coffee. "It may surprise you, but I would like to marry again one day, but I don't trust my own judgement."

"What do you mean?" Bubs asked.

"I think perhaps I go too much for physical attraction. It seems to me there should be more to it than that. Mother and Father were great friends as well as husband and wife, and they had such a lovely relationship. That's what I'd like."

"Mm, I know what you mean, Derek and I were good friends, but the other side was almost non-existent. Just do what you have been doing. Have a few dates and see what happens—and enjoy the process."

They laughed and finished their coffees.

"Come on, let's look round the shops."

They picked up their bags and went to look at what was on offer.

Bubs sat silently as Belle drove off the ferry and followed the other vehicles on to the French roads. Before they left Calais, Belle filled up with petrol and then she had to concentrate because she needed a different road to the last time she was here. Bubs had expressed a strong desire to go to the Normandy beaches, as she had lost two uncles in the second World War and they were buried there. She had managed to find out where their graves were amongst the many thousands along that coast. So, they drove away from Calais and turned in a westerly direction. Belle had booked a motel in Caen and it was early evening when they turned in to the motel car park. Pleased that they had already eaten a substantial meal at one o'clock, the two weary travellers made their way up to their room on the second floor. They had bought sandwiches and crisps on the ferry and there were hot drink facilities in the room, so there was no need to go out any more. They could just relax and plan the next day.

They set off the next morning, and, with the information Bubs had managed to obtain, they found the cemetery where her two uncles were laid to rest. At the entrance they both stopped and just stared. So many graves, and this was just one cemetery out of hundreds.

"Isn't it beautifully maintained?" Said Bubs.

Belle gazed at the straight rows of headstones and the neatly mown grass. Many of the headstones were set in flower beds, and although it was now mid-September there were many flowers and roses still in bloom. Bubs was silent, her face sad and her eyes downcast as she walked slowly along the rows of graves. She consulted her information, then walked further on before stopping, she stooped down, tracing the wording with her finger tips.

"Here's Uncle Joe." She looked up at Belle, her eyes glistening with tears, "He was only eighteen. Oh, it's so sad. What a waste." She stood and gazed at the headstone for a few minutes, then walked on until she found Uncle Cyril's grave. She stooped down again and touched the wording.

"Uncle Cyril was twenty two. He was married and had a baby son he never saw. Oh Belle."

She could not continue and let herself be comforted in Belle's arms. After a few minutes she wiped away her tears and blew her nose.

"I don't remember them. I was only a baby when they died. But I still feel so moved, and close to them somehow. I'm so glad we came Belle."

They slowly made their way back to the car, looking at a monument on the way. Belle had also found it a moving experience and had shed a few tears herself.

After leaving the cemetery, they went down to the coast to see all the artefacts left over from the war. There were tanks, gun emplacements and the remnants of floating pontoons. They were quiet as they read all the information and dreadful details of the battles that had taken place there. Although they remembered their parents talking about the war, some of it had been forgotten over the years. Now it all came back, and it was incredibly sad. They left Arramanche and made their way back to the motel at Caen. It had been an emotional and exhausting day and they needed to have a relaxing evening and a good night's sleep. They hoped to get to Tours by midday tomorrow, to give themselves a day and a half to explore the Loire Valley.

The journey went well until they got to Tours, where they got completely lost trying to find the motel. But by asking at several garages, and with the help of the road atlas and some very bad French, they finally arrived at five minutes to one. After booking in and unpacking they ate a light meal at the restaurant next door and headed out into the countryside. With Bubs navigating, and by taking smaller roads they followed the river on the North side, stopping often to take photos. Then, taking a different route, they meandered back to Tours and their motel. Later, as they sat outside the motel with a glass of wine, they chatted about the day.

"Gosh, the Loire river is huge isn't it?" Said Bubs, "I never expected it to be that big."

"It certainly was very wide in places." Belle replied. "And such pretty countryside. We'll go South of the river tomorrow. What do you think?"

"Yes, that's a good idea." Bubs pointed at the atlas. "There appears to be lots of villages to visit, it should be interesting."

"And look Bubs, what's that?"

"It's an abbey, it's called Fontevrault-le-Abbaye. We must go there."

As they were using the same chain of motels, the layout and décor in each was almost identical. Although Bubs said she could 'sleep on a clothes line' Belle was not so lucky. But she found the similarity in the rooms made them sort of familiar and this helped her to sleep well.

The next day was wonderful. The sun shone from a clear blue sky, but it wasn't too hot. They called into a local shop and bought snacks and drinks and set off. As they drove along the road which followed the river, the scenery was spectacular. As Bubs pointed out, it was marked on the map as a tourist route and it certainly was pretty.

In less than an hour they were at the abbey. They parked and went in. It was huge and consisted of a square of buildings with a large courtyard in the middle.

The gardens were criss-crossed with neatly trimmed box hedging and the beds themselves were full of colourful, late summer flowers. Everything was immaculate, the gardens and the buildings. They had picked up a guide book in English and looked at everything, the tombs, a model of the whole place and the beautiful, ornamental stonework. There was a banqueting hall which you could hire out (If you were very rich) for special occasions. Belle and Bubs spent the entire morning at the abbey, then moved on to have some snacks and a drink.

After they had eaten they continued to drive alongside the river until they were almost at Angers, then, turning sharp left, went in the direction of Doue-la-Fontaine.

"Do you know anything about this place Bubs?"

"Not a thing, we'll just have to wait and see."

As they drove into the town it appeared to be just a normal small urban area, then Bubs noticed a sign.

"Oh, look Belle, there's a zoo. Gosh, I haven't been to a zoo for years. Shall we go and have a look?"

It was quite small by English standards, but all the creatures seemed to be well cared for. After looking around for a while they came across a restaurant called 'The Giraffe'. Belle glanced at her watch and then grinned at Bubs.

"I know it's only four o'clock, but those snacks are long forgotten. How about having a meal here?"

"That would be good, if they are still serving."

Food was still being served, so they ordered jacket potatoes which came with four or five accompaniments on the plates, all beautifully laid out. It was delicious.

Now it was time to head back to the motel and plan the next day. With a cup of coffee to hand, they studied the atlas.

"I'm not sure how far it is to Toulouse Bubs. It's in kilometres and my maths isn't that good. But very roughly I would think between 350 and 400 miles."

"Crumbs, that's a long way. We'll share the driving. The roads look good, motorways most of the way I think. That makes such a difference."

They arrived in Toulouse early evening, having eaten a main meal on the way. The journey had been good again, without any problems and this time the motel was easy to find. They were to spend just one night here and then head for Spain. Bubs had been to Spain twice before, but she had flown and both times had stayed on the Costa del Sol. The Costa Brava would be quite different, and she was looking forward to exploring it. Belle had rented an apartment in Lloret de Mar for one week.

They set off promptly the next morning. They didn't have quite so far to go as the previous day and once more it would be mainly motorway.

"As soon as we cross the border I want to stop for a while." Belle said "I've been looking forward to seeing Spain so much."

"Well these little diamond shapes on the map mean rest areas and there's one about seven or eight miles beyond the border. That will have to do Belle."

By early afternoon they crossed the border and gave a cheer. The roads here were as good as in France and the kilometres sped by.

"When are we going to see the sea Bubs?"

"Not until we are at Lloret de Mar I'm afraid, you'll just have to be patient. Pull in at the next rest area Belle and we'll have a coffee and then I'll take over the driving for a while.

By five o'clock they were there. The apartment was part of a hotel complex and overlooked the sea and was surprisingly spacious. They dumped their cases and bags on the floor and opened the French windows on to the balcony, then stepped out and took in the view.

"Wow." They said together, then chuckled.

"I want to go out and look around." Belle said eagerly.

"Please let's rest for fifteen minutes or so. Don't you ever feel tired?"

"OK then. Fifteen minutes but no more." Belle responded with a grin.

They slipped their shoes off and reclined on the beds, chatting quietly about the day's journey and what they could do this evening.

"I must introduce you to tapas, Belle. They are small dishes of local food and there's usually a good choice on offer. You can have hot or cold dishes and you have one or two if you're not very hungry, or five or six or more if you are starving. It gives you a chance to try lots of different things. They are usually delicious."

"Mm, that sounds good. We'll unpack in a minute, then I need to wash a few things through. They'll soon dry on the balcony or in the bathroom, then we'll go out, have a look round and find somewhere to eat. Is that OK?"

As it was a warm evening, Bubs chose to have cold tapas and Belle decided to have hot dishes. That way they could sample each other's.

The next morning, they both enjoyed a hearty breakfast in the hotel's restaurant before gathering bags and cardigans together from their room and walking out into the sunshine.

"Can we just wander up and down the promenade please Belle? Or are you going to drag me off somewhere to explore?"

Belle laughed. "Am I really that bad? Actually, I'll be quite pleased to take it easy today, after all the driving."

They walked in silence for a while. Bubs was the first to speak.

"I bet you noticed that handsome young waiter at breakfast. When are you going to ask him for a date?"

Belle giggled. "I'm old enough to be his mother, you naughty girl. It's more likely to be those two elderly gentlemen who were sitting near us at breakfast. Did you see them eyeing us up?"

"Oh crumbs, that's just what we need." Bubs commented, "Two love starved old men."

"Oh Bubs, don't be unkind, I thought they looked nice--and very respectable."

"I'm not that desperate." Bubs replied.

"Shush. Look Bubs, here they are, coming towards us."

The two men approached and seemed ready for a chat.

"We meet again ladies. It's a lovely day, isn't it, and so pleasant to walk along the front?"

They chatted for a few minutes, commenting on the hotel and the excellent breakfast. The girls explained that although they were in one of the small apartments attached to the hotel, the facilities were quite basic. Because of that, they were using the hotel restaurant.

"By the way, I'm Noel and my friend is Jack."

Noel was tall and slim, and Jack was short and rather plump.

Belle replied. "I'm Belle and my friend is Bubs."

Noel raised his eyebrows, but made no comment at the unusual name.

"Would you allow us to buy you a coffee, ladies?" Asked Jack.

Belle and Bubs exchanged glances.

"Well, I don't see why not." Said Bubs.

They all turned and walked towards a nearby bar, the girls uncertain whether they were doing the right thing. Still, no harm could come to them in broad daylight, in the middle of a busy resort. They decided to sit outside as it was a lovely day. The sea sparkled in the sunshine and the sky was blue from the horizon to the mountains behind them. The two men disappeared inside to order the coffees before returning to join the ladies at the table.

"How long are you here for?" Noel asked.

"Oh, just one week." Belle replied, but didn't add that she might stay longer—on her own.

"Same as us." Replied Noel.

They fell silent for a few minutes as their coffees arrived. Then Noel continued.

"You see, our wives, who are sisters, are into all this classical stuff, and we're not interested, so we have one week each year when we do our own thing. They go to concerts and art galleries and we go away for a week, although this is the first time we've been abroad without them."

"Well that seems to be working well for you." Belle commented.

"Yes, it does. How about you ladies. Have you left your fellows at home?"

"No, we don't have anyone at home, but we are quite content as things are." Bubs said. "I'm divorced and Belle is a widow. I must say, you're wives are very trusting."

"They know there's nothing to worry about, we like the company of ladies, but we will never stray." Said Jack, "They are great girls and we are lucky to have them."

They sipped their coffees and watched other holiday makers wandering by.

"Have you been here before?" Belle asked.

"No, never. How about you?" Noel queried.

Bubs explained that she had been to Spain several times, but not to this area, and that it was the first time for Belle.

"We haven't been here before either." Said Noel. "We shall hire a car for a few days and have a drive around. There are a few places I'd like to visit.

"Mm, we will do that as well probably. We drove down, so we have got my car here, and so it would be rather silly not to make use of it."

"Do you mean, you drove all the way from England? Gosh, you're brave. How long did it take you?"

Noel sounded very surprised and Jack's mouth just dropped open.

"Well we took our time." Belle said airily, "We looked at this and that on the way down." She nudged Bubs under the table. "I'm quite used to driving in Europe."

'I mustn't laugh'. She thought to herself, but struggled not to. But it was too much for the pair of them and the giggles started.

Jack looked at them. "What's the joke then?" He asked.

Bubs got herself under control. "Shall I tell them Belle?"

"If you want to Bubs."

"Well, fifteen months ago, Belle's husband was still around, and Belle was a quiet, obedient little wife. The furthest she had ever driven was down to the local supermarket. She had never flown, never been abroad, never eaten anything other than English food, never even been in a pub for just a drink. Then Bernard died, and Belle was re-born. Now, there's no stopping her."

Noel and Jack listened, fascinated, their gaze going first to Bubs, then to Belle and back again.

"Well, I don't know what to say." Noel started, "I'm sorry you lost your husband, but you seem to have found a way to get over the sadness."

"Yes." That's all Belle could say.

The two men asked lots of questions about the journey down from England, the places they had visited, and the route they planned to take on the way home.

"We haven't decided yet." Belle said, "We'll probably just get in the car and go where the fancy takes us."

It was now after midday and Bubs announced that she was hungry. They all went into the bar and to the girl's delight, there was a selection of tapas along the counter. They all chose what they wanted and then sat down again at their table in the sun to wait for the food. The girls had declined a glass of wine, preferring to wait until the evening. It was after three before they parted company from the men, and by then they were like old friends. Belle and Bubs wandered back to the hotel to write some cards and decide what they wanted to do the next day.

Belle said. "I didn't want to suggest it in front of Noel and Jack, but how would you feel about going for a drive and inviting them along? I'd feel safer somehow, if we were with them."

Belle looked at her friend to get her reaction to the suggestion.

"Yes, I don't mind. How will you feel about having them in the back though?"

"I don't think it will bother me, as long as they are not back seat drivers." She grinned at Bubs.

They turned in to the hotel.

"I'm going to put my feet up for a while after we've done the cards, and relax." Bubs said. "How about you?"

"Yes, that's a good idea. I'll do the same and we'll ask the men about joining us when we next see them."

But that evening there was no sign of them in the restaurant.

"We'll see them at breakfast I expect." Belle said, as she piled her plate with food from the buffet. "We'll suggest it to them then."

The next day the sun shone from a cloudless sky again. Noel and Jack were choosing their breakfast and called a cheery good morning. They were finished sooner than Belle and Bubs, but as they got up to leave, Belle called them over.

"Sit down with us for a minute. We had a thought. Have you hired a car yet?"

The answer was a shake of the head.

"Well, would you like to come for a drive with us? We are going inland today, and you are welcome to join us if you wish."

They both jumped at the chance.

"I've never driven abroad before." Jack said, "Noel has once, but he's not very confident. But the only problem is, we really wanted to go to Llagostera. Apparently, it's a nice drive there and an interesting town, so friends have told us."

Belle smiled in surprise. "Well I never! That's exactly where Bubs and I want to go as well. We've finished eating now. How about we meet you out the front in twenty minutes?"

The men agreed, and Belle and Bubs hurried upstairs to get ready.

The route followed the coast for a few miles, twisting this way and that. Belle concentrated on the driving, but there were lots of 'Oohs and Aahs' from the passengers. She thought to herself that it would be nice to do this drive again and find somewhere to stop, so that she could enjoy the views as well. Maybe later in the week. They turned inland, climbing steadily, the road following the contours of the hills. When it was possible to stop, she did so and they all climbed out and enjoyed the views. Everyone had cameras, so lots of photos were taken before getting back in the car.

By the time they reached their destination, a coffee was the priority. It took some while to find somewhere to park. Spanish towns and villages were built long before motor vehicles were around, and the roads were narrow, but at last they were seated in a rather quaint café, with a cup of coffee and a doughnut each.

"I say, this is all rather nice." Noel said, "This is what I like, exploring inland, away from the busy coast and tourists."

Belle smiled at him. "So do I, probably more than Bubs. I just want to see as much as I can because I've had a late start with travelling and there are so many places to see."

They strolled around the town, looking at the contrast between old and new. From time to time the vista would open out before them and it would be time to stop and just look and take pictures.

It was with some surprise when they suddenly realised it was nearly two o'clock.

"Gosh, I'm hungry." Said Jack.

"You're always hungry." His friend replied with a chuckle.

There were plenty of cafes, bars and restaurants open now and wonderful aromas were wafting out into the street.

"This looks nice girls. What do you think?" Noel looked to the girls for a response.

"It does look rather nice." Bubs said, "But I bet it's expensive."

"Oh, don't worry about that. We'll treat you for being our tour guides, won't we Jack?"

"Yes, it will be our pleasure." Said Jack.

So, the ladies accepted and they all stepped inside. A waiter came forward and showed them to a table. He spoke a little English and asked them if they would like a drink. Noel was a bit of a wine buff and he chose a red wine which he said was good. As they waited for it to arrive they looked around at the restaurant. The building was obviously old and the décor complimented it with it's furnishings and ornaments. The walls were covered in dark wood panelling and the chairs were covered in a soft, dark red fabric. The lighting was discrete and it took a while to adjust after the bright sun outside. The waiter appeared with the wine and glasses. He poured a little for Noel to try, which he did, and declared that it was very good. The wine was poured and the waiter left briefly, then returned with the menus.

"Oh, thank goodness, it's in English as well as Spanish." Said Bubs, "I do like to know exactly what I'm eating!"

It was three thirty by the time they left the restaurant. The meal had been delicious and the service exemplary. The men had paid at the bar while the ladies were finishing their coffees. They all stepped outside, squinting in the bright sunshine. Bubs wanted to visit a museum and Belle had seen a church she wished to look at, but Noel and Jack just weren't interested in either. So, they parted company and arranged to meet back at the car at five o'clock. However, they all got rather lost and it was twenty past five before they were all back together. The sun was getting low in the sky and Belle was a bit nervous about finding her way back to their hotel. The drive down to the coast was simple enough, but then there was a town to get through. Once they got through that Belle didn't foresee a problem, so as they got nearer Belle told everyone to look for the signs pointing South, to either Lloret or Barcelona. It was now dusk and Belle slowed down and looked for road signs. She realised she was hot and her hands were damp, but she didn't want anyone to know how unsure she was.

"Come on you three." She called out cheerfully, "You're not helping."

Suddenly Jack said. "Next left Belle."

Belle did as she was told and ahead could see more signs and a bigger road. A few minutes later they were on a dual carriageway and heading out of the town. Belle relaxed and accelerated, in fifteen minutes they would be back at the hotel.

Belle and Bubs called out a friendly goodbye to the men and headed for the lift and their apartment. Once there, they relaxed in their easy chairs.

"You did well today Belle." Bubs said. "I can't believe how confident you are."

"Oh Bubs, if only you knew. I was terrified going through that town. But I knew it had to be me driving, if that doesn't sound big headed, so I just kept going."

Bubs looked astonished. "I had no idea. You hid it very well."

"Well I didn't want the men to know. The trouble is, I always find the dusk slightly difficult to drive in. Anyway, here we are back, safe and sound."

Bubs got up and gave Belle a hug. "My clever friend." She said.

Although they had all got on very well, no arrangements were made to go out together again. The next morning the courier came up to them and asked if they would be interested in a trip to Barcelona the following day.

"It will be a fairly early start." She told them. "Breakfast at seven and leave at eight o'clock sharp."

They looked at each other.

"What do you think Belle?"

"I'd like to do it."

"So would I." Said Bubs

The courier put their names down and moved on to speak to some other members of their group.

"Let's just take it easy today." Bubs suggested.

"Good idea, I agree." Said Belle.

The weather was not so good although it remained dry and quite warm. So they just walked and window shopped and relaxed on seats overlooking the sea. They chatted about other holidays in the past, and places they would like to visit in the future. They also talked about the decision that Belle must make at the weekend. To head for home or go further down the Spanish coast. She was finding it so difficult to decide. Her enthusiasm to explore other places, against the pull of her home and family. In the end she just shrugged her shoulders and said there was plenty of time to make her mind up.

The sun was back the next day and they were up bright and early. As is always the case, someone was late at the coach, but they were on their way at just ten minutes past eight. They had a good journey down the coast with no holdups.

Belle said. "It makes a nice change not to be driving, I can look at the views."

Noel and Jack were on the coach and were sitting just behind the girls. The driver pulled into a rest area on the outskirts of Barcelona and everyone piled out for a refreshment break, before continuing to a coach park in the city. The courier was very knowledgeable and helpful. She told them all that there were lots of things to see and do, and gave them some ideas.

"I'm sure that everyone will want to walk up and down Las Ramblas. There are plenty of places to eat there. For those who are more energetic, I would recommend getting to the Sagrada Familia. It is the most amazing building, as yet unfinished after more than a hundred years. I can honestly say there is nothing else quite like it anywhere in the world. It's a long way from Las Ramblas and it may be best to get a taxi. Whatever you decide to do, enjoy your day. I'm going to Las Ramblas now, so those who would like to join me, wait outside the coach."

She handed out maps of the city with places of interest marked on them, and the coach park with a red circle round it.

"I must have everyone back here by five thirty. We will be stopping at a restaurant on the way back to Lloret for a meal. We hope to eat at seven."

The coach pulled away and the courier switched on her microphone.

"Did everyone enjoy Barcelona?"

There was an enthusiastic and positive response.

"I want to thank everyone for getting back to the coach promptly, and now I'll let you relax until we get to the restaurant."

"What a great day." Bubs said, "I'm so glad we came, but I'm really tired now. What was your favourite thing Belle?"

"Oh, the Sagrada Familia, without a doubt. How about you Bubs? What did you enjoy the most?"

"The same as you, although I loved all of it. It's such a lively place, isn't it?"

"Mm, but I'm the same as you, really tired. I may even nod off." She smiled, then closed her eyes.

The meal was very good and Bubs and Belle had been joined by the two men. After talking about the day, Belle asked them if they would like to come for a drive up the coast the next day. They eagerly nodded and both said, "Yes please."

"I've looked on the map and it's marked as a scenic route." Belle continued, "Should be a nice day out."

Jack grinned. "I hope it's not going to be another early start."

"Well we mustn't be too late. How about nine o'clock? Is that too early for you?"

"No, that's just right, isn't it Noel?"

"Yes, that's fine. You have to remember we're just two old pensioners, not young like you two."

They all laughed and then stood up and made their way back to the coach.

The trip up the coast proved to be as beautiful as they had predicted. The road twisted this way and that, up hills and down the other side, with views of the sea appearing and then dropping from sight.

"It's very green isn't it?" Belle said. "I didn't know Spain was like this, it's lovely."

"Yes, it's quite dry and barren in some places, but we are in Northern Spain don't forget. It's cooler and they have a lot more rain up here." Bubs informed her. "It's drier on the Costa Blanca."

They continued to drive North, not hurrying, and stopping whenever they got the chance. They had decided they would eat back at the hotel in the evening, so they stopped at one o'clock for a snack and a break. Afterwards they turned around to make their way back to their hotel. They arrived back a little early for the evening meal so decided to go for a short walk along the seafront to stretch their legs after having been in the car for most of the day. The men went off to find a phone box to ring their wives for a chat and the girls continued along the front. It was now quite dark, but very pleasant. The moon shone on the sea and the stars twinkled in the sky. A lovely end to a most enjoyable day.

Now it was Friday and their last day. Belle still hadn't made a final decision about whether to go North or South. They spent a lazy day around the hotel and beach, buying gifts to take home and making a start on the packing. They were not late to bed as a prompt start was planned for the morning. Bubs was getting a coach that would take her to Barcelona airport and it would be leaving at eight fifteen.

CHAPTER 23

Bubs alarm woke them both up very early Saturday morning. They both groaned and crawled out of their beds. The week had flown by and Bubs holiday was at an end. The week had been relaxing, but also quite busy at times with the trips. Bubs worked full time and had a responsible job, so she had needed to take it easy and recharge her batteries, so that's what they had done. Belle had to leave the apartment today but had booked one night in another hotel while she decided what to do.

After breakfast, Belle said goodbye to Jack and Noel, who were also going to Barcelona on the coach, and then helped Bubs with her bags down to the coach, which was waiting outside.

"When do you think you'll be home?" Bubs asked.

Belle shrugged. "I've no idea. I'll sleep on it tonight and decide in the morning. I've got no reason to rush home, apart from the family."

"But you know you get lonely on your own."

"Yes, you're right. I've had my little fling so I don't think I'm looking for a man friend."

"That's what you tell me, but I'm not sure I believe you."

Belle slapped her leg. "You've got me all wrong Bubs. Anyway, have a safe journey. I shall miss you like mad. I'll write or phone and let you know what I'm doing and where I am. Bye Bubs."

They hugged and Bubs climbed aboard. Belle waved until the coach was out of sight.

Now it was time to collect her belongings, put them in the car and drive to the hotel just down the road. After she had booked in she put the car in the secure underground car park. Picking the atlas up, she found a café with seats outside and ordered a coffee. Twice she took a breath to say something to Bubs before remembering that she wasn't there. She felt very undecided. Half of her, no, more than half, wanted to carry on and drive further down the coast. But she was also nervous and there was no one to discuss it with. She finished her coffee but didn't move, her mind going backwards and forwards. Go home or carry on. Impatient and cross with herself, she got up and walked back to the hotel. The restaurant wasn't open until eight thirty and that was too late for her, so she turned around and went back out again, heading towards the town. She knew that the tapas bar they had used earlier in the week was open from mid-morning until very late, so she would eat there, then relax in her room and hopefully come to a decision.

Belle slept well and woke feeling more positive. She would continue down the coast towards the Costa Blanca. She looked at her Spanish atlas and the motorway seemed to go all the way down, avoiding all the major cities and towns.

'Thank goodness," she thought. She dreaded finding herself in the middle of one of those. Her confidence had grown enormously over the last fifteen months, but she didn't think she would ever be able to tackle a big foreign city. She decided to drive as far as possible on the first day and not do any sightseeing. By doing so she found herself about forty miles North of Valencia by late afternoon. Tired and keen to find a hotel she took the next exit and made her way to a place called Moncofa. It was a smallish town on the coast and quite flat. The many roads were in a grid system like a crossword puzzle. She drove right to the front and sat there for a few minutes looking at the sea and the buildings along the front. As she had hoped, there were several hotels. Finding a parking area, she paid and put the ticket in the car, locked it and strolled up the street. The first hotel she looked at was rather tatty, but two others were much nicer. Neither seemed to have a parking area. With her phrase book at the ready she enquired whether they had a room, how much was it, and where did she park? The first hotel had a vacant room and a small car park at the rear, so without looking at the second hotel Belle booked in, parked her car and went up to her room. It was quite small, but perfectly adequate and spotlessly clean. She hung up a couple of items of clothing for the next morning, then went back down in the lift and out into the early evening sunshine. She needed a walk after a day in the car. She strolled along the front until the buildings ended and then back along to the other end. There were no restaurants open, but a small snack bar seemed to be still serving. She ordered a tuna bocadillo and a coffee. Within a few minutes the food was brought to her with a small dish of olives. It was all very tasty, and Belle was hungry. The sun was low in the sky as she made her way back to the hotel, but the walk and the food had done her good.

The next morning after a simple breakfast of coffee, toast and peach jam, Belle set off once more. Taking the road around Valencia, past Denia and on to the city of Alicante. Here, the motorway ended and became a dual carriageway, but it took her quickly and safely beyond the city. She had been following the signs for Murcia, but with the city of Alicante behind her, she turned once more towards the coast. Almost immediately she was passing building sites with tall cranes and other machinery busily at work. Then a finished, but obviously new estate of houses and on through the old original part of the town to the sea front, where she discovered she was in a resort called Torrevieja. She parked and wandered along the front, looking for somewhere to have lunch. Very soon she came to a café and went inside. They had a small selection of tapas and Belle ordered some of those, with a coffee, and sat down. As she ate her meal it became obvious that there were people of several nationalities also eating there. She could pick out what sounded like German and Scandinavian, also Spanish of course, and English. Quite a cosmopolitan place and obviously very popular. After she had finished her meal she left the café and stood outside, dithering, not sure in which direction to go first. Just at that moment an English couple came out of the cafe. Belle smiled at them and they returned the smile.

"Excuse me." She said, "Are you familiar with the area or are you just on holiday?"

"We know it quite well. Can we be of any help?"

"Yes please, I've just arrived and I need somewhere to rent, like an apartment or a small villa. I may be here some time, so I don't want to go to a hotel."

The woman looked at her companion, "How about Pete? He'd be the best bet, wouldn't he?"

"Yes, definitely." He pointed along the road, "See that tall building? Turn right there and his office is just a few yards along on the left."

"Thank you very much, that's very helpful."

A few minutes later Belle stepped into a small office. A middle-aged man sat at a desk, a pile of papers in front of him. There was a door at the rear of the office and Belle could hear the sound of a typewriter coming through.

"Can I help you?" the man enquired with a smile.

Belle told him what she was looking for, and added. "I'd rather have a villa so that I can keep my car off the street."

"I've got a couple you may like to look at. A small, one bedroom villa, and a larger two bedroom. Just a moment." He walked to the door at the back. "Gerry, could you take a lady to look at a couple of villas? I thought number twelve and number forty-two."

A lady of similar age to him appeared at the door, car keys in her hand, and greeted Belle.

"Come with me, one is just around the corner, but the other is about a mile away."

The first one turned out to be the smaller villa. There was just room to get the car in the drive and close the gate. The villa had a balcony along the front and a small strip of garden, which was gravelled. Gerry unlocked the door and they stepped straight into the living area. She then went over to the window and raised the blind and sunlight streamed in. The room was square and a reasonable size. It was obviously the kitchen, dining room and lounge in one, which was what Belle had at home in England. However, this was about a third of the size of that. A kitchen area took up one end, very small and basic, with a table and four chairs.

"Why four chairs Gerry?"

"Well, the settee opens up to make a bed, so four people could stay here, but I have to admit, it's a bit cramped. Plus, of course, people may like to have friends in."

"Yes, of course." Belle was trying to keep an open mind. Gerry took her through to the bedroom and once more raised the window blind. This window looked out on to the front balcony, as did the one in the living room. There was a double bed, a single door wardrobe and a chest of drawers. There was also a narrow shower room at the rear with no window, but an extractor fan to take away the steam.

"So how do you get to the back of the villa?" Belle asked, puzzled.

"There is no back." Gerry patted the wall, "This is another villa. They are back to back."

"Oh, I see." Belle felt she could make do with this villa, but she was keen to see the other one before coming to a decision.

Gerry closed the blinds and they stepped outside. Belle admired the veranda going along the full width of the villa, while Gerry was locking the door.

A few minutes later they were at the second property. As with the first, it was in a terrace and from the front, it appeared smaller, certainly narrower. There was slightly more garden at the front and the balcony was deeper, but only went half way across the front. Still adequate for a table and four chairs. The entrance to the villa was from the balcony and led straight into a lounge-cum-dining room, which was adequately furnished with everything she would need, including a 'put you up' settee and easy chairs. At the rear was the kitchen, with a unit partially dividing it from the lounge area. Belle looked with interest at the fixtures, fittings and equipment, it was much better than the other villa. There was a door leading from the lounge to a small, square hall, and off this there were two bedrooms, both double, and a bathroom. As before, Gerry had raised all the blinds, and Belle could see immediately that there was a nice little rear garden. At the back of the kitchen there was a door leading outside. They stepped out onto a paved area. Once again, the gardens to the front and rear were either paved or gravelled, although there were several shrubs in the rear garden. Belle really liked this villa and decided there and then to take it.

"The only problem Gerry, is that I don't know how long I want it for. It could be a couple of weeks or more, or it could be all winter."

"Yes, that does make it more difficult for us. I'll have a chat with Pete and see what he says. You see, we may refuse a longer booking, and then you go home and we've lost out."

"I understand. But whatever you decide, I love it and I'll certainly want it for the next few weeks."

They walked back through and Gerry closed the shutters. As they stepped outside a car pulled up next door and a lady climbed out and opened the gate. Her husband drove in and turned off the engine. As they turned to walk into their villa, Belle realised it was the couple who had helped her earlier.

"Well, hello again." The lady said with a laugh, "What a coincidence. Are you our new neighbour?"

"Well I hope so." Belle said.

Pete said if she was prepared to pay for a month, he would not take any more bookings, so Belle agreed. She moved in that afternoon and at four o'clock she was sitting on the veranda with a glass of water. She had been surprised to see several small radiators in the villa. She had assumed that heating would not be necessary, and that the sunshine would keep the villa warm, even in winter, that was certainly the case at the moment.

Now she needed to shop. She had no groceries, not even a pint of milk. She decided to knock on her neighbours' door and ask where the nearest supermarket was. She had picked up her car after sorting things out with Pete and Gerry. She tapped lightly on the door and it was opened almost immediately by the lady.

"Sorry to bother you, but could you tell me where the nearest supermarket is please?"

"It's no bother. You've got to go back towards the old part of town I'm afraid. We haven't got one here yet, although they are building one. You can't miss it, there's a car park at the rear."

Belle thanked her, grabbed her handbag and drove off. Three-quarters of an hour later, she was back, loaded with shopping. She had been tempted to study everything in the store, but it had been a tiring day, and a quiet evening and an early night was what she needed. Now to test the oven. While it was heating up she put the shopping away, then popped a pizza in for her evening meal.

The next morning, she had a light breakfast and then took her tea out to the veranda with a notebook where she had been making notes. After a while her neighbours' door opened and the lady called out, "Good morning."

Belle put her pen down and returned the greeting.

"Would you like to come around for a coffee dear? We can tell you where everything is and what there is to do and see."

"Oh yes please, that would be lovely." A time was arranged, and Belle duly arrived on their doorstep.

"Come in dear, we're in the garden." She led the way through to the rear of the house and out into the garden

"We ought to introduce ourselves. I'm Vi and my hubby is Harry."

Belle held out her hand to each in turn. "I'm Belle, it's very nice to meet you."

"Coffee alright for you Belle?"

"Yes, thank you."

Vi disappeared inside to make the coffee and Belle smiled at Harry. "So, do you live here?"

"Yes, we do, we've been here eighteen months now and we feel quite at home."

"That's good. I thought that was the case. You've made it really homely."

"You mean all Vi's bits and pieces. She does love collecting things. I'm just glad I don't have to dust them all. The dust is awful here, what with the dry sandy soil and all the building work going on."

Vi returned with three coffees on a tray and some biscuits.

"So, did you get your shopping done dear?"

"Yes, I think I've gone a bit mad. I had a job getting everything in the fridge."

Vi chuckled, "Well, I've probably got a bigger fridge than you. I can spare you a corner if you're stuck. Now then Belle, we'll tell you a bit about the area. It's still being developed and there will eventually be all sorts of things here. They are planning a community centre and a church. There's already a supermarket nearly completed, and a row of small shops are going to be built along the coast road. But a lot of the villas are already occupied and a lot of those are British. About a third, wouldn't you say Harry?"

"Yes at least a third."

Vi continued. "So, things are being done to keep people happy and busy. We have an expats club in an old building just up the road. We do all sorts of things to raise money so that we can build a new one. Fortunately, it's cheap to build here. We've got a committee, which I am on, and we arrange lots of activities like card evenings, bingo, dancing and outings. There is a small charge to join and for some of the activities, and it all goes towards the new centre." She took a deep breath. "So, if you're going to be here for some time, you might be interested."

"She won't be happy till she's got you roped in." Said Harry with a grin.

Belle told them of her concerns about being lonely. That she was a widow, but she wanted to travel and that's why she was here.

"You see, I'd never been abroad until Spring this year and I was longing to see Spain."

"Never been abroad?" Vi looked puzzled but was too polite to ask why.

"Anyway Vi, I would be interested in joining your club. When is the next meeting?"

"Oh there's something on every night. We've got a bar you see, and a darts board. Harry and I don't go down every night, usually a couple of times a week.

There's a notice board down there with a list of what's on and you can pick and choose. What are you interested in?"

"I don't know really. I don't go out much you see. But I'm quite sure that I'll find something."

"Well, we're not going down tonight, but tomorrow we've got a card evening. Would you like to come down with us and we'll introduce you to everyone and you can see what's on over the next couple of months?"

"That would be lovely, thanks." Said Belle.

She went back to her own villa feeling happier. She didn't feel so alone and the pull of home was not quite so strong.

The next morning Belle went back to the supermarket. She didn't need anything except for perhaps some more milk, but she had been too tired to take it all in yesterday. Now she wandered around at her leisure, and despite her best intentions, picked up several interesting things to try. She had left some washing on a clothes airer in the back garden and when she got home it was dry. She smiled with satisfaction and put another load in the machine. While it swished away she had an early lunch, then walked in to the old part of town and did some exploring. She was surprised how big it was. Ancient buildings, new shops, cool plazas, all quite different from anything at home. She bought a sun hat and some post cards, then popped into a 'farmacia' for some paracetamol. Soon it was time to walk back to the villa, have something to eat and get ready for her evening out.

Belle could see that a lot of hard work had been done to make the old building usable. The walls had been painted a pale eggshell blue which brightened the interior up and made it seem cooler, even if it wasn't. One club member was a retired carpenter and had made the bar using pieces of wood other members had donated, then applied varnish to finish it off. It looked rather good. Chairs and small tables stood about, few of which were matching, but it didn't matter.

Vi and Belle sat down while Harry went and got them a glass of wine and a beer for himself. As people came over to say hello to Vi, she introduced Belle to them. Some members were playing cards and at another table four men were playing dominoes, a popular game in Spain. There was constant chat and laughter and a friendly atmosphere. After a while a woman called for silence, and when she had everyone's attention she began to speak.

"Can I remind everybody about the walk on Wednesday. We've only got six names down so far, so if anyone else is interested, please let me know. We are going inland this time and it will be approximately four miles. It would be advisable to bring water and snacks because we are unlikely to be going anywhere near cafes or shops. Secondly, Chas is going to book a coach for a day trip to Benidorm. It will be on the third Thursday in October and we need to know as soon as possible who would like to go, so that we can decide on what size coach to book. By next Tuesday please. There will be a piece of paper on the notice board where you can write your names. That's all for now. Thanks everyone."

The buzz of conversation started again, and Belle turned to Vi.

"I'd like to do the walk and the trip, they sound like fun."

"So, you think you'll still be here in October?"

"Well—I'll decide over the weekend. Do you have someone to lead the walk?"

"Yes, there are three people who sort of take it in turns as leaders. I think it's Chas on Wednesday."

"Who is this Chas who is so involved? Is he here tonight?"

"No, he's not. He's just a nice bloke. He gets roped in for a lot of things because he's younger than most of us and he's got no commitments."

Belle began to relax as the evening wore on. She put her name down for the walk and then joined in a card game. At ten o'clock sharp everything was tidied up and packed away and the hall was locked up. The end of a pleasant evening.

On Sunday, Belle was invited out for lunch with Vi, Harry and another couple. They all managed to squeeze into the same car and set off at twelve-thirty for the restaurant. Belle watched the road from the middle of the rear seats. The route took them this way and that, past olive groves, down tiny roads and over canals. They arrived at last in a small village and turned off down a bumpy lane and into an even bumpier car park. The restaurant was a sprawling, single storey building with the outside painted a brilliant white. A babble of voices greeted them as they pushed open the door. A woman called out a greeting to them from behind a small bar.

"Hello everyone, a table for five isn't it? How are you Vi, and you of course, Harry?"

"We're very well thank you. This is Ruby and Don, who you may have met before, and a newcomer to this area, Belle."

Smiles and greetings were exchanged and then they were led through the first room, which was already full of diners, to another room beyond. The rather rustic, tiled floors were on several different levels, a couple of steps down here and a step up there. Belle took care not to trip. The lady led them to a table, nicely laid for five, close to a large window overlooking a garden. Another young lady came up to them.

"Hello. Would you like to order some drinks?"

When the orders were placed, and the waitress had gone, Belle turned to Vi.

"Everyone is English. I didn't expect that, it all looks so Spanish here."

"Yes, and it's English food here. Spanish food is lovely, but sometimes, when you live here, you long for a good old English roast or something similar."

The drinks came, and each person was given a printed menu to study.

"Well you know what I'll have love." Said Harry.

Vi rolled her eyes. "Roast beef for you then, the same as always, I'm going to have lasagne. How about you Belle?"

It was difficult to decide, but Belle never had roast at home. It was too much bother for one, so she chose the roast beef as did Don. Ruby decided on the salmon. Belle was very curious.

"So, do English people own this place Vi?"

"Yes, and most of the staff are English too. It's very popular. If you want to come on a Sunday, you have to book a table in advance."

"What's it called? I didn't notice a name on the way in."

"It's called the Countryside Inn, it's nice the way they have done it up on the inside, don't you think?"

"It certainly is." Replied Belle.

The meal was a leisurely affair and it was almost four o'clock when they finally arrived home. Harry had taken a different route back which had made it more interesting.

On Wednesday, Belle waited on her veranda for a lift to the start of the walk, car sharing was the norm. Vi and Harry didn't do the walks as Harry had a 'dodgy' hip, but Don and Ruby were going, and they would pick her up. There was another single lady called Mary, who sat in the back with Belle. It only took them twenty minutes to get to the start, and a small group of people were already parked, and ready to go. A tall man was chatting to the group. Fair haired and slim, he was dressed in casual trousers and a checked shirt. Belle guessed this must be Chas and that proved to be the case as introductions were made all round. There were eleven walkers altogether, four couples, Belle and her companion in the car, Mary, and Chas. She thoroughly enjoyed the walk and the company. Most of it was level and easy going, with a few ups and downs. They stopped halfway and sat on rocks or wherever they could and had something to eat and drink, then moved off again. As often happens when walking with a group, for a few hundred yards you find yourself walking with one person, then you cross a bridge or go through a gate and you have a different companion. By the time they had completed the walk, Belle felt she knew everyone. After the half way break she found herself walking with Chas for a while. She found him pleasant to talk to, but it left her curious. Later, as they drove home, she asked Mary.

"Tell me a bit about Chas. What does he do for a living? Is he married?"

"No, he's single. He says he's not the marrying sort, although he likes the ladies! As for work—he doesn't, he's a gentleman of leisure. Although he's very friendly, he seldom talks about himself, we can only speculate. Some people think he's won a lot of money on the lottery, or maybe his father is a Duke or something and they have a huge family estate somewhere. Who knows?" Mary chuckled. "We often come up with these ideas. Somebody said the other night, perhaps he's a retired film star or a model."

"Well he's good looking enough, although I prefer tall, dark and handsome myself." Belle said with a laugh.

Belle soon got into a routine, although she was lonely at times, it was no different to being at home in England, where a large part of the day was spent in her own company. If she was bored she did what she would have done at home, climbed in her car and drove off somewhere to explore. She had bought a large-scale map of the area and was finding some interesting places to visit. Quaint villages, huge reservoirs and vast areas of orange and lemon groves. Sometimes she would get a bus into the city of Alicante and explore there. But she never went to the beach. Strangely it was the place where she felt most lonely.

Every week she would take a purse full of change and find a telephone kiosk and phone home, taking it in turns to phone either Chris, Rose or Bubs. She would ask them to pass on all the news to the others. The phone calls were not long, but she also wrote and then she would tell them every little detail. The post was quite reliable going to England, but coming the other way, it was rather erratic. It could take a week or two and sometimes it would never arrive at all. But it was good that she was settled in the villa and she could give them an address to write to.

Belle enjoyed going to the club. There were so many different things to do. So, no matter what your interests were, you could always find something to enjoy. She was aware that Chas was making an effort to include her in things and thought how kind he was. At the beginning of November, a Guy Fawkes night dance was arranged in the hall. It was preceded by a short but extremely noisy firework display, then everyone went back into the hall and hot dogs and drinks were served. Chas brought some food and a glass of wine over to the table where Belle was sitting.

"Thanks Chas, no wine for you then?"

"No, I don't drink, I'm quite happy with a glass of coke. It's not just that. Call me strange if you like, but I like to be in control. I think there's nothing more off-putting than a civilised person falling about and slurring their words. Rather undignified. But that's just my opinion."

"I know what you mean, and I think I agree. There was a time when I used to have a little too much brandy, but that was when my husband was being particularly trying. I usually just have one glass of wine now, occasionally two, but not often."

Chas looked at her with a smile. "I can understand that." He paused, and then asked. "Have you finished eating?"

"Yes, I have thanks."

"Then let's dance." He led her on to the floor and they found a small area free amongst all the other dancers and he pulled her close. After a couple of tunes had played on the old Hi-Fi, Chas took her back to their table. Almost at once, Harry appeared and demanded a dance, and for the next forty minutes Belle didn't stop until Chas rescued her and led her back to her chair. He bought her another glass of wine and another coke for himself.

"Just drink as much as you want to Belle, I don't want to be accused of getting you tiddly."

She was thirsty after all the dancing, so she drank half the wine quite quickly, making her feel a little light headed. Chas pulled her back to the dance floor for a slow number. As he held her close, she became aware that there was some chemistry between them. Chas looked down at her.

"I'd like to take you out for a meal Belle. Would you like that?"

"Yes Chas, that would be lovely."

The dance ended and they sat down and agreed on a day that would suit them both.

"I know a little place on the outskirts of the city. I'll take you there. I'll pick you up at seven."

And so, they drifted into a close relationship that Belle hadn't wanted at first. But it was nice to be taken out, to be driven everywhere and looked after.

As they were walking one Wednesday, Belle told him a little about her marriage, and how she seemed to fall for the wrong sort of man.

"It always seems to be someone who wants to tell me what I should or shouldn't do."

Chas looked taken aback. "I don't think I do that, do I?"

"No, you don't Chas, and I must thank you for that."

"Forgive me for being blunt with you Belle, but I hope you're not getting umm---too attached to me, are you?"

"Oh Chas, you're very sweet, but I'm not in love with you, if that's what you mean."

"I'm glad. You see, I've never been in love. I'm forty-six now and it's not going to happen. I think for some reason I am incapable of falling in love. That's why I've never married."

Belle looked at him in surprise. "Never been in love. Gosh, that's sad. But don't think it will never happen. And I bet when it does, you'll fall head over heels, you wait and see."

Chas threw back his head and laughed. "I don't think so, but it will be interesting---me and marriage? Mm."

During her phone calls to home, Belle had been trying to persuade the family to come and visit. She didn't want to go home yet and face the English Winter, but she was missing them all, so when she phoned Rose the following weekend, there was a lovely surprise for her.

"I'm so glad you phoned Mum. I've got some news for you. I've got a really cheap flight out to Alicante in two weeks' time. Please say it's OK."

"Of course it's OK. It's more than that, it's brilliant! I don't do anything that can't be cancelled. Give me the flight details and I'll make a note."

"What clothes shall I pack? Will it still be hot?"

"No, not hot, but pleasantly warm. Just bring medium weight things and pack cardigans, you'll need them in the evenings."

Rose gave Belle the time of her flight arrival and Belle said she would pick them up.

"Are the children excited?"

"Madly excited and they are counting the days. They have a chart on the wall and they tick off each day as it goes by."

The next two weeks flew by. There was another walk and a couple more things on at the club. Also, the new supermarket opened, and compared to the little Spanish one on the edge of the town, this one seemed huge. But Belle was limited for space, having only a small fridge with an ice box and one cupboard for food. But at least the shop was close by and she could shop every day if necessary. She managed to get some more linen and blankets from Pete for the 'put you up' and although it was still pleasantly warm, he reminded her how to put the heating on, and adjust it, just in case.

CHAPTER 24

The downside of the cheap flights was the timing. The children had to be woken at three thirty in the morning. They were reluctant to wake until Rose reminded them where they were going, then two excited children leapt up, got dressed and had some juice and biscuits to keep them going. By the time they got to the airport and were in the building, they were ready for breakfast. In fact, they all were, but Dave cautioned them not to eat too much as there would be another breakfast on the plane, which amused the children. The flight was a little late leaving, but the pilot told them that there was a tail wind and the time would be made up on the journey. The upside of the early start was that at ten-thirty they were in arrivals at Alicante and looking out for Belle. Gary was the first to see her, and before anyone could stop him, he was under the rope barrier and running into Belle's arms.

"I've really missed you Nanna." He hugged her back, then looked concerned. "Why are you crying?"

"Because I'm a silly old Nanna. I'm crying because I'm so happy to see you. Megan, give Nanna a hug, did you like flying in the aeroplane?"

Megan nodded. "It was a bit noisy when the brakes went on, but it was good."

Belle reached for Rose and held her close. "Oh, it's so good to see you all."

"Hey, don't I get a hug from my glamorous mother-in-law?"

Belle turned to Dave and greeted him with a hug. "Of course you do."

Then they all walked along beside him as he pushed the trolley out into the sunshine, across a pick-up area and into the car park.

The children had slept for most of the journey and now they were full of energy. When Belle unlocked her villa door, they ran in and explored every room, bounced on their beds and then asked to go out in the rear garden.

"The villas' nice Mum, not very big, but just right for you."

"Yes, it is, but there's room for visitors although it's a bit squashed. The only problem will be the bathroom. We'll have to decide who showers in the morning and who in the evening."

Rose said. "The only thing is, I'm a bit worried about where you're going to sleep Mum. We'll be in your bed."

"Oh, don't worry about that Rose, the settee is a 'put you up' and it's very comfortable. I actually tried it yesterday afternoon and fell asleep."

The children ran back in from the garden.

"We're hungry Nanna."

"We'll have a drink and a biscuit. Then after Mummy has unpacked, we'll have lunch, and then you must decide what you want to do this afternoon."

"Go in the sea." The children chorused.

They stayed for a week and during that time Belle took them to the castle and the street market. On one of the days they went for a drive in the surrounding area and visited the huge reservoir which supplied their water, but most of the time was spent on the beach. In the middle of the week, Chas took them all to the Countryside Inn for lunch.

"So, what did you think of Chas?" Belle asked Rose and Dave later that evening.

"He seems to be a nice man." Dave said.

"And good looking." Rose added.

"But---." Dave hesitated. "A bit dull. You can imagine him always playing safe. Do you know what I mean? Never taking a chance. I imagine you'll soon get bored with him Ma-in-law."

"Yes, I have to agree Dave. But I feel completely safe with him, and that's important. I've got no wild emotions clouding my judgement."

Rose listened to this exchange of opinions.

"So, you won't be moving out here permanently Mum?"

"Goodness me, no. I'll probably be going home in early spring."

Rose had brought a letter from Chris with her, and in it she asked if she could come over for Christmas and the New Year, if Belle was still there. So Belle wrote a reply and said that would be lovely, but to book flights soon, while there were still some available. She gave the letter to Rose to be posted in England when they returned.

The week flew past and in no time at all Belle was driving them back to the airport. As she waited with them in the queue, the children were subdued.

"I wish you were coming home with us Nanna." Gary said.

Belle was too emotional to answer, she just hugged them close. But once she had waved goodbye and returned to her car, she shed a few tears, because she had the same wish.

But on Wednesday she was glad she had stayed, because Chas had planned a walk which would take them right into the Spanish countryside. He had checked it with a Spanish friend the week before and as it was a more arduous walk, only seven people had put their names down to go. They were advised to take food and drink with them, and Chas had a small first aid kit in his backpack, just in case. To begin with, the route took them along an easy stretch of path beside some irrigation canals, and then they left them behind as they climbed up a rough track. They passed abandoned buildings, jumped over streams and trekked around large pools. All the time they climbed steadily until Chas called a halt.

"Right, we'll stop for twenty minutes for a drink and a rest, but first, turn around and look at the view."

There were gasps as everyone looked back. They were high up and looking down over villages and towns and the city of Alicante, with the Mediterranean sparkling in the sunshine in the distance. The air was crystal clear with just a faint haze over the city. Those with binoculars passed them around for others to have a look. Then everyone found some flat rocks to sit on while they enjoyed refreshments. Chas had them walking again after the twenty minutes were up.

"OK everyone, the next couple of miles is fairly level but the path is rough so please take care. We will then turn back towards the coast and after another mile or so, we come to an area which is used by the Spanish on hot Summer days. There are trees for shade, with seats as well. Also, you will see several barbecues and some children's play areas. Because it's high up, it's cooler, and often there's a breeze coming up from the sea. We'll have lunch there."

They set off once more, taking care not to twist ankles, or stumble on the stony path. As they approached the public area, Chas held his hand up and brought everyone to a stop.

"Quiet please everybody, if you look at the top of that conifer tree ahead, the one with the cones. I think there may be crossbills feeding there."

Binoculars were raised, and it was confirmed. There were two or three keen bird watchers with them, and they were very pleased. After ten minutes they moved on to find the benches and seats, and have lunch. As it was mid-week, the area was deserted with just one parked car, but no one in sight. They stayed there for forty-five minutes and then threw their wrappers in the bin provided before setting off again. This time the footpath was well used and never far from the road. It only took an hour to get off the hill and nearly another hour to get back to the cars.

Belle felt invigorated by the walk and decided to join a walking club, if possible, when she got back to England.

The next few weeks passed quickly and once again, Belle found herself at the airport, waiting impatiently in 'arrivals'. But the flight was delayed by over an hour because of bad weather in England. She wandered off to get a coffee and wait in comfort. At last they arrived, Chris with a big smile on her face at seeing her mother.

"Chris, you're here at last." Said Belle. She turned and hugged Steve, once Chris had released her and they headed for the car park.

"It's so cold at home Mum, you're in the best place here."

"It's quite cool here actually. I put the heating on a week ago, just mornings and evenings."

"You've got heating?"

"Oh yes. People think it's warm here all the time, but it's not. And the houses don't have cavity walls like they do at home, so they get very cold. A bit like being in a caravan actually."

She unlocked the car and opened the boot. Steve stacked the suitcases away and they all climbed in.

"How long will it take to get to the villa, Mum?"

"About forty minutes, we'll soon be there."

Chris and Steve had arrived the day before Christmas Eve and were going home on January the second. Belle had made lots of plans after being advised by Chas. She wanted to make it a Christmas to remember.

Then, although she had not mentioned it to anyone, she was going home early in the new year. Everyone here was friendly, but it just wasn't the same. She needed familiar surroundings and her family close by. All her life she had lived in the same area and her roots went deep.

But it wasn't to be. They arrived back at the villa and Chris and Steve disappeared to have a look round and unpack, while Belle put the kettle on.

"Here you are Mum, English teabags, as requested."

"Oh, thanks Chris, the ones I buy here are rather weak."

They sat down with their tea and some delicious Spanish biscuits.

"I've got two surprises for you Mum. The first one is, there's a baby on the way."

Belle leapt up and leaned over Chris to give her a big hug, a delighted smile on her face.

"Hey, I helped, can I have a hug too?" Steve said with a grin.

"That's wonderful news. Well done, both of you."

"Do you want the other bit of news Mum?"

"Yes, but you can't top that." Belle said, still beaming with delight.

"You have another visitor, end of Jan."

Belle had to hide her disappointment and look pleased.

"Who is it? Is it Bubs? I didn't think she had holiday leave left."

"No, it's not Bubs. It's Uncle Rob."

Belle was surprised to say the least, although it

would be nice to see him. For a few minutes she said nothing, not sure how to respond.

"Aren't you pleased Mum?"

"Yes, I am, I just didn't think it was his sort of thing."

"Well neither did I, but Rose has a theory. You know what she's like. She thinks he's jealous of this chap Chas, and he wants to warn him off."

"Oh, honestly, what would you do with her. Does she think there's going to be a duel at dawn? Both of them are far too civilised for that. Anyway, there's nothing really serious between Chas and I. We're just company for each other."

"Is that all?" Chris asked with a grin.

Belle laughed. "Well, sort of!"

"I've got a letter from Rob Mum. Perhaps you could write an answer and I'll post it when I get home." She handed the letter to Belle and she ripped it open.

Dear Belle

I'm really missing you, so I thought I would come out and see you, if that's OK. I've already booked a flight for the last Saturday in January and I'll be staying one week. Perhaps you would be good enough to book me in somewhere, close to you if possible. I shall come anyway, even if you don't want to see me. I can easily keep out of the way. Please give your reply to Chris. I would appreciate it though, if you could pick me up at the airport.

Fondest love, Rob.

Belle immediately wrote a reply and gave it to Chris to put in her suitcase until she got back to England.

Dear Rob

It will be lovely to see you and I insist that you stay with me. I have two bedrooms as I'm sure Rose has told you. You will not be in the way, I can assure you. Chas is a good friend, but very laid back. There will be no problem there. I look forward to seeing you.

Lots of love, Belle.

On Christmas Eve, Belle took Chris and Steve into the town centre where there were huge models of the nativity scenes laid out and lit up. The whole place looked stunning, with displays of poinsettias everywhere, on lamp posts and even on roundabouts. There was a chocolatier in the square, selling steaming mugs of delicious hot chocolate and doing a brisk trade with all manner of chocolate merchandise for Christmas gifts. After they had looked at the nativity models, they just had to try the hot chocolate. It was served with a small dish of churros to be dipped in the hot drink.

"This is just so yummy, Mum." Chris licked her lips. "I'm going to get some chocolate as well, for everyone at home."

Later, as they sat down to a simple meal of plain white fish and mashed potato, Belle told them the plans for Christmas Day.

"I've kept tonight's meal simple, because apparently, according to Chas, we will be having a huge meal tomorrow."

"We're eating out, are we?" Steve asked.

"Yes, and I know no more than you. Chas has arranged it and of course he will be with us. He's picking us up at one o'clock."

"But if he's driving Mum, he won't be able to have a drink. Can't we have a taxi?"

"Chas doesn't drink so he'll be happy to drive."

"Not ever. He never has a drink?" Steve looked surprised.

"No, never. He always goes to this restaurant at Christmas because he hasn't got any family. There will be other people we know there, walkers and neighbours. It's very popular."

"Well it sounds great and something quite different. We are usually at your place Christmas Day Mum. Lovely though that is, this sounds like it will make an interesting change."

As they walked in to the restaurant, the noise hit them. It was a huge room, more like a community hall than a traditional restaurant. Tables, mostly seating at least eight people, were placed as close together as possible and they were rapidly filling up.

"Gosh Chas, how many people are here, do you think?" Belle was as amazed as Chris and Steve.

"About two hundred and fifty I believe. How would you fancy catering for this number then?"

"Mm—not much." Belle said with a chuckle.

Bottle after bottle of wine was brought to the tables, reds and whites, and passed up and down for people to help themselves, then more appeared as the bottles emptied. After twenty minutes or so, large platters of food were placed down the middle of the tables and people took what they wanted. Each course consisted of several choices of just one thing. It may have been breads, fish, vegetables or meat, but it just kept on coming.

Along one side of the room was a solid metal hotplate, probably twenty feet long. There was a pile of burning wood at one end, and the red-hot embers were dragged along under the hot plate as they were needed. Almost every hot dish seemed to be cooked on this. Behind was the kitchen area where other food was prepared. There were, it seemed, dozens of staff, and they never stopped. More wine and more food just kept coming to the tables. Finally, the desserts arrived, followed by the coffee.

"I've just counted up." Said Chris "That was eight courses!"

There were different nationalities enjoying the food. Spanish, English, German and Scandinavian, and the babble of voices was almost deafening. Next to their table was a Spanish family. All ages, from small children up to elderly grandparents. Suddenly a couple of people at the table started singing 'Happy Birthday'. Gradually the whole restaurant joined in. A little old lady stood up, a rather bemused smile on her face. It was obviously her birthday they were singing for. The atmosphere was something they would all never forget. It felt like the true meaning of the Christmas spirit.

Over the next few days Belle and her visitors relaxed, taking gentle walks along the sea front and drives into the countryside. Plus, of course, a visit to the castle at Alicante, obligatory for any visitors! Chas stayed away for most of this time, but one evening they were invited to his villa, where he cooked them a very tasty paella. He had a very nice home. The villa was set in quite a large garden and was detached with three bedrooms and two bathrooms. He had every comfort. The kitchen had been refitted the previous year by a German company and it was superb. Quite different to Belle's basic little villa.

On New Year's Eve he took them to a local Chinese restaurant. This was always very popular, and Chas had booked it as soon as he heard about Chris and Steve's visit. Unlike Christmas day, this was the size of an average restaurant, but once again, as many tables as possible had been squeezed into the space.

There were just a mere five courses this time, but it was more than enough. The one that impressed Belle the most was the main course. Two whole pineapples were placed on the table between the four of them. The top had been sliced off to make a lid and it was filled with chicken and pineapple in a delicious sauce. As midnight arrived, everybody in the restaurant began to sing 'Auld Lang Sine'. But their voices were completely swamped by Chinese crackers going off just outside. They were so loud, Belle put her hands over her ears, but Chas laughed at her.

As he drove them home Chris said. "I'm still deaf. I've never heard anything so noisy."

"It's because they were in an alleyway between the two buildings. But that's how they like it, the Spanish and the Chinese, the noisier the better."

When Chas dropped them off back at the villa, Steve shook his hand.

"I want to thank you for three fabulous evenings. It's been good to meet you. I don't think we'll ever have a better holiday."

"Well thank you Steve, I've enjoyed it as well." He looked at Chris. "I hope you are happy now you've met me. You know I'll take good care of your Mother."

"Yes, I do. It's put my mind at rest."

Once more, as Belle saw Chris and Steve off at the airport, she felt very emotional. If it wasn't for Rob coming over in a few weeks time, she would have got in the car and driven home the next day. But then she was soon back in the routine of seeing Chas, going to the club and joining in the walks. She often saw Vi and Harry and enjoyed shopping with some of the ladies while the men were playing golf. The days were mainly bright and sunny although with a cool breeze. Belle had to smile to herself because sometimes, despite her home sickness, she even thought of staying until the Spring.

The weeks seemed to fly by and suddenly there were only a few days to go before Rob arrived. Belle tidied the garden, which didn't take long as it was designed for low maintenance, and then started on the villa. Everything was cleaned from front to back and the spare room beds aired. Then it was Saturday midday and she was back at the airport yet again. Her heart gave a little leap of pleasure at the thought of seeing Rob. The flight was on time and obviously not full, as the passengers were very soon coming through to be greeted by friends and loved ones. Belle spotted Rob from about fifty yards away and began waving with a big smile on her face. She was soon enveloped in a big hug, then given a kiss on each cheek.

"Oh, Rob, it's so good to see you, did you have a good journey?"

"Yes thanks, quick and smooth and as you saw, it was on time too."

They walked out into the sunshine and back to the car park. Rob was looking around and taking everything in, but clearly delighted to see Belle again. As they drove out of the airport and joined the busy coast road he was also impressed with Belle's driving skills. She was competent and relaxed. He marvelled again at how she had changed. She looked beautiful and happy, and he was pleased for her.

When they got back to the villa she followed the usual procedure. Kettle on, then show the new visitor the villa and their bedroom, then leave them to unpack while she made the tea. They took their drinks out to the rear garden which was sunny and protected from the cool breeze. Rob took a sip of tea, then to Belle's surprise, he took her hand.

"You have no idea how much I've missed you, Belle Johnston."

"I bet it's just my tea and biscuits that you've missed." She said with a laugh, trying to keep things light. She was remembering what both her daughters had hinted at—that Rob was in love with her. The last thing she wanted was to hurt him. But she didn't feel that way about him---did she?

Rob told her about the things he would like to do and the places he would like to visit, and they made a few notes.

"We'll go and look at your castle, I understand it's compulsory." He said with a grin, "But I prefer the countryside and the beach to busy towns. I've had a hectic few weeks and I feel a bit jaded. One of the reps had an accident and I've been covering for him. I thought I would have to cancel the holiday, but he came back last Wednesday, thank goodness."

"We'll do whatever you want, but I would like you to meet my friend Chas. He makes a fabulous paella and I've asked him to do one for us. We're going around to his villa on Tuesday evening. Is that OK with you Rob?"

"Err—yes that's fine." He sounded doubtful.

"He's just a good friend Rob, charming and harmless and actually, rather boring. He just takes me around and keeps me company. You'll like him, I'm sure."

"Well, we'll see." Was all Rob said.

On Sunday they kept to the local area, strolling down to the beach and having a light lunch there in a beach side café. Then they walked along to the edge of the town.

"I'll take you back through where all the building work is going on. There are going to be hundreds of new villas. They have just opened a big new supermarket and there are plans for many more shops and a church for all faiths. Plus, there will be green areas and playgrounds. It should be nice when it's matured. I'll have to come back in ten years time." She said with a smile.

"Mm, maybe I'll come with you." Rob replied.

They came back via the supermarket and Rob chose the food for the evening meal.

It seemed very strange having Rob in the spare bedroom and it took some while for Belle to drop off to sleep.

The next morning over breakfast they decided to 'do' the castle.

"We'll go on the bus." Belle said, "It saves looking for somewhere to park."

Despite Rob not really wanting to do the city, he seemed to enjoy the whole thing, even the bus ride in. He chuckled at Belle's attempts to tell the driver they wanted to be dropped off near the castle, but then he apologised.

"I shouldn't laugh, I can't speak a word of Spanish."

"No, you shouldn't mock me. I do just fine in the shops and cafes and they seem to understand me."

"I'm sorry. I'm actually very impressed. You never cease to amaze me my dear. Isabelle has gone forever, and Belle has taken her place. To me, it seems like two completely different people."

"Well Rob, this is the real me. Isabelle was just a possession belonging to Bernard, not a normal person at all. I hope you don't mind the real me, I would hate to lose your friendship."

"That's never going to happen. I'll always be here for you." He squeezed her hand and then tucked it through his arm, "Right, which way now?"

They must have been at the top of the castle for nearly an hour and by the time they were back at street level they were ready for a tapas lunch. As they strolled back from the bus stop later, Vi and Harry were sitting on their front veranda.

"Have you had a good day then?" Vi called out.

"Yes, great thanks." Belle said, "We're going down the club tonight, will you two be there?"

"No, not tonight dear, but come around for a coffee tomorrow morning."

"Thanks, that will be nice, we'll see you then."

Rob seemed quite relaxed that evening, chatting easily with everyone and enjoying a game of darts. As they left and were making their way back to the villa, he said what a nice bunch of people they were.

"I can understand why you don't want to come home. But don't stay too long Belle, we all miss you."

"Don't worry Rob, I'll be home by the Spring. I feel happy here most of the time, then I'll be hit by home sickness and I want to wave a magic wand and be back in my home."

The next morning Belle listened to Rob chatting to Vi and Harry over coffee and chuckling at something Harry had said. Bernard would have been out of his depth, she thought. Small talk and laughter had been beyond him most of the time. Rob was quite different.

As they went for a stroll after lunch, Rob told Belle that he needed a phone box, just to make a quick call to work. Belle sat on a seat in the winter sunshine, quietly thinking about Rob and Chas and her new life since Bernard's death. When Rob had finished his call, they wandered back to the villa, comfortable in each other's company.

This was the evening they were going to see Chas and he wanted them there by six o'clock so that they could enjoy a pre-dinner drink in the garden, if it was warm enough.

"You'll love his villa Rob." Belle said as she backed out on to the road. "It's big and beautifully furnished and the kitchen is wonderful."

"So, he's a good cook then?"

"Yes, but he really enjoys cooking and I think that helps."

"Does that mean he is overweight?"

"Gosh, no. Chas cares about his weight and his appearance. He always looks smart. Well, you'll soon see won't you?"

As soon as Belle pulled up outside his house, Chas stepped out of his door and put up a hand in greeting, before coming down the villa steps and opening the gate for them.

"Hi Chas, this is my dear friend Rob." Then she giggled and turned to Rob and said, "And this is my other dear friend Chas."

The two men shook hands and Chas kissed Belle on the cheek.

"Come in. It's too cool outside, we'll have a drink in the lounge. Are you enjoying your holiday Rob?"

"Yes I am. Belle is spoiling me and it's been relaxing and interesting. So many new places to go and things to see."

As they sat in the lounge, Rob looked around.

"Belle said your villa was nice, and it is."

"Thank you. Would you like to look around it?" Chas asked.

They put their drinks down and stood up. Belle watched them leave the room and listened to their voices as Rob made comments or asked questions, and Chas responded. She sighed with relief. For some reason she thought they might have been awkward with each other. Silly really, as they were both friendly, easy going men.

As they drove home later, after a very pleasant evening, Rob told Belle he felt easier now he had met Chas.

"And he certainly makes a delicious paella." He added.

On Wednesday Belle took him South, stopping here and there for a coffee or to admire the view. They finally ended up in the big port city of Cartagena. Belle found a nice restaurant where they had lunch, then they had a short look around the city before driving up into the hills above. They found themselves looking down over the harbour, where large cargo ships were anchored, prior to unloading. They were surprised how the sounds from the ships floated up to them in the clear air. After taking in the views they decided on a long scenic route back to Torrevieja.

"I can't believe it's Thursday and your week is nearly over Rob. I'm really going to miss you when you go home." Said Belle, as they strolled along the promenade.

"It's a good job you've got Chas then, and of course, Vi and Harry."

"Ye—es, I suppose so." Belle didn't know quite how to respond to his comment.

"I'm glad we have taken it easy today." Rob grinned at her. "Where are you taking me tomorrow then? I'm sure you'll have something up your sleeve!"

"Well I need a few bits from the supermarket, then we'll have an early lunch because I want to take you to a reservoir later, which I think you'll find interesting."

"OK" said Rob. "Sounds good to me."

The next morning, they drove out into the countryside to an enormous reservoir, and Rob got out of the car to enable Belle to pull in close to the barrier as parking was limited. Then they walked down a rough path to the edge of the water, where they found a flat rock and sat down in companionable silence, looking out over the water to the trees in the distance. To their right was a huge dam and to the left the water curved round and out of view.

Belle sighed.

"What's the matter my dear?" Rob looked concerned.

"I'm not sure. I suppose I don't want you to go home."

Rob slipped his arm around her shoulders, neither of them spoke, but Belle was aware that his eyes were on her. She turned, and they gazed at each other for a long moment, then Rob leaned over and kissed her lightly on the lips. She was aware that things had changed between them and she wanted him to kiss her again, properly. He did, and so engrossed were they, neither of them noticed that the sun had gone in and a huge black cloud hung overhead. Suddenly there was a flash of lightning and almost immediately a loud clap of thunder. Belle screamed as the heavens opened and the rain poured down on them. They leapt up and ran towards the car, Belle fumbling in her pocket for her car keys. She pulled out as quickly as she could to allow Rob to get in, then they looked at each other and laughed. Belle's hair was clinging to her head and her clothes were rather damp, but Rob was soaking.

"Let's get home and get you dried out." She said.

On Friday they went into the town and Rob bought presents for his colleagues and insisted on buying something for Chris, Rose and the children. When Belle said that it wasn't necessary, he replied.

"They are the kids and the grandchildren I never had."

There was nothing Belle could say to that, so she just squeezed his arm.

"And I'm taking you out for a meal tonight, for looking after me so well. Chas recommended somewhere, but you'll have to drive I'm afraid. But actually, why don't I get a taxi, that would be better, and don't argue, I've made up my mind. Oh dear, I hope I don't sound like Bernard." He pulled a wry face.

"No, you don't." Belle laughed. "But I'll do whatever you say, just in case."

As they browsed around the shops, Belle decided to buy some presents as well, as she might not visit the town again. Rob bought his presents with help and advice from Belle.

"Could we pop into the supermarket again on the way home?" He asked.

"Of course. What were you after?"

"Just a couple of bottles of wine, it's such a good price. I actually noticed some in cartons at a ridiculously low price. They would be safer to take home."

"Mm, I've tried that and I rather like it. Tell you what Rob, buy as much as you like and I'll bring it home in the car, whenever that may be."

So, on the way back, that's what they did. Rob bought a dozen bottles and cartons and Belle bought six more, then they headed back to the villa to rest for a while before getting ready for their evening out. Rob leaned back in the armchair and to Belle's amusement, was soon fast asleep. It gave Belle time to think. She gazed at that dear, familiar face and admitted to herself that she loved him. But did he love her? Could what the girls have said be true? She couldn't possibly say anything unless she was certain—and she wasn't, but the thought of him going home in the morning made her heart plummet.

'Oh well.' She thought, 'I suppose I'll soon get back in to the swing of things. Out with Chas and up to the club. And there's a lovely walk planned for next week'.

But she just couldn't work up much enthusiasm.

Later, as they were shown to a table in the restaurant, Belle could not dispel that feeling and they were both rather quiet. A couple of glasses of wine didn't help. It just made Belle feel emotional and several times she felt close to tears.

Rob's flight was at one o'clock so there was plenty of time for him to pack in the morning. They left the villa at ten o'clock and drove to the airport, where Rob booked in.

"There's time for a quick coffee before I go through, but the flights' on time so I mustn't be too long."

They sat down with their drinks and gazed at each other.

"Don't be too long coming home." Rob said again.

"No, I won't, I promise."

With the coffee's finished, Rob picked up his cabin bag and headed for the door to departures. He dropped his bag and held Belle close for several minutes, then kissed her gently before letting her go. He picked up his bag and made for the door that would take him away from her. Just before he disappeared he turned and waved, his face serious and unsmiling. Belle returned his wave and blew him a kiss, but already her eyes were full of tears. She felt as though a part of her had been torn out, and she wouldn't be whole again until they were back together. She hurried back to the car and sat for a while until she had her emotions under control, then blew her nose, took a deep breath and started the car.

She happened to know where there was a piece of high ground where you could watch the planes coming in and going out. There were always a few plane spotters there and Belle found herself a parking space and turned off the engine to wait for Robs plane. As she sat there she made a decision. She was going to set off home tomorrow! She mentally planned the rest of the day. Go home and pack, take the left-over food next door and then pop down to see Pete and Gerry and inform them. She could leave the key in their mail box in the morning. Her spirits lifted at the thought of going home, not just to see Rob again, but also her family and friends. Now she was impatient. If it had been possible she would have turned her car towards home right then and there. She glanced at her fuel gauge and it reminded her she was low, so she must fill up with petrol as well.

She was so engrossed in her plans that she almost missed Rob's plane taking off. She leapt out of the car and waved like mad as it flew over. Then she chided herself for being silly. The chances of him seeing her were slim. As the plane disappeared behind some light clouds, Belle took a few deep breaths and started the car.

'I'm coming home darling Rob. In just a few days I'll be there'.

Then she remembered Chas. She wasn't looking forward to saying goodbye. He had been good to her and she was fond of him. She blushed to think she had even enjoyed their love making.

'Oh well'. She thought with a smile 'I've had a couple of flings, and why not? But now I hope I can settle down again. That's what I really want'.

She decided to call in and see him first and get it over with. He was in, thank goodness and welcomed her with a kiss on the cheek.

"Come in Belle."

She followed him in and sat down in her usual chair.

"Did Rob get away OK then?"

Belle nodded.

"Chas---." She hesitated.

Chas smiled at her. "You're going home aren't you?"

Belle just nodded again.

"That guy's mad about you, and I think you feel the same. Am I right?"

Belle felt very tearful and just nodded yet again.

"Then go home Belle dear. Go back to your Rob and be happy. I've enjoyed your company and I'll miss you, but it's the right thing to do."

They stood up and held each other for a long moment.

"Thanks for everything Chas. Look after yourself."

She turned and left the villa without looking back, got back in her car and with a last wave, headed for the office of Pete and Gerry. Soon she had said her goodbyes to them as well. Now she just had to go to the garage to fill up with petrol.

As she stepped inside the villa door her first thought was, where to start? She made out a list, but it seemed as soon as she crossed something off, another job was added. Rob's bed linen and towels went in the machine first, then she went out to the car and made sure that was tidy, with no rubbish on the floor or in the door lockers, because she would need every bit of space. She made a quick decision about what clothes she would need for the journey, then packed the rest into her largest suitcase. That went straight in the boot of the car. As she stepped back and closed the boot, a voice hailed her.

It was Vi. "You're not leaving us are you Belle?"

"I'm afraid so. I'm glad I've seen you Vi. Please don't be offended, but would you like to come and help yourself to any food or cleaning stuff I've got?"

Vi wasn't proud and she came around immediately.

"What about your journey Belle? You'll want to make up some sandwiches won't you?"

Between them they sorted out what Vi wanted, what Belle needed for the journey and what could be thrown away. Vi didn't stay long, knowing that Belle had lots to do, but it was agreed that she would go round that evening for a farewell drink. Belle had finished packing as much as she could, cleaned right through and had a bite to eat by seven fifteen. She popped next door and sat down thankfully with a glass of wine.

"We shall miss you Belle, you've been a lovely neighbour. You will come back and see us some time, won't you?"

Belle said she would. But as much as she liked Vi and Harry, she was exhausted. A nice shower and her bed were calling her, after a restless night thinking about Rob. She soon said goodbye and there were more hugs.

Oh, how she hated goodbyes, and that was all she seemed to be doing at the moment. It was with great relief that she stepped back inside her own villa and locked the door.

Belle woke and looked at the clock. It was six thirty but not yet light. Still, that didn't matter. She wanted to be away as soon as possible. While she ate her toast and drank her tea, she made her sandwiches and the last few bits of food were packed away in a cool bag with some ice blocks. She dressed and brushed her teeth. The clean linen was folded up on the table for Gerry to pick up and her dirty linen was in the machine to be taken out later and put on the line. When that was done she would be ready to leave. She left quickly and quietly, not wanting any more goodbyes. All she had to do now was drop the keys in to Pete's letter box and find the motorway.

CHAPTER 25

Belle heaved the last suitcase up the stairs and thankfully closed the door. Nobody knew she was coming home so she could sort everything out in peace, then think about making some phone calls. As always, there was laundry to go in the machine and a cup of tea was vital. She had done a small shop on the way home, so she had the essentials. When all was done she made a sandwich and sat down to go through the heap of post. Most of it went straight in the bin. Anything important had been sorted out by Dave, with her permission. Then she picked up the phone.

"Hello Rose, it's Mum. I'm home."

Rose was absolutely delighted, and Belle also had a chat with Gary. Rose said yes, she would love to come to Sunday lunch, and she would bring a dessert. Next, she rang Chris and then Bubs. All were pleased to have her back and luckily, they were all free on Sunday. Belle didn't chat long. They could hear all about it on Sunday, then she would only have to tell it once.

Then, heart thumping, she rang Rob's number. She looked at her watch. Just after seven, he should be in, but he wasn't, so, somewhat down hearted, Belle left a message.

'Hi Rob, I'm back home. Everyone is coming to lunch on Sunday. Hope you can come too'.

She hoped he would ring back, but he didn't and she went to bed a little worried and disappointed.

The next day she threw yet another load of washing in the machine and sat down to toast and tea. Rose and the children were coming around after school, so the day was hers till then. She decided what to cook on Sunday and made out a shopping list. It was Friday, so she had plenty of time to make some cakes and clear the ironing. At nine o'clock she slipped a coat on and picked up her handbag and shopping bags. Then the door buzzer sounded and made her jump. Who would this be? Surely not Rose. She looked out of the window. Rob stood below, his face turned up towards her. She waved and let him in, swiftly taking her coat off as she waited for him to come up the stairs. His face was serious as she let him in. He hugged her briefly and sat down as Belle put the kettle on.

"How was the journey?"

"It was OK thanks, but tiring. Why didn't you ring me back last night?"

"I was out till late. There was a meeting in Birmingham and it dragged on." He said.

"I was worried, but you are alright, so that's good. Although you don't look very happy. Is it post-holiday blues?" Belle tried to make it a joke, but it fell rather flat. She put his tea and the biscuit tin down beside him. Sitting down opposite him, she said.

"What's wrong Rob?"

He looked at her for a long moment, then started to speak, and Belle was stunned by what he told her.

"Belle Johnston. I've run out of patience. Have you any idea how long I've been in love with you? How long I've stood on the side lines while you were married to Bernard, then you went off to France and got tied up with that man Frank. Then there was Chas. Well I need answers. I love you, I have for about eighteen years and if you don't feel anything for me I'm sorry, but I had to tell you—" His voice trailed away.

"H-how long?" Belle gasped.

"Do you remember?" Rob began. "What a terrible time you had with Chris when she was in her early teens? Bernard just made everything ten times worse and I just wanted to take you away from all that. Then I realised I loved you. Oh Belle, it's been such a long time. Please say you care for me."

Belle looked across the table, then reached over and took his hand and held it tightly.

"Rob, I love you dearly. I realised it in Spain when you left to come home."

Simultaneously, they both stood up, and fell into each other's arms.

The next couple of hours were spent talking, laughing and crying with joy. Discussing their future together as man and wife, and looking forward to making up for all the lost time they could have shared.

Belle said. "You know, the girls will be unbearable. It will be— I told you so Mum." But they will be thrilled to bits as well."

Rob grinned.

"Shall I make an announcement on Sunday? If

you're happy, we won't say anything until then. I'll bring some champagne. Then when we are all around the table, I'll pour it and tell them we are going to be married."

Belle laughed. "And the place will erupt."

At this point Rob said. "I really must go and make some calls and let you do your shopping. I'll get here as soon as I can on Sunday morning."

Belle slipped her coat on and they went down the stairs together, before reluctantly going their separate ways.

Sunday arrived, and Belle, wearing her favourite sky blue tee shirt, was busy preparing the roast dinner. Rob had been there since ten o'clock and was helping. People began to arrive. First Bubs, then Rose and family and finally, at noon, Chris and Steve. Rob carved the joint and brought it over to the table. Once everybody had been served with their meal, he produced the bottle of champagne and walked round the table, pouring a little in to each glass.

"Don't worry, there's another bottle, if anyone wants a top up."

"What's all this about then Rob?" Dave asked. "What are we drinking to?"

Rob stood at the head of the table and raised his glass.

"Ladies and gentlemen." Everyone laughed. "I have an announcement to make. Belle has agreed to become my wife and the wedding will be soon."

He had to shout the last few words because, as expected, the room erupted. Rob's hand was shaken, Belle was kissed and hugged, and Rose burst into tears of relief!

When everything had quietened down and the family were busy eating, Gary suddenly said.

"Does this mean I've got another Grandad now?"

Rob said. "Yes, it does."

It was late evening. Everyone had gone home except Rob. They sat close together on the settee with Rob's arm around her shoulders.

"I don't think I've ever actually asked you to marry me." He said. "That was very remiss of me."

He stood up and then dropped on to one knee before her.

"Darling Belle. Please, please say you will marry me."

"Oh Rob, of course I will, and whenever you like."

Rob stood up and pulled her into his arms.

'This is where I belong.' Belle thought. 'I've come home.'